A SMILE

DJ Mendel

ELBORO

ISBN: 978-1-7321817-5-5

Published in New York by Elboro Press

Elboro Press books may be purchased in bulk for educational, business or sales promotional use. Please address enquires to:

office@elboropress.com

Elboro Press
779 Riverside Drive, Suite B25
New York NY 10032

A Smile Shy

The First Book of Weezal, called GENESIS

In the beginning he said, "Let it be a whiskey." And it was a whiskey. A good whiskey.

He cracked the seal on his pocket-sized bottle of Jim Beam and took a whiff. A deep whiff. It was a good whiff.

On the second day he took his first sip. A small sip. Mm, good sip.

"Things," he said, "will never be the same." And they weren't.

The third day found him two shots along the way and eating peanuts. "Nothing," he declared, a bit tipsy now, "is more satisfying than eating peanuts and drinking whiskey." And when he said this the earth shivered with a drunken chill, acknowledging this truth.

The fourth day, a third shot.

The fifth day, a fourth.

And on the sixth day he went ahead and bought himself a fifth.

Alone in the heavens, save for a pack of Pall Malls and an old George Jones record, he drank the whiskey, slowly getting stoned. The peanuts were long gone so he chewed on his bottom lip, which became swollen and sore.

He closed his eyes and the earth began to spin. It spun wickedly out of control and circled the sun. The spirit curdled in his belly. Fermentation in the Firmament!

He erupted.

He puked up galaxies and planets. He puked up continents and oceans. He puked up Adam and Eve. He puked up flowers and trees and mountains and rivers. He puked up philosophy and mathematics and politics and athletics. He puked up everything he'd eaten since the beginning of time: the stars, the moons, the dust, the tears, the broken bones and bruises. He puked up the possibilities. He puked up the mortgage. He puked up the pickup. He puked up nostalgia and vice. He puked up every aching muscle and every ancient excuse. He puked up the breakup. He puked up a lifetime of wasted opportunities. He puked it all up and kept puking it up until he couldn't breathe. Then he puked up some more.

And on the seventh day he was completely fucked. His head pounded relentlessly behind his swollen eyes. His mouth tasted like battery acid and metal. His lips were chafed and crusty. His guts were burning a hole from the inside out.

So he rested.

Where It All Ends

Planted in the hill and abandoned like a crop gone bad, the trailer park grew wild and smeared across its rotten terrain. This place was spoiled. You could see it in the faded aluminum sidings. You could smell it in the trash collecting in the burning barrels, in the shit seeping into the soil from a busted septic. You could taste it, if you wanted to, by taking a big gulp from the fetid creek water.

The overgrown weeds and crab grass were crawling, spreading like an infection over the blacktop roads and stripped-down/jacked-up automobiles. The sheds and carports were sagging and rusting and rotting. Housing wildlife. The sun was constantly beating down on the trailers like an angry, drunken mother. Angry because she never wanted any of this. Angry because it was too late. Angry because love, the love she always wanted, never found its way into her life.

None of the clothes on none of the lines suggested it was 1998. In fact, they all looked '78 or '68, everything a size or three too small. All the hems had been let down, all the taken-ins, taken out. Some of the used-to-be white tube socks had become so black and blue with age they could now be worn proudly to church with the dress slacks. The reds, the yellows, the too many shades of green had all faded into the same dull color: pale. And everything creaked: old trailers, old furniture, old pipes, old people. It all creaked. It all moaned. And when the wind picked up it was anybody's guess as to when the whole damn trailer park wouldn't just keel over, curl up and die.

Screen doors missing screens. Windows without glass. The blacktop was gray. And you could just see it in every bloodstained bed sheet hanging limply from the clothesline, see it in every mangy dog, feel it in every moment of time, time that lingered in the air like a stale fart in August, this place was spoiled.

But it wasn't called, "Spoiled Trailer Park," it was called, "Big Bass Lake and Mobile Homes," with a subheading explaining, "an alternative lifestyle."

Big Bass Lake was now bone-dry puddle. A poor design and three summers of drought had left the man-made lake nothing but a dusty playground for twelve-year-old boys and their dirt bikes. Everything up and evaporated: the water, the bullfrogs, the dreams of catching bass— big ones.

The trailer court was jammed into the side of a 66-foot high, nine-acre wide hill. It was sectioned off into three 22-foot high tiers. Each tier was given its own poorly laid blacktop road. Each blacktop road connected a dozen quarter-acre plots. Each quarter-acre plot was the site for a trailer. Each trailer was parked in the same catty-corner direction, northeast. The last trailer was dragged in and planted on July 4, 1972.

This place had no charm. There were only three wind chimes and two welcome mats (both of which had been worn away to read, "w lc me"). It had come to look like what it was intended to be—a festering pest-hole for those infected with poverty. The decay had begun the minute the last plot was sold and the last trailer parked. "Them poor some-bitches," thought their families and friends, all the while stretching back their jaws into the same tight smiles they used in the wedding pictures, saying things like, "Quaint, charming, good luck."

The plots situated on the top tier were the most expensive on account of the view. It was a pretty view, a view that forced your sights away from the trailer court, away from the truth, away from the present. A view that could calm you down after getting off the phone with J.C. Penney's or the Pennsylvania Power and Light Company or the bank handling the mortgage, all of them telling you that you ain't worth a damn. All of them talking like they never make mistakes. Like their ends always meet.

Looking east you could see a good twenty miles of Polk Mountain's ridge. Polk Mountain was a smooth, gentle mountain peaking at about 1800 feet, dressed green in a fluffy spruce. The pines were all leaning down the mountain, falling into the Effen River, which hugged the base, disappearing around a bend to the south.

Directly across from Big Bass Lake and Mobile Homes, due north, was the McGraw farm. A small twelve-acre deal that rotated yearly between corn, alfalfa and sunflowers (there was one potato year, apparently disastrous). This was an alfalfa year.

Also from the top tier you could see all 3.8 miles of Goddfree. Not much existed in Goddfree. So little, in fact, that a quick list could tell all:

* Big Bass Lake and Mobile Homes
* The 12-acre McGraw farm
* 2 Weeping Willows (both more wailing than weeping)
* 26 Chevys, 67 Fords and 1 Volkswagen Rabbit (Diesel)
* 1 Church (With a sign that read: "Yes! There is God in Goddfree! Lutherans - 8 am, Catholics - 9 am, Presbyterians - 11 am and BINGO - all Christians Welcome at Noon")
* 2 Highways (Rt.'s 209 and 715), 7 auxiliary roads
* A Revolutionary War fort designed by Benjamin Franklin, where he developed a national lottery to help pay for the expense of war. (Incidentally, the very first winning lottery numbers were: 23-9-28-12-16 and won by Mrs. Freda Koganburger who, at the age of 102, used the money to buy a gun and kill herself. True story.)

All of that existed in Goddfree and not much more.

If you stood at the highest point on the highest tier, which happened to be a lookout tower built and displayed proudly as an added attraction, a special feature, but was now used mostly by beer drinking, hickey sucking teenagers, you could also see most of Effen. Effen was the only surrounding village for a good twenty miles that was developed enough to be called a town. Like you might say, "I'm goin' into town," and that would mean you were going into Effen. It had your basics: gas, food and strip mall.

Polk Mountain blocked the view of the four villages on the west side of the mountain: Dunkletown, Monkey's Paw, Sugar Hollow and Joe's.

The bottom tier was the most dangerous. Every morning a thick, sticky fog would roll down from Polk Mountain (as would most of the garbage from the upper levels) and smother this tier, trying to kill it. But it takes more than that to kill the poor and eventually the fog would clear and there they'd be, watching their stories, drinking their beers and humping like rabbits. Great big smiles on their faces. If you lived on the bottom tier you didn't hike up to the top tier to see the view. You just weren't welcome. Class wars in the trailer court!

The worst tier, however, was the middle. Nothing but trouble either way you looked, "knee deep in horse shit and over your head in debt." Weezal Peterson, who lived on this tier, spent most of his day staring straight ahead, out his kitchen window, trying to forget.

The Great Big Sign

It was a joke told in bad taste. The gold, golden letters had lured them there. Gold, golden letters bursting from an electric blue background:

Big Bass Lake and Mobile Homes
An alternative lifestyle

It sizzled with excitement—those glittering letters of gold—paradise promised in every contract. The small print said something about trailer parks being disaster magnets (tornadoes, floods, famine, Tupperware parties) and that the builders couldn't be held responsible. Acts of God and whatnot. The small print was a formality. Who reads the small print? But now the gold, golden letters had become dirt, dirty brown, a brown so dirty it had no real name (Weezal's hair was this same color brown) and every year another letter would fall from that great big sign at the entrance to the trailer court and now all it said was "BIG."

For two years (1980 and '81) the "B" from Bass and the "L" from Lake were the only two letters missing and the great big sign at the entrance of the trailer court said, "BIG ASS AKE." And every morning going to work, and every evening coming home, they'd see that great big sign at the entrance to the trailer court and it would remind them that their pipe dream had rusted. Maybe it froze up in the middle of a cold winter's night. Maybe that old pipe dream had sprung a leak. Maybe they were holding it all together with a couple of rolls of duct tape. Sooner or later, though, they knew that sucker was going to burst.

And like a joke told in bad taste (say, telling a mongoloid's mother: "These two retards walk into a bar...") that great big sign at the entrance to the trailer court was hard to swallow.

A Rough Dray to Drag
Over The Ground

Faded yellow like the color of dried-up dog piss on a fifteen-year-old newspaper, Weezal's trailer sat in the middle tier surrounded by a quarter acre rhubarb patch. The deep greens of this August morning rhubarb screamed at the piss yellow trailer to get a paint job. But, like Weezal, the trailer was too hot, tired and weak to even think about such activity. It felt fine just the way it was.

Dawn was yawning, rolling over and opening the shades. Night crawlers were digging deep into the soil. The thick, leafy rhubarb sat motionless, sagging in the humidity like a field of ninety-year-old breasts. The gnats and horseflies were busy inspecting something rotting in a burning barrel that was planted at Weezal's front door. The creek that used to move water down from Big Bass Lake through the trailer court (halving the rhubarb patch) was gasping and choking and praying for rain. All cotton mouth. Bones of a stray cat were sandwiched between two rocks. The last eyeball recently plucked by a crow. And the piss yellow trailer was quiet, sleeping, or perhaps pretending to be asleep.

"Hot enough fer ya?" was heard echoing, bouncing between the trailer park and Polk Mountain. The low rumble of a tractor coming from over at the McGraw farm broke through the silence and then died. Nothing was going to move this morning, not even something with wheels. The piss yellow trailer had flat tires and hadn't moved in ten years. Today would be no different.

Weezal was asleep on the kitchen table. The table was actually an old door that was propped up on cinder blocks and covered with an American flag tablecloth that was soiled with coffee stains and Jim Beam dribbles. A filthy, dust covered electric fan was humming him a lullaby. Somewhere, the alcoholic breath Weezal exhaled with his last snore was floating toward a sleeping child. That child will wake up in a frightened sweat, convinced that he or she had been molested. That's the nature of an alcoholic breeze. The fan was blowing this breeze in gentle circles around the trailer, the alcoholic mist forming clouds of poison over the plants. And they were wilting. They were plastic plants and magazine cutout pictures of plants, but they were wilting. The Slim Jim wrappers and watermelon rinds surrounding the garbage can were covered with ants. Ants drunk from breathing in the stink.

And, man, could these ants drink! One ant was playing an Irish drinking song on his plywood violin. It was a scratchy violin that his grandfather had given him. He'd announce, "My grandfather was a Native American Ant. He was robbed of his fertile land by the white man and offered this," pointing to the Slim Jim wrappers and the empty Jim Beam bottles, "in return!" And then, with a tear rolling down his cheek, he'd play. And, man, could this ant play. He scratched and ripped and gnawed his way through a hundred tunes. The other ants knew the words to every song he'd saw.

The Slim Jim wrappers really started steaming up when the little ant whores went to work selling their bodies to the libertine ant daddies who were pissing away their welfare checks, trying hard not to think about their little ant wives and their little ant kids back at the home front. All of them hungry. "Fuck it," they'd say, "tonight, I think only of myself." And that's when the Slim Jim wrappers got good and greasy.

Rancid air was the first thing that he smelled. His eyes were closed and he tried to place the odor. It was his breath. A thick paste was coating his tongue and every time he swallowed it stuck to the roof of his mouth. His eyes were crusted shut. The smell of his breath was making him nauseous. He tried exhaling hard and fast, blowing the sour odor out across the room but his lungs were weak and the exhale lingered just under his nose, taunting him, until he was forced to turn away. He turned away three times. He scratched at a mosquito bite on his thigh. He could feel his overalls sticking and rubbing at his flesh. He was soaked with sweat. Jim Beam was leaking out of his pores, covering him like a winter quilt. He heard the ants running away and he wondered why.

The roaches. The roaches came a-yodeling in like wild Apaches, ripping holes in the Slim Jim wrappers and conquering the watermelon rinds. The ants were scared. So they ran. The roaches were ready to party.

His eyes were still closed. His nose was packed with snot forcing him to breathe through the acerbity of his mouth. It tasted like shit. He could feel a slow ooze of puss seeping out from where his littlest toe used to be, but he wasn't in pain this morning. In fact, he had no feeling in his foot at all. He half wanted to take a baseball bat or a broomstick and give the foot a good whack to see if it was still there. But he didn't move. He stayed still in the stench and the sweat. For once not feeling any pain. It was a banner morning.

Weezal was about to smile when a tickle got caught in the back of his throat. He threw a coughing fit. The fit cramped him into a fetal position on the chair and filled his head with blood. His eyes ripped open, tearing through the crust, and the early morning sun shot through his pupils, blinding him. The cough ended in a scream. A scream the neighbors had become familiar with.

He closed his eyes again, exhausted.

The sweat was beading on his forehead and on the back of his knees.

He scratched. It felt like bugs were crawling on him, everywhere. But there was no pain this morning, just discomfort. A low moan began in the bottom of his belly and forced its way up and out of his throat, exiting as a yawn. Time to get up. Then he heard the roaches running away and he wondered why.

The rats. The goddamn rats scurried in and started eating the roaches. They were eating the roaches, the watermelon rinds, the Slim Jim wrappers and one of Weezal's good socks. Weezal stared a moment, trying to focus. He spotted the creature. He took hold of an empty Jim Beam bottle and whipped it at the rat nibbling on his sock. Nailed him. The stunned rat casually shook his head, gave Weezal a curious look and then sauntered under the sink. The other rats followed. This party was over.

Weezal gave himself a shove off of the table. He needed to pee.

The smell of elephant shit was everywhere in the trailer. It was obvious that the circus had come through, though Weezal couldn't remember when. His burning, bloodshot eyes made it impossible to distinguish between piles of garbage and piles of elephant shit, so he carefully stepped over everything.

Weezal unbuttoned his overalls and pulled out his pecker but decided it would be easier to sit and pee, so he unlatched the whole contraption and sat down. Anyway, he hated how sticky the floor got when he missed. Once sitting down, and this happened to him a lot, Weezal realized he also had to shit. While shitting, Weezal would think.

He thought about his dead father. He thought about his dead cousin Earl, his dead grandmother, his dead grandfather, his dead dog Bruno and finally his dead mother, Sarah. His dead mother, Sarah, was always the last thing he thought about. He thought about how he loved her. A long time ago. Weezal couldn't remember his father's name but he knew that it rhymed with Casper. So many things forgotten.

"Just now," he thought, "I'd like to be born again."

Weezal caught whiff of a meatball and it made him smile. His shit didn't smell like meatballs, it was coming from somewhere else. It was coming through the bathroom window. He took another deep breath but this time could only smell his waste. A minor disappointment. No toilet paper. A major disappointment. He flushed.

Weezal stopped to look at himself in the mirror and saw a letter taped to the glass. He stared blankly at it for a few seconds before slowly pulling it from the glass. He started to read:

Forget it. Forget it not. Forget it. Forget it not. The infection is rising up and over your stinky swollen feet. You didn't take the boots off last night. Forget it. Forget it not. Forget it. Forget it not. One toe short of a perfect foot. One toe that has probably rotted and decayed by now. One toe that may have become squirrel food. One toe chopped off while trying to carve wood with a chainsaw. You screamed and yelled and carried on like a little baby. Then, like an even littler baby, you ran away and left the toe behind. Forgot it.

Then you buried your books. Books had nothing to do with your toe. You buried all your books because you were afraid to read. Afraid you had forgotten how. But now you are reading this and thinking that you probably made a big mistake. You can't mutilate your feet to keep from walking into disaster. You can't bury your books in hopes of forgetting what you know. Forget it. Forget it not. Forget it. Forget it not.

Weezal looked everywhere for the author of the note. He checked down the drain, behind the shower curtain, in the medicine cabinet, but no one was around.

The handwriting on the note looked exactly like Weezal's but he was sure that he hadn't written it. His handwriting was generic and easy to forge. He was convinced there was an imposter. Maybe someone, at this exact moment, was walking around in a pair of ragged overalls, smoking Pall Malls, swigging Jim Beam, writing letters in his hand-writing—ultimately pretending to BE Weezal. He wondered if this fraud was happily married with a good job and a couple of kids. Made him sore to be so close to a good thing. He wondered if the author of the note wore the same size shoe. He wondered if the author was missing a toe.

Weezal was missing a toe, it was true, just a little pinky toe—nothing to keep him from dealing day to day with the empty mailbox, the sour stomach or the leaky roof. Sometimes when he was sober and depress-ed, he'd wish his whole damn foot was gone.

And this wasn't the first letter, there had been many throughout the years. Weezal knew them to be fakes because of their rudeness. No date, no signature. Weezal had dated and signed every letter he'd ever written. Example given:

May 13, 1981
My dearest Wilma,
My nights are filled with sweaty, endless turning.
My days are crammed with yearning.
My afternoons, while napping,
are filled with dreams of you.
Love always - Forever and a day,
Weezal

Moreover, the ink on the note was still fresh and Weezal hadn't lifted a pen in over ten years. Ink gave him the creeps. A whole world of bad memories associated with ink. Things he couldn't exactly remember. It was most assuredly a fake.

Weezal limped out of the bathroom and continued to search through the trailer. He swept his hand along the backside of the refrigerator. It kicked up dust, making him sneeze. He checked under the kitchen sink but not too well because it stunk under the kitchen sink.

"Cocksucker!"

He sat at the table admiring the artistry of the counterfeiter. This was a professional job. The t's crossed just so, the i's dotted a smidgen ahead of the letter (suggesting a hope of better things to come), and the W's, Weezal's specialty, all narrow valleys and curly peaks. Perfection.

"Weezal, you dumb fuck," he thought, "this is the handwriting of your dead grandpa."

It didn't bother Weezal that the fresh ink made this impossible. He needed to get a handle on the situation. He felt comfortable knowing someone he had once admired had written the letter. Dead Grandpa had been dead since long before Weezal was born, which is why he thought of him, quite fondly, as Dead Grandpa. And although he'd never met the man, he had heard stories about his big hands and loud voice. Stories about how he built stone houses. He sounded like a good man, a man to admire, so he did. It was Weezal's father's father. Sarah's father was known only as Grandpa and he wasn't admired.

"Weezal, you dumb fuck," he said again about to denounce Dead Grandpa as a possibility. Instead he drifted into a memory. He had so few these days, he let it unfold:

A girl is picking strawberries for her mother. She's blind but has a curiously supernatural ability to pick the ripest berries in the patch. The little blind girl insists the secret of her talent lies in an extremely acute sense of smell. But little Weezal figures she's just faking her blindness. (He didn't think that at the time, he only thinks that now, interjecting it into his memory because he's become skeptical of the handicapped. You become bitter when you're one toe short of a perfect foot, four toes shy of a cripple.) The memory slips and fades with this interjection and Weezal catches another smell of meatballs. This time, though, the smell doesn't brighten his morning. The mysterious letter, the foul breath, the humidity—alright, alright: the hangover—had put him in a bad mood.

He thought about maybe walking into Effen and getting some Pop-Tarts, maybe some more liquor. Maybe stock up on both so he wouldn't have to leave the trailer until autumn.

"You fucking coward, come out and face me!" he shouted. But the dirty dishes didn't respond. The green linoleum, curling at its edges didn't respond. Nothing. Just the rattling gurgle of the electric fan.

It was the paragraph about burying his books that bothered him most. Yes, he buried his books. Yes, he was trying to forget all he ever knew. But that was his business. And no, he didn't think he'd made a big mistake by burying them. He felt just fine about it.

His head started to bob and bounce. It had been a laborious night of searching for something. He couldn't remember what. Forget it. Forget it not. His eyes fluttered once and his head fell hard against the window on the table. He kind of felt it hit. It kind of hurt. But he was too tired to react. He lay quietly with his mouth open, a dribble of drool dripping out.

It was getting hotter and flies were beginning to circle the dirty dishes. One flew over to Weezal and landed on his hand, but Weezal was asleep and didn't feel it.

¼ Cherokee Indian, ¼ Czechoslovakian, ¼ Irish and ¼ Hobo

Maisey's blood was a survival cocktail. Straight blond hair and a square jaw framed her flattened, broken nose. Just above—eyes the size of chestnuts. Her chestnut eyes were blue and her skin was fair. Her features talked of her Slavic background, the Irish and Indian parts of her only conversed behind closed doors, the lights dimmed, something romantic playing on the stereo. No one had heard these parts in three years. Three years ago she was twenty-one.

Maisey shared her last name, Walker, with her father and two brothers. She shared the house she lived in with her father. The two brothers were long gone. One in San Diego, a member of the Air Force. She never heard from him. The other was living in New York City—this week a sculptor, last week a photographer. She only heard from him when he needed money.

Walker wasn't the real family name. It was originally Walcheroitocsky but had been shortened at Ellis Island's receiving desk because the gentleman there thought that Walker would be easier to pronounce. And although her great-grandfather was upset by the name change, Maisey (Lazy Maisey, Crazy Maisey) couldn't have cared less. Walker was what she knew and was comfortable with. A simple name. And, besides, it wasn't as if the Walcheroitocsky coat of arms was lined with royalty or riches, and these were the things Maisey had turned her attention to.

Her mother was half-Indian and half-Hobo and so, as if it was written in the stars, one day she got drunk and ran off. That's how her father (Irish/Czech) explained it. Her mother ran off (drunkenly) when Maisey was five. Maisey had often wanted to run away, too, but being only one quarter-Hobo, she never got past the driveway.

Raised Catholic. Her confirmation name was Mary. She wanted to use Carmella, which was her mother's Christian name. Her mother's real name was Crooked Knee, though she didn't have one. Crooked Knee was not confirmable because it wasn't the name of a saint and Carmella was refused by her father with a simple, "No." So, Mary, her father's choice, was how she was confirmed. She made a point never to use that name. Her father used Mary when he prayed for her. He hadn't had a prayer answered in three years. Maisey was just fine with that.

PRAY: Dr. William Pray: File No. 363588

"No way," she thought, "Maisey Walker Pray." It sounded like a demand from her father.

She was sitting alone in a small office at the county courthouse, a stack of manila folders on her table. She opened the file. This is what she learned:

* Dr. William Pray of Monkey's Paw, 213 Meixler Valley Road.
* Sued Driggs Pharmaceutical for the sale of bogus penicillin.
* Dr. Pray's suit is in response to malpractice suits that were filed

against him.
Investigation: ON GOING.

Too risky. She went to the next file:

PRAZZINSKI: Joseph Prazzinski: File No. 354579

* A construction worker with the Pennsylvania Department of Trans-
  portation. Congestion Coordinator.
* A break down in radio transmission leads to an accident involving
  eighteen-wheeled vehicle.
* Court Awarded: $173,000 per year, until deceased.

That sounded like some good change but there was a catch—he had
no legs. And, she wondered, if he had no legs, does he have a... It gave
her the heebie-jeebies. She went to the next file:

PROCTOR: Arthur Proctor: File No. 367783

* A former high school History teacher and football coach. Severe
  head and neck injuries during a football practice. A collision with
  student/player. Snapped spinal cord.
* Full recovery from physical injury. However, for reasons beyond
  current medical knowledge, Proctor is unable to remember anything about American History.
* Awarded: Pay for new training.

UPDATE FILE NO. 367783 PROCTOR

* Proctor has no ability to remember anything at all.
* Jury Awarded: $21,000 plus 3 1/2% increase per year, correspond-
  ing to salary at Happy Valley High School.

Twenty-one thousand wasn't nearly enough. Hell, she made almost
that much folding laundry at The Polk Mountain Hideaway, the honeymoon resort where she worked.

A bit disgusted, Maisey grabbed the seventy-four files she had gone through that afternoon, slipped her purse over her shoulder and headed for the reception desk. The receptionist saw her coming and let out a moan.

"Now, Ms. Walker, I've asked you nicely a hundred times. I need these folders back by quarter to five. I have an appointment tonight and now I'm going to be late."

"I'm sorry," Maisey said, surprised that it had gotten so late. She was in a hurry herself now. "I'd help but..."

"Go on, get out of here," the secretary said, "but next time I'm not kidding. Four-forty-five and not one minute later."

"I promise, Mrs. Furlong." Maisey dropped the pile of folders on the desk and headed for the door.

"Hey, Maisey."

"Yeah?"

"Any luck?"

"Nothing. But you'll be the first to know. You'll hear me screaming from the back room. See you Monday." Maisey blew her a kiss before slipping through the door.

Irish Meatballs

Marty McGraw was leaving his wife and kid again. He was walking slowly up old Route 209 toward the trailer court and away from the house that he had built with his own two hands. He had built that house, brick by brick, through the cool spring mornings of 1981. Marty had fond memories of that spring, but he wasn't thinking about those days as he walked away from his house toward the trailer court. He was thinking about getting drunk.

He was also thinking about his daughter but because she was so young and not much help around the house, he could only think of her as a pet. He remembered patting her on the head saying, "Good girl," when she called him daddy for the first time. Then he thought about his wife, Darlene, and how much he loved her.

They had met at the big state university. It was called Big State University and was located in the sprawling farmlands of central Pennsylvania. He remembered, fondly, how they'd watch foreign movies and eat ice cream. Marty enjoyed French movies. Darlene preferred

Italian. They both liked vanilla ice cream. English was their major, though Marty's main interest was writing and Darlene's was reading.

They had met at the Shakespeare Bar and Grille, which was a favorite haunt of the university literary crowd—a place where students and professors would mingle and fall in and out of love. Darlene worked at the bar, earning thirty dollars a night as a belly dancer. Marty liked belly dancing and Darlene danced well. As their love affair blossomed, Marty became jealous. He didn't like Darlene belly dancing in front of his friends. He never told her this because Darlene hated jealousy. She did quit dancing shortly after their relationship began, however, because an appendix removal left her dancing belly scarred and less jiggly.

Nowadays, Darlene did the laundry and taught freshmen English at the Effen High School, home of the Effen Effectivists. It used to be the home of the Effen Swashbucklers, which Marty thought was a pretty intimidating name. That was the problem. High schools throughout the northeastern region of Pennsylvania had begun receiving flack from activist groups claiming names like Swashbucklers, Bears, Fighting Cardinals, Braves, Cavaliers, etc. were, "chauvinistic, unnecessarily aggressive and racially problematic," and that, "in view of the changing times, with a stronger emphasis being placed on diversity, rather than the culturally limiting 'melting pot', it was time for serious re-evaluation." The activist groups (which included: Mothers Against the Melting Pot and Teenagers Against Being Identified with Aggressive Nicknames), demanded that the high schools change their nicknames to, "something more suitable and characteristic of a kinder, gentler and more intelligent society." Thus, the Effen Swashbucklers, which Marty thought was a pretty intimidating name, had become the Effen Effectivists and on Friday nights they'd hit the gridiron and battle teams like the Stroudsburg Competitors and the Lehigh Valley Opportunitists. The mascots were stripped of their headdresses, pirate uniforms and bear claws and were now donning color coordinated outfits that, to Marty at least, resembled military uniforms. It gave Marty the creeps. The marching bands were performing halftime extravaganzas highlighting Irish jigs, Slovakian folk tunes, African tribal numbers and Eastern meditation music. The cheerleaders were chanting like this:

The Cookie Monster says that the Effectivists are
the most Efficient cookies
at the top of the jar.
And the Cookie Monster says that the Opportunitists are
the wasteful, artificial ingredients
at the bottom of the jar.

Marty didn't like any of it. Darlene's only comment was, "a rose by any other name..." And she was always doing that, quoting somebody. It went with her job. Marty didn't mind because he was well read and recognized most of the quotes, but sometimes at dinner parties she would annoy the guests.

Marty loved to read. He said it was the second most important thing a human being could do. Breathing was first. Fucking was third. Eating didn't appear on the list until seventh, preceded by sleeping, drinking and cooking.

And he cooked a delicious meatball. The best, most likely, in all of Goddfree. He'd take his time and cut the onions up so small you'd need a microscope to see them. He'd cook the sauce slow like, letting it simmer for five days over a dozen burning candles. After three days of simmering, the entire town of Goddfree (and the outskirts of Effen) could smell Marty's meatballs. It always meant the same thing: Marty was depressed. It happened every month. Always on a Tuesday.

On this humid August morning, Marty's meatballs were just beginning to choke the trailer court hillside. Marty was not far behind, making his way to Weezal's. Marty smiled at the sight of Weezal's dilapidated trailer and overgrown rhubarb patch. He liked the way his meatballs smelled from Weezal's trailer as much as he liked Weezal's company. Weezal was Marty's only friend. And vicey-versee.

Weezal opened his eyes, surprised that he had fallen back to sleep. He stood up and his bones creaked. Leg bones, backbones, neck bones, they all creaked. He walked to the kitchen sink and got himself a glass of water. Cool water. He looked out the window, squinting into the sun, and could see Marty shuffling up the road. Marty was carrying a shave kit and a bag of groceries. Weezal didn't understand why Marty always brought the shave kit. Marty had a wild, unkempt beard and he never shaved. Weezal was happy to see Marty and it made him think of the first time they'd met. Marty had arrived unannounced and pounded on Weezal's door. Weezal, whose first instinct is to hide when strangers arrive, dove behind a couch and waited for Marty to walk away. But Marty kept right on banging until it was clear to Weezal he wasn't going to leave. Weezal cautiously opened the door.

"Hi, my name is Marty. Marty McGraw. And every third Tuesday of every month, I get fat. I shed my skin, feathers grow from my belly and fireworks shoot out my ass. It's only appropriate that you should meet me now, and see me at my most obese. And if you would put me up, maybe fix me a drink, I promise that I'll be skinny by tomorrow and out of your hair."

"So you're thirsty?" Weezal asked.

"A little." Marty replied.

"Okay. I got some drink. But I have to tell you, you don't look fat at all," Weezal said. And he meant it.

"Thanks, but my wife insists that I am fat and I love and respect her opinion, so I'm afraid it's true."

"Maybe she just said that to get your attention," Weezal said, recalling something he had once done.

"Perhaps. And if so, it worked. But I won't be fat for long. Just a day, really."

"Okay," said Weezal, "come on in."

"You're a good man. And mark my words with green spray paint and frame them in a piece of mahogany, I will only stay the night. Tomorrow I shall be skinny and on my way!"

Weezal enjoyed Marty's odd phrases and manner of speaking. He found it playful rather than pretentious. Maybe it was the unkempt beard or the dingy, fraying sweater and baggy pants. Maybe it was the muddy boots or the dirt under Marty's fingernails—whatever it was, Weezal never thought of Marty as pretentious.

That first night they drank Jim Beam and got drunk. Marty told Weezal he had watched him working in his rhubarb patch, admiring his long, skinny frame. He said that he'd promised himself that he would make a point to meet Weezal but figured he'd wait until he was depressed and needed a friend. That was the third Tuesday in January of 1985. Weezal liked to remember that first, third Tuesday on hot summer mornings. It had been so cold.

Weezal drank another glass of water and watched Marty poke his way up the road. He liked the way Marty walked. He waddled. A fat man's walk. With the right music playing, Marty's walk would have looked like it came straight out of an old silent film.

Weezal was the kind of skinny that never got fat. His mother, Sarah, was that kind of skinny, too.

Marty stepped in a tempo that followed the rhythm of the poems he was composing in his head. Weezal liked Marty's poems, they were gentle. They were poems about life and death disguised as vegetables. Weezal's favorite poem was one of Marty's shortest. And although Marty's poems were never written, and Weezal's memory had gotten very weak, he could remember this one word for word. It went:

Tomatoes
tomatoes, ripe and bleeding
squashed underfoot
i cried as i sucked every last
seed and
swallowed

Weezal thought it sounded like the description of a blowjob. Marty insisted that it was about the birth of his daughter, Rose. Weezal wanted to know why he composed a poem about his daughter, Rose, called "Tomatoes" and Marty said, "that's just the nature of poetry." "Besides," he added, "too many poems have been written about roses and not enough about tomatoes." Weezal could see the logic.

Weezal burped, scratched his balls and went into the bedroom to change his overalls. He slipped into a pair of shorts and left his chest bare. As he pulled a comb through his long, thinning hair, he heard the first knock on the door.

"It's open!" he shouted. But no one came in. Marty liked to be received.

Weezal opened the door and began his greeting, which was the same every month:

"You fat bastard."

"'Tis true, 'tis true."

Marty handed Weezal the bag of groceries, walked over to the couch, sat down and kicked off his boots. Weezal saw that a roll of toilet paper was at the top of the bag.

"I'll be right back," he said and disappeared into the bathroom.

Marty closed his eyes and thought about why he was depressed. It was always the same thing: Darlene hated farming. She thought he was wasting his time and talents. She thought of their twelve-acre corn-alfalfa-sunflower field as his hobby. She was able to think of it that way, too, because she was bringing home the paychecks, paying all the bills. The farm had not made one dollar in its thirteen years of existence. In fact, it had lost a total of $17,343.00. But Marty loved that farm. He couldn't imagine himself doing anything else. He had to be outdoors. In the nature.

He only had two occupational interests: farming and writing. (He never wrote about farming, though. He said it was like dancing a clarinet.) He quit writing to have a wife and kid. And once a month Darlene would try to steal farming away from him. And once a month he would tell her he had to "get away and clear his head." He'd tell her he was going somewhere to "think about life. His life. Their life." Then he'd come back and say that he couldn't give it up just yet.

But his farming days were numbered. In fact, that number was 365. Darlene had given him one year to choose between raising a crop and raising a family. She swore on the bible and on her dead father's grave that if he didn't give up his "gardening" she was going to leave him. And she used the word "gardening" to get his goat. Marty packed his bags and went to Weezal's.

Weezal came out of the bathroom and sat next to Marty on the couch.

"I'm going to quit, Weez. I'm really going do it this time."

"I'll miss the sunflowers."

"You don't like the alfalfa?"

"Not as pretty as the sunflowers."

"Yeah, I think you're right. I'm going to miss the sunflowers, too."

He had planted those sunflowers because he loved Darlene and Darlene loved sunflowers. But he had ruined them for her. She told him that. Sunflowers always reminded her of the fields of France, where she and Marty vacationed after college graduation. And now, after four sunflower cycles—all failing to produce a single dollar, he had ruined them for her. She would be happy if she never had to see another goddamn sunflower as long as she lived. That's what she said.

He had ruined many things for her over the years. He ruined her favorite dress by spilling red wine all over it. He ruined her smile by slamming a door in her face—accidentally, of course. He ruined her self-esteem by laughing at her when she directed the high school production of *The Glass Menagerie*. "Way too sentimental," he told her, "and a serious lack of understanding of what Tom, as a writer, was going through. Too much emphasis on the cripple."

He didn't mean to do any of it.

"I fucked up, Weezal," he said.

"Probably," Weezal replied, figuring everybody did.

"You ever been in love?"

"Sure," said Weezal, "a long time ago."

"What happened?"

"Family problems,"

"What sort?"

"She was my sister."

"Too bad. That's some tough luck."

And Weezal looked away. It was a long time ago and he was different then. He imagined Marty and Darlene were different when they fell in love, too. He imagined Marty as a young college boy, clean shaven and neatly dressed. He realized he'd never seen Marty without his beard. Then he thought, "Maybe he was born with that big bush." And that made him laugh.

"What the hell's so funny," Marty asked,

"The thought of you being born with that beard," Weezal said and Marty laughed with him.

"My dad was a hairy son-of-a-gun. Hair all over his back, shooting out of his nose and ears, everywhichwhere. Ma used to say that's why she left him. Too goddamn hairy." They laughed again and let it fade into a summer silence.

Weezal had a comfortable couch. It was the kind of couch that you could sit in for hours without saying a word. It had been broken-in and Marty was happy to sit there, saying nothing.

Three hundred and sixty-five days seemed like a long time. He felt bad about ruining the sunflowers for Darlene. He loved her, now. Really. He hadn't always loved her like this. When he was younger, he chased a more eccentric skirt. Darlene was plain. But it was the kind of plain that you could always run back to. He found the more adventurous women too much of a spiritual, sexual and emotional challenge. They were competitive and dramatic. Marty didn't like dramatics and usually after a month of these turbulent romances, he would crave the plainness of Darlene. She loved Marty and always took him back. Always.

It seemed the table was turning, as Darlene had predicted it would. Now he wanted her more than she wanted him. He didn't think she was craving a new romance, but she certainly wasn't interested in theirs. "Why did I have to kill the sunflowers?" he thought. He had always counted on them to help raise her spirits. Now there was nothing.

"You want a drink," Weezal asked, knowing the answer.

"Yes," said Marty, predictably.

Weezal went into the kitchen and got two glasses. They would start civilized. He opened the freezer and scraped some ice off the side. He put the slush into the glasses and walked back to the couch. Marty was waiting with the bottle of Jim Beam already opened. He poured two healthy glasses. Half-empty for himself, half-full for Weezal. They nodded.

"Tell me about your lover," Marty said.

"I didn't say she was my lover. I said, I loved her."

"Was she pretty?"

"Beautiful."

"Plain?"

"As dry toast."

"And you loved her?"

"A long time ago."

Marty took a sip of whiskey. He wasn't settled yet. He wiggled around on the couch searching for the sweet spot. He found it.

"It's hot," he said.

"Yup," said Weezal with his first swallow of the day. It burned.

These meetings always started slowly. Weezal liked how slowly they started. Marty would have preferred a quicker pace but he was always too depressed to mention it.

Weezal wondered what Marty was like when he wasn't depressed. He tried to imagine him making love to Darlene. Weezal guessed that their lovemaking was long and quiet. Darlene didn't seem the type to holler. Weezal figured they learned to make love by watching French movies, which wasn't a bad place to learn how to make love. Better, he thought, than watching dogs, which is how Weezal learned. Weezal liked to make lots of noise and he loved to sweat. He couldn't imagine Marty and Darlene sweating. He just couldn't.

Weezal once asked Marty what it was like to make love with Darlene and Marty said it was like carrots and that her vagina tasted like red beets. Weezal loved red beets so he ended the conversation, a slight blush filling in his cheeks.

Marty took another suck on his whiskey. So did Weezal. This one hurt, too.

"Too hot," Marty said.

"Yup," Weezal said and coughed.

The smell of Marty's meatballs was starting to fill the trailer. They both could smell it but said nothing. They didn't talk about Marty's meatballs. It was a rule.

It couldn't have been more than ten or eleven o'clock, Weezal thought, as he looked down at his empty glass. He poured himself another. Marty sucked down his last swallow and held out his glass for a refill. They nodded at each other and took a sip. This one didn't burn.

"Something's up. You're too quiet," Marty said. He knew Weezal pretty well.

"I found a letter this morning."

"Another one?"

"Yup. An exact duplicate of my handwriting."

Marty thought about the letters, the love notes and poems Weezal had been finding throughout his trailer. He didn't know what to make of it.

Neither did Weezal.

"What's it say," Marty asked.

"Doesn't make any sense. Talks about my bad foot. Says I'm pathetic."

"Let me read it."

Marty reached into his shirt pocket and took out his glasses. Marty hated these glasses because they were too small for his face and they made him look fat. While Marty read the letter Weezal finished his second glass of whiskey and poured himself a third. Marty held his glass out for a refill without looking up from the letter. Marty got a queer look on his face.

"Weezal, you wrote this letter," Marty said so matter-of-fact that Weezal was offended.

"Your meatballs smell good," Weezal shot back in a childish retort.

And though it sounded like a compliment, it hurt Marty. The smell of his meatballs meant he was depressed. But it wasn't just the comment that hurt Marty's feelings. It was something else. All of the poems, the love letters, the secret messages Weezal had been finding recently, tacked to his mirrors, scotch-taped to his forehead, all of them, were obviously being written by Weezal himself. Probably in a drunken stupor. It made Marty jealous. This drunk—this skinny little drunk— was a writer. The writing wasn't particularly good but it wasn't expected of Weezal to be particularly good at writing and it was more words on a page than Marty had written in ten years. The whole goddamn thing pissed him off.

What had he been doing this past decade? Gardening! What happened to that young, energetic author that he once fancied himself? The poet? Where'd he go?

Weezal was upset with Marty's silence and began to feel bad about commenting on the meatballs. He wanted to apologize but he couldn't remember how. He knew it had something to do with the word "sorry" but he wasn't quite sure how to use it in a sentence. So he said it the best way he could, simply and with feeling:

"Sorry."

"Don't be. You're right. They do smell good."

Marty folded the letter and finished his drink. Weezal was never one to push anything. He knew Marty would talk about the letter when the time was right. He poured them both another.

Marty thought about Weezal burying all of his books. It used to be that Marty looked forward to inspecting Weezal's surprisingly experimental collection of literature. Surprising because as far as Marty could tell, Weezal had never been schooled—not at a University, anyway. And how the hell else do you come to appreciate the experimental? But just now he didn't want to talk about the letter. Or books. Or anything.

And that was fine with Weezal. He trusted Marty's opinion when it came to the letters and poems because Marty was a writer. He knew he could count on Marty's honesty and criticism to help him find the author. Marty was the only writer Weezal knew. It didn't surprise Weezal at all that the only writer he knew didn't write. That was the kind of luck Weezal seemed to have all his life. All sorts of things that seemed to be wonderful possibilities and potentials—but all missing one vital ingredient. One missing toe. One missing tooth. But his luck was changing. December seventh was coming and things would be different.

December seventh was the anniversary of breaking his bedroom mirror. Weezal had never been superstitious but seven years of bad luck had made him so. Seven years of bad luck that included the chopping off of that toe, rapid thinning of his hair and many other things. Seven years of bad luck and it was all coming to an end.

"Cheers," Weezal said, raising his glass for a toast.

"To what?"

"To new teeth, new hair and a new toe."

"And to sunflower fields that have never been planted."

Weezal poured the remainder of Beam into Marty's glass and stood up to get another bottle.

"While you're up, why don't you grab some breakfast," Marty called out, remembering that he hadn't eaten yet. The Jim Beam was taking effect and some breakfast, he knew, would slow it down. He wasn't in a hurry. He had his shave kit. He had a change of clothes.

Weezal walked to the table and started unloading the grocery bag. He pulled out the Pop-Tarts and threw them over to Marty. He pulled out two flimsy steaks. Lean. He pulled out a box of Slim Jim's. He grabbed a basket of strawberries and it made him want to cry. He looked toward the ceiling and blinked his eyes fast to stop the tears. He reached to the top of the fridge and pulled down a fresh bottle of Jim Beam. He joined Marty on the couch.

Marty was head back, feet up and eyes closed enjoying his Pop-Tart. Weezal grabbed a package and tore it open. Cinnamon-Apple. This was his favorite flavor. Both he and Marty liked to eat Pop-Tarts raw. It was just one of the many things they had in common. They also liked Loretta Lynn and horseshoes.

"Did you ever read *The Sun Also Rises*?" Marty asked.

"Sure," Weezal said, "did you?"

"Read it? Hell, I once wrote it."

A picture of Marty sitting in his college apartment. A ratty old manual typewriter. He had gotten the rinky-dink machine at a flea market for five bucks. He carefully took it apart and cleaned it. He cut long strips of cloth and soaked them in ink to make the type ribbon. Then he started to write. He stayed in his room for eight days, occasionally coming out for a piece of lightly buttered toast or to take a piss.

A picture of Marty admiring his own efficiency. Admiring his dedication and discipline. A picture of Marty writing glorious passages. Passages from another era, another generation. And it wasn't until the fourth and final edit that he realized he had traced the entire 275 pages of *The Sun Also Rises*, word for word, sentence for sentence. Copied old Hemingway better than Hemingway was able to copy himself in later years. Horrified, he immediately put the whole manuscript into a trashcan and burned it. It was his final assignment. He quit college the next day, three credits shy of a Bachelor's degree in English.

"Why'd you trace the novel?" Weezal asked.

"It was an accident. I was young and didn't know any better."

Weezal could accept that answer because when he was young, he thought, he didn't know any better either.

Weezal was drunk. He took a mouthful of Beam and swished it around, flushing out the Pop-Tart sticking to his teeth. The whiskey started to burn his tongue so he swallowed, took another sip and swished some more. He wondered how long it would be before they were just sucking straight from the bottle. Probably a couple of hours, he thought.

"I wish I knew you before you were drunk," Marty said, sucking straight from the bottle.

"And I wish I knew you before you were depressed," Weezal said with a suck of his own.

But they both knew a meeting like that could have only taken place years ago and back then neither of them had anything to talk about. Except the future. And they both hated to talk about the future. It made Weezal want to drink and it depressed the hell out of Marty.

"You probably weren't so ugly back then," Marty said.

"And you probably weren't so fat."

"I've always been fat."

"I don't remember if I've always been ugly."

"Maybe we can call someone and find out. Call an old friend or something." And when Marty said, "call" he didn't mean on the telephone, Weezal didn't have a telephone, he meant to stand at the front door and call out into the hills, in a loud rumbling voice, "Was Weezal always ugly?"

"We could but I don't think anybody would answer."

Another summer silence followed. Weezal gazed out the front bay window of the trailer. He had an urge to get up and go outside—maybe kick some dirt. Something to remind him that life outside the trailer, though dirty and decrepit and failing and hot and humid, was still life—still living. The earth was living and breathing. The air was moving. The molecules and atoms and the spirits of the dead and of God were floating and drifting and it was all within his grasp if he'd only get up off of the goddamn couch and explore it. If only he'd open himself to receive it. Instead, he sat—the urge not quite strong enough to set himself in motion. A long summer silence.

"What will you do if you quit farming," Weezal asked, drunk enough to get things started.

"This trailer stinks," Marty said, not drunk enough to answer.

"The circus came through," Weezal said.

"You better be careful. It's going to sneak up on you."

Weezal knew that Marty was talking about drinking. But he also knew that it had already sneaked up on him.

"My sister was never my lover, although I wanted her to be," Weezal said, "and I think she loved me, too. But I never told her how I felt. And the truth is she wasn't really my sister. She felt like a sister—like family—and that was the problem."

Marty poured himself another drink.

"It was illusive. The first opportunity I had, I grabbed it. I grabbed it like a lightning bug and smeared it on my finger. I smeared it on my finger and danced around the driveway, presenting it to her as a wedding band. She didn't take it.

"Eventually, the light went out and all I was left with was a dull slimy glow, wrapped around my knuckle. I tasted it and imagined that the guts of the lightning bug were toxic. I died for her that night, eating the poisonous wedding ring, and all she had to say about that was, 'You're gross.'

"It was hard to tell her that I loved her because it seemed false. It wasn't poetic. Just me and this sister. She was sitting on the front porch. I was chasing lightning bugs up and down the driveway. I was trying to get her attention. I'd start talking, then stop. I was carefully building pauses."

Marty poured himself another drink and thought about torching his alfalfa field.

"I built pauses and watched them collapse into particles smaller than her smallest toe. I watched the particles of these pauses turn into water, then into gas, which is when the breath of her sigh blew them out across the driveway. I chased them, these pauses, stumbling on the loose gravel, but they were illusive."

"You're drunk," Marty said, wanting to break the story long enough to pour Weezal another drink.

"Yes," Weezal said and took a sip. Just enough to wet his tongue.

"I jumped onto the porch and held her. I could feel her underarm sweat. I wondered if it was me that she was sweating for. I was strong then and not so skinny. She squeezed my arm and could feel my sweat. I wondered if she knew my sweat was for her.

"And right then is when I should have said it. But I couldn't remember the words. I'd said those words a thousand times a day with thoughts of her—I love you—but when I needed to, I couldn't remember. I knew it was only three words so I searched. I searched every spelling bee, every book I'd ever read, every conversation I'd ever had and still, I could not find those three words.

"Something yanked on my tongue. I could feel the weight of three words teetering there, waiting to fall out. And out they tumbled, 'You're my sister.' Those were the only three words I could find. I said it twice to be sure there was nothing else, 'You're my sister.' She stroked my hair. And kissed me on the cheek. Family."

Weezal took a bigger sip now, this time to wet his entire mouth. Marty's glass was empty but he was feeling fine.

"Her eyes were swollen. My mother, Sarah, had those same eyes. Eyes that housed a thousand tears waiting for an excuse to flow. They'd use any excuse. A dying dog. A stubbed toe. A lonely morning. They didn't need much provocation. Her shoulders were a perfect match for those swollen eyes. Broad, curved and ready for consoling. A '57 Chevy. Round and smooth.

"When she stopped stroking my hair I got up and walked away. I walked to the end of the driveway and leaned on the mailbox. It was a mailbox pocked with a thousand tiny holes."

"A mailbox that held a thousand love letters that you probably sent her," Marty said, swigging now from the bottle.

"Probably. I don't remember. I probably perfumed those letters with aftershave. I probably sealed them in wax that I melted down with crayons. I probably pretended that I was Romeo and she was Juliet. I probably hid in the bushes watching her undress. I probably sat silently, masturbating, waiting for my cue, my chance to tell her that I loved her. But I was probably too scared and stayed in the bushes, near the barbed wire fence until I came.

"And as I stood, leaning on the mailbox, the one that had been ruined by a violent redneck boyfriend of hers, a boyfriend who had forgotten that she was as soft and squishy as a barefoot surprise, a boyfriend who dismounted his shotgun from the rack in his truck and blew holes into the mailbox that was probably holding love letters from me, love letters that I probably wrote left-handed so I would be sure to take my time and choose my words carefully, as I stood, leaning on that buckshot mailbox, she was falling asleep on the porch."

Weezal swallowed a shot.

"I carried her to bed that night, kissed her cheek."

"Where is she?"

"Don't know. Out west probably. She always liked the setting sun."

Marty was thinking about Darlene and all of the things he had ruined.

"I just wanted to carry the umbrella," Marty said.

"Drop her off and go park the car," Weezal added.

"Go get the car and pick her up," said Marty.

"Hold her tight in a thunderstorm," added Weezal.

"Get along with her father, who she hates but wants me to be."

"Laugh at all of her jokes."

"Attend, happily, family functions."

"Have interesting conversations."

"Sit in silence when she didn't want to talk."

"Massage her feet."

"Satisfy her sexually."

"Surprise her with flowers."

"Leave when she is ready to go."

"Stay when she is not."

"Plan for the future."

"Which would include trips to Europe."

"But none of this," Marty declared, "I was able to do with much success!"

Marty and Weezal held their glasses high.

"To Satan," Marty said. "Because Satan is a lady. A fine looking lady with long legs and a saucy mouth!"

They swallowed.

How It All Got Started
"Are you kidding me?"
—Thomas Jefferson
August 2, 1776

The inkhorn was full. But it hadn't come easy, the filling of the ink-horn.

It was the excitement. The rush and bustle, the spiritual and emotional vertigo experienced when preparing to sign divorce papers. Divorce from tyranny. Divorce from oppression. Freedom! A revolution won. Big, old meanie England drank a bit too much of the spiked punch and when he tried to get it up realized that the crown, the family jewel, had become a shriveled appendage, an impotent nub useless to these American colonies in heat.

And it was in this heat (this yowling in the night) that someone forgot to buy the ink. Adams blamed Franklin. Franklin blamed Morris. Morris blamed Lightfoot Lee and so on. Finally, Jefferson, annoyed at the whole lot of them, decided to go and get the ink himself.

It was a quick jaunt to Market and Third Street, to an unassuming ink shop (Jefferson did go) where he purchased an ordinary bottle of black ink. Nothing fancy. (Jefferson didn't like fancy. He said so. Said, "I don't like fancy.") He tried to persuade the gentleman running the shop to relinquish the ink free of charge, "in the name of freedom." The gentleman said, "I don't want to know from freedom." And Jefferson, not willing to haggle at such an important moment in history, forked over the cash. ("I'm always getting stuck with the tab." —Thomas Jefferson, on numerous occasions)

And now the inkhorn was full. An air bubble floating atop the ink, winked, bursting into oblivion. Seconds later the papers were signed and America put on her slinkiest dress (the one she had been saving all those years and, god love her, could still squeeze into) and went out a-dancing.

And that unassuming ink shop, through no effort of its own, was about to join the party.

There was no way for John Penn (North Carolina) to know that the ink he used to put his John Hancock on the Declaration of Independence was bought from a company bearing his name. There was no way of him knowing this because it was pure coincidence that the little run-down ink shop on the corner of Market and Third, was called Penn Ink. (Incidentally, nor was this Penn of Penn Ink in any way related to the Penn of William, founder of Pennsylvania.)

This Penn (of Penn Ink) was one Donald Penn, a drifter, a ne'er do well, a ramblin' man who emigrated to America in 1762 to escape the life of hard work he surely faced back home in his mother country, Holland.

Donald had heard stories about America from his friends. No doubt these were grossly exaggerated stories—for Donald's friends were a mischievous, slothful lot, forever sniffing out schemes that would keep them from having to earn an honest, sweat-covered guilder. But these stories filled Donald with hope and he knew that the only way he could afford a life of ease and riches was to move to America.

The death of Donald's father was a fortunate surprise.

A sudden heart attack left Donald in sole possession of his father's estate, which included a substantial savings account and seven thousand acres of valuable real estate. It should be noted that the sudden death was fortunate for had there been a last will and testament, Donald, who hadn't spoken to his father in five years, would have received nothing. Donald sold the land, packed his bags and within three weeks of his father's funeral (a cheap memorial, buried in a casket made of the cheapest pine) he hopped a ship to America.

In America he quickly acquired a building at the corner of Third and Market Street in Philadelphia. The building had a small storefront where Donald decided he'd open an ink shop. The shop, however, was merely decoration. A way to meet people. Donald was not, at all, interested in building a solid career or business. He had come to America for what he had been told would be a life of pleasure. Ease. A place where the locals were brewing a concoction of revolutionary teas to fight for their God-given right to pursue happiness. A pursuit Donald believed in—God granted or not.

So, to invite the curious, he threw an inkwell and one piece of paper in his storefront window. The paper said, "We Sell Ink." And that was the total of his advertisement and signage.

The hours of operation were Monday through Thursday from 11am - 3pm. He was failing miserably, of course, but it didn't matter to Donald. His inheritance was enough to last him, he was sure, until his death. His gambling had subsided so his debts were few.

His folly now was fishing. He spent the afternoons, and every weekend, waist deep in the Delaware River. Often he'd spend weeks at a time in the river paying some local boy to attend the shop. It was never a concern that the boy knew nothing of ink for, after all, neither did Donald. He merely purchased ink, added three and a half percent to the price and sold it. No paper. No feathers. No nibs. Just ink. Black ink.

This curious conduct of business gained him the reputation of an eccentric. He enjoyed this reputation and encouraged it further by taking long strolls through the streets of Philadelphia several times a day, each time donning a different outfit; a purple satin robe and yellow stockings in the morning, a mint green, eight-sided hat and peacock feathers (a full bouquet, mind you) exploding from his coat pockets in the afternoon, and in the evening, a pair of pink knickers and a walking cane made from human bones.

And, of course, there were his parties! Late nights of dancing and drinking and laughing and fucking (that no one—hm, hm—of course attended).

Aside from the fanatically religious or the socially insecure, Donald was well liked. His peculiar behavior was a breath of fresh air. Philadelphia was so stuffy, after all. Too much like London.

As the years passed on, it was his reputation that brought customers to his shop; some curious, some wishing to join his circle of indecency, some who genuinely enjoyed his company and none leaving without a purchase. This, of course, infuriated Donald because he was getting busier and was soon forced to keep his store open five days a week, so as not to offend anyone.

To balance out the five-day workweek, Donald began the practice of closing down the ink shop for three weeks every two months. Then he'd go fishing and dream of closing the shop forever. But after a few weeks in the wild and with a belly full of trout he'd return refreshed, open the shop, throw a party and start griping about how busy he was all over again.

By the late 80's he was forced to open two new shops (further north in Pennsylvania—to keep the workload in Philadelphia to a minimum.) He hired capable gentlemen (which was not his intention at all) to run the two shops and never inquired about their success or failure. He paid them handsomely and they never bothered him with details. Just the way he liked it. And off he'd go, wading through the Delaware River, pursuing his happiness.

The years passed.

Penn Ink continued to grow (through absolutely no effort of Donald's and much to his dismay) and on July 4th, 1786 he threw an enormous party to celebrate FREEDOM. It had been his intention to close the shop forever in '86. Freedom! Perhaps he'd host a daily luncheon. Freedom! Let it ring! Freedom! And as paradoxes go—that night, while drunk and deeply into his celebration of Freedom, he met Harriet Bayles.

Harriet Bayles was the youngest and only daughter (seven brothers) of Alice and George Bayles, a small farming family from McKungie, Pa. An excellent fisher and hunter herself, Harriet snared the eye of Donald Penn, wrapped it in some old newspaper and tucked it next to her bosom. It was an ample bosom. Donny was safe and snug. The plans for closing the shop would have to be put on hold. Harriet had an agenda that involved getting away from the family farm.

Six months of silent knee-deep-in-the-river courting and they got hitched. Just like that. The newspaper said it was "a delightful ceremony, a bit odd because Mr. Penn insisted on wearing hip boots above his tuxedo, but well attended and fabulously catered."

Exactly three hours and sixteen minutes after the last couple left the reception (The McMurphy's—can they ever leave a party sober?) Harriet Bayles-Penn began her inquiry into the accounts of Penn Ink North, Penn Ink South and the home base, Penn Ink Philadelphia. She wanted all the numbers. All the books. All the details. Donald, of course, had no books, had no numbers and, least of all, any details.

"You know nothing?"

"Nothing."

"But how does the company survive."

"My dearest, Harriet, if only I knew, I'd put a stop to it, I assure you. As a matter of fact, I've been thinking of closing it down for good."

"Like hell. I'm going to do a little research."

"Please don't."

And that was that. Harriet decided she'd take control of the company and turn it into an American institution. Donny got scared. He ran away. Disappeared for six days. The police searched the riverbanks but found nothing but one of his fishing hats. He was presumed dead in two of the local papers when finally Harriet received a letter postmarked from New York City. It said:

My Dearest Harriet,

It is important for you to understand that the success of Penn Ink interests me not at all! At this point in my life I wish to fish. I wish to entertain. I wish to entertain the fish. That is all. I've enough in real estate and inheritance to take us, quite comfortably, into the next world. In the meantime, I wish to enjoy this one. Please don't make me work. As far as any children we may have—I say, let them fend for themselves. It's the land of opportunity, is it not? Please, I implore, I beseech. Try to understand that my eyes are weak, my back is soft and my mind is feeble. There seems to be no time in my schedule of fishing and entertaining for meaningless paperwork.

Forever Yours and Deliciously Rich Without Ever Having to Lift a Finger,

Donny.

Harriet sent word to New York immediately that she was not expecting him to work. She was more than happy to make all the decisions, sign all the papers.

Donny came home. Great big smile on his face.

He threw a party. And cooked some fish.

Twice Married, Twice Divorced
and Twice Acquitted of Murder

Maisey wasn't new to the courthouse and was on a first name basis with most of the personnel. She called the secretary Mrs. Furlong out of respect—she was, after all, seventy-three years old. Her ability to access the files at the courthouse so freely was due largely to the favoritism displayed her from Judge Rinehart. The judge felt sorry for Maisey. She had been through some rough times. In return, Maisey brought him a fresh pack of Red Man chewing tobacco with each visit because she knew he liked it and his wife forbade it. It was a small town, Monkey's Paw, and the little things made a difference.

The Monkey's Paw courthouse served all of the lowland area, which included the towns of Dunkleville, Burger Hollow and Joe's. The sheriff's office was located in the back of the courthouse.

The Sheriff's name was Bill Kunkle and he liked Maisey, too. But, unlike Judge Rinehart, Sheriff Bill also liked her in a romantic way and had often brought flowers to her house. Maisey wasn't interested in Sheriff Bill because he was a married man. He also didn't make enough money. She kept her mouth shut about him bringing the flowers around, though. She wasn't looking to get anyone in trouble. Just looking to get herself out of it.

Maisey was watching Monkey's Paw, town proper, fade away in her rear view mirror. Wishing it was the last time she'd see that picture. A picture of sad, sagging buildings, weathered and gray. Faded paint and rotting wood everywhere you looked. Old farmhouses going down, making room for strip malls and banks. So many goddamn banks. Ain't enough money in these parts to keep those banks filled. Bakeries closing down. Plenty of fat people to keep the bakeries open. That's why she had to get out. Nothing made sense anymore.

Maisey gripped at the steering wheel of her '69 Plymouth Valiant, rubbing hard, massaging her palms. She drove with her left foot resting on the dash. She pushed the accelerator to the floor, trying to gather steam, the energy it would take to climb to the top of Polk Mountain. She instinctively lowered her foot from the dash. The winter nights, the icy roads had always made her nervous and she felt safer with both feet on the floor. There was no ice, of course, but ever since she drifted into the bank, halfway up the hill (or halfway down depending on how you saw things) thinking she was heading over the edge, straight into the Effen River, she's lowered her foot. And it has always felt safer.

She had climbed this road, Burger Hollow Road, through two solid winters when she lived at the top of the hill with her first husband, Jack Korger. They lived in a little two-bedroom ranch number they got for twenty-two thousand dollars because it had only three windows and no heat. A cabin, really. A fixer-upper. As is. The cabin was situated on five nice acres (those acres, alone, were now worth sixty, seventy thousand dollars) of thick fury pines. A maple sprinkled here and there. In the winter, with the pine needles carpeting the ground, it was quietest place she had ever been. The sound was thick with silence, swallowed by the needle bed.

Her screams should have echoed, bouncing down the mountain and into someone's living room but instead they were sucked up and silenced by those dead pine needles.

"Kiss my ass."

The end of their property, western line, came to a point, a jutting extension of Polk Mountain, a rock ledge measuring fifteen feet in width. A natural balcony overlooking Effen and Goddfree. A stargazer's paradise. A make-out point.

Often Maisey had stared through binoculars at life on the other side of the river. It was pretty well known that Effen and Goddfree were filled with rednecks and welfares. Unless something extremely urgent brought you there, you had no business traveling through these parts. Staring through her binoculars Maisey noted that life on the other side of the river looked much the same as life on this side: depressed as all hell.

The Valiant struggled to climb the mountain. The engine screaming, whining, carrying on. The chassis shaking like a dog trying to shit a peach pit. She kept the accelerator pinched to the floor.

It was a good car. Bought it for fifty dollars when she was eighteen. There had been problems throughout the years but nothing Maisey couldn't fix herself: a break line carburetor alternator water pump timing belt. Aside from the currently missing muffler, this car was 165,345 miles young and sober. Valiant. Slant Six. Just can't beat 'em.

As she neared the top of the hill, she eased off the gas and stroked the dash. "Good girl," she said. The muffler quit bawling enough for her to make out the song on the radio. She didn't like it. She turned it off.

She came to the curve at the top of the hill, bearing right, and was once again on flat land. She eased off the gas, a cool thirty miles per hour.

She rolled slowly past the "Dead End" sign that marked the beginning of her old driveway. The "For Sale" sign was now weathered and torn. No one wanted to live in a house with bullet holes in the bathroom. And they never did fixer-up. She was still as-was.

The house was starting to droop on all four corners. Getting round in its old age. The cheap wooden shutters Jack had installed to keep out the winter winds were faded now, hanging by a few screws. The hinges failed. The trees she decorated on the holidays, by the porch, were now towering over the house, their peaks swaying a good ten feet above the roof. It looked all spooky and Halloween.

Maisey threw the car into park, rolled down the window and reached for a cigarette. She always liked the smell up here on the mountain, away from the cars and shops in the Monkey's Paw shopping district. The Lowlands had become so crowded in the past ten years with New York and New Jersey folk looking for their paradise in the country. None of them finding it. Up here it still smelled like her childhood: leaves and dirt. Earth. The living, breathing earth.

She lit her cigarette and killed the engine. The silence and hum of her body relaxed her. She leaned her head back against the headrest.

It was easy to see how she got conned. This was a great place to start a family. And she wanted all that when she first got married. She was eighteen then, just out of high school. He was thirty-two, an age difference her father would never have supported save for the fact that Jack Korger was the pastor at the Lutheran Church in Dunkleville.

Maisey sucked on her cigarette, thinking how she once teased him, sucking on a cigarette (eighteen, teasing, sucking, cigarette), licking her lips, rubbing his thigh, exhaling her smoke as she blew softly into his ear. She thought about how he'd moan, a playful moan, saying, "You're killing me," but he'd refuse to touch her. Wouldn't go near her.

The Lord. What's right. Respect. You're so young. All sorts of bullshit.

Wouldn't go near her. Scoot way over by the driver's side door. Would have put his feet up and pushed her back had she been more aggressive. But she let it go. Didn't know how she felt anyway (eighteen, unsure, sucking, cigarette).

Finally, she demanded. She said, "You have to. I need to know before we're married." She was thinking that a lifetime was a long time not to know whether or not it was going to work at bedtime. And he gave in. He had to. Asked for forgiveness afterward. Asked for fucking forgiveness for fucking. Said the Lord would understand, but no one else would, so keep your mouth shut about this. And she did. Who was she going tell? Besides, it had embarrassed her, confused her, to see him repent a blowjob, repent a fuck.

And the joke of it? How gentle he was. How careful. How he took his time, easing her tension, the butterflies, the nausea from nervousness. How everything was slow and sweet. Apple butter. Kissed her from top to toe. Teeth only lightly touching her skin. All lips and tongue. The fucking joke of it, really. Biggest lie he ever told. And he told plenty.

"Shit luck," Maisey said, exhaling out the window.

Their honeymoon was a short weekend getaway to the Poconos, a honeymoon town sixty miles north of Monkey's Paw. Tennis courts, horseback, swimming pools, champagne glass shaped hot tubs designed for knowing. And in a twelve-foot champagne tower hot tub, she experienced his violence for the first time. She'd almost drowned in the bubbling water. He held her under while he came. She threw him off of her, gasping, water flooding her eyes. Was she crying? Screaming? Don't cry, baby. Don't scream. It was an accident. I wasn't prepared for the excitement it would cause: Your fat. Beautiful. Pussy.

And the accidents kept happening until she was afraid of knowing him. He liked that she was afraid. He'd rape her and beat her and pinch her and grab her and he didn't care about her fear, he liked it. He encouraged it. He'd sneak up on her. She'd scream. He'd laugh. He encouraged it. He'd tie her down. He wanted it. And he'd beat her with a belt, a yardstick, a piece of rope, a wet towel, his own cock, whatever. He wanted it. And she was afraid.

She held back the tears. She didn't scream. Because that's what he wanted. But then he'd beat her harder, saying, "If I'd wanted something like that, some quiet little church mouse, I'd've married one of them old fucking maids always kissing my ass down at the church." He wanted, "a whore, a spicy fuck, with a fat, beautiful pussy."

She tried to tell her father but he was afraid of the Lord, of men of the cloth, of the church, of anything negative coming out of Maisey's mouth about the church and he was sick and tired of her whining, complaining and sinning.

"Shame!" he would holler and she didn't even know what in the hell he meant by that.

She'd try easing into a conversation with her old man by saying things like, "He smacked me the other night because his dinner was cold." And her father, without looking at her, it was difficult looking at her swollen bruised eyes, her scabbing lips, her father would say, "Try harder, Maisey. He's a good man. You gotta try."

And this is when she missed her brothers the most. But they were gone. They left because they never wanted to have to deal with those kinds of stories again. They never wanted to be called upon when. They had seen enough of the bruises, the beatings. They'd heard enough of the screams.

And she did try to make it work. She attended church. She listened carefully. She read the books he wanted her to read (sex books, fetish books, pornography). And she read them out loud to him, because that's what he had wanted. Then he'd rape her. She cooked the dinners and did the laundry and never looked him in the eye when they were in public, unless he asked her a question. And still a beating. And still a raping.

She was trying to grow, to mature. She'd say, "Why? Let's talk." Then he'd cry and ask Jesus and her for forgiveness. She always gave but hoped Jesus wouldn't. And who the fuck was Jesus anyway? Or even God? She had her doubts. Jesus wasn't getting beaten. God wasn't getting raped. And if he really was a jealous God, a vengeful God— why didn't he kill this motherfucking brute?

She flicked her cigarette out the window and got out of the car. She walked to the front bay window they had installed and scratched away three years of dirt. The house was bare except for the broken couch. She didn't want the couch. So much semen and blood spent into the cushions of that couch. Wanted to burn it. But just walked away. Only taking a box of her mother's old jewelry. Didn't come back for two years. Then, out of curiosity, and a pining for the smell and silence, she went back. She liked how it felt, so she did it when she needed to be reminded of why she was spending so many hours at the courthouse. Needed to be reminded why she never wanted to be in love again. It always worked.

She walked around to the back of the house where she had planted an azalea bush. It was a twig when she got it. She had to put an orange flag in the ground to keep from running over it with the lawnmower. Now it was fat. Bigger than the Valiant.

She looked at the bathroom window. Bullet blasted through it, still torn wide open. The blood now colored in with the dirt, no telling the difference. Ashes to ashes.

She looked away from the window, trying to follow a path of where the bullet might have traveled. She grabbed the bullet shell she wore as a necklace and gave it a tug, pulling the clasp to the back of her neck. Making a wish. The bullet shell was a souvenir from the trial. She wore it to remind herself. She wore it as a warning to other men who might be thinking about hurting her, hitting her, talking dirty to her, grabbing her ass. The men in Monkey's Paw kept their distance.

Maisey walked back to the Valiant and jumped up on the hood. She laid down and looked up past the tops of the trees. It was a cloudless day.

She remembered Judge Rinehart's voice.

"He was a son-of-a-bitch and an animal. I have never, in my twenty-eight years on this bench, heard such a disgusting story of cruelty and injustice. Miss Maisey Day Walker, and I assume you will be taking back your name, you have done this community a great service. That scoundrel was not human, not by any standards I know, and next to castration, death was what he deserved. This case is closed." And the courtroom agreed and cheered at the decision. Jack Korger had no family to speak of so there was no major commotion against the judge's remarks.

The prosecuting attorney was not angered because he knew, once discovering the literature, the sex toys and torture devices, after seeing the pictures of Maisey tied up and brutalized, tortured, he knew that his dead client deserved what he got. He fought hard because that was his job. But he, too, congratulated Maisey. And on her way out of the courtroom, he handed her the shell.

"Trophy?"

"Sure," she said, and then smiled for the first time in two years.

Maisey's father, ashamed for not listening to his daughter's pleas for help, for not protecting her from that filth, that blasphemer, begged her for forgiveness.

"There's no such thing," Maisey said.

Maisey lifted her hand to block the sun.

It was so easy to pull the trigger. Never a second thought. He didn't drink so there was no chance of killing him when he was drunk. But the routine was always the same. He'd come home, eat, shower and if he was in the mood, rape her. Three years. Beaten and bitten. Three years of screaming. This is why he wanted to live so high up in the mountains. The pine needles soaking up her screams. Three years before she finally realized that her screams weren't getting past the driveway.

And on the final day he pushed her face down and spread her legs, tying each ankle to the bedpost. Then he took out his loaded .44 caliber Magnum and used it for a show. He liked the threat it posed. He'd use it on her sometimes, loaded like that, sticking it in her ass, her pussy, rubbing it over her, making her suck on the barrel. Loaded. Ass. Mouth. Pussy.

That night he mounted her and drove, drove, drove like the constant drone of an autistic hum. Sweaty-browed and eyes set far apart, looking at what? She never knew. But his eyes staring and rolling around like a live current is being sent through his body. Drove and drove like that into the night, away from the family and friends, toward something, something. Drove and drove so far away, up on that mountain, getting farther as he drove and drove. Oblivious to his surroundings. Drove and drove until he neared orgasm. Then he'd climb off her (this was always the routine) and go into the bathroom where he could finish himself off by hand. Rub himself down while muttering apologies to God. Finish himself off because it was cleaner that way. Finish himself off because the last thing he wanted was children. Propped on the toilet, her scent fresh on his fingers, he'd rub himself down and scream at her, "Devil's cunt! Devil's whore!" Scream it at her and it would drift out the window and snuggle up with her screams in the thick pine carpet of their front lawn. Stars shining down just like on sleeping children.

The final night there wasn't a second thought. She untied her ankles, took the .44 from the nightstand and walked to the bathroom door and listened. She listened to the constant driving of his hand. Driving, driving, quicker like a boy late for supper. And she waited. She wanted to catch him right before he came, wanted to send him to hell on the verge of an orgasm.

And then his screaming stopped and she knew that it was time. She kicked open the door. His face was red, eyes closed, he was leaning on the back of the toilet, hand driving, driving, mouth slightly open, eyes squinting harder now and she squeezed, squeezed the trigger one time. And the bullet flew through his head. His head exploded. He slumped over and fell on the floor. It seemed long after he fell to the floor that she heard the bullet shatter the window glass. She stared at his body, limp on the floor, a puddle of urine forming at his knees. She rolled him over with her foot. No sperm. His hand still wrapped around his cock. His cock still hard. But no sperm.

She walked out of the bathroom and into the kitchen. She poured herself a glass of milk. Strawberry milk.

She thought about calling someone. But who? So few friends.

She finished her milk and went back into the bathroom. The blood was starting to flow toward the door. She closed it, packing a towel at the crack to stop the blood from running into the hallway, ruining the carpet.

Tonight she'd get some sleep. She needed it. She'd call the sheriff in the morning. Right now she just needed to get some sleep. So she slept.

Maisey let her hand fall back to the car. Three years he'd stolen from her. Made her hard and pessimistic. Afraid to touch her own body. Three years. If he were here, right now, she'd kill him again. She wasn't so young anymore. She wasn't so young.

Two weeks after the trial ended Maisey got an official divorce because her father didn't want Maisey to be in any way associated, spiritually, with the soul of Reverend Jack Korger.

Maisey sat up on her car. It was getting late. The cloudless sky was pink now. Little boy blue, go blow your horn. The sun was sneaking down behind the mountain, taking with it anything left of a summer breeze. A chill caught her by surprise. Maybe a storm was on the way. She thought about taking her sweaters out of storage when she got home.

Maisey got back into the Valiant and started it up. She tapped the dashboard with affection. She rolled up the window, leaving just a crack and lit another cigarette. She backed out of the driveway and headed down the hill.

"Hey mom, if you're listening, I've got something I want to ask you."

She had gotten into the habit of talking to her mother when she was seven. There were times when she believed she could hear her mother's voice.

"Did any man really love you? I'm starting to think you left me some shitty gene, some bad blood. Maybe it's your fault. Maybe not, maybe it's me, but tell me, did any man ever really love you?"

And just as Maisey had suspected, her mother said, "No."

Miracles and Parables
of our Maudlin Doppelgangers
Weezal and Marty

*Translated out of the original Drunken Tongue
and into a language we can all understand*

The earth spun and now it was dark. Marty and Weezal were asleep on
the couch. Their glasses of Jim Beam lay empty, spilled on the floor. It
was 9:00 p.m. and they had been sleeping for six hours.

Darlene looked up toward the trailer court and could see the twinkle
of front porch lights and the constant blue flicker of the trailer park's
twenty-seven television sets. She wondered how Marty was doing and
she wondered if he was drunk yet.

The trailer court was watching TV, relaxing after dinner. The neigh-
borhood kids were trying to squeeze a few more hours out of the day by
kicking a soccer ball around. But it was over. Everybody knew it. The

kid who owned the ball picked it up and walked away. Nobody pro-
tested. It was a dark night, new moon, and it was quiet.

A lot of tired fathers and husbands were beginning to snore. A lot of
tired mothers and housewives were folding the laundry. A lot of dull
conversations were being spoken. "Tomorrow you have to pay the
phone bill. Ask them if we can send fifty now and fifty next week."
"Honey, could you take a look at the refrigerator, it's leaking again."
"You better talk to that son of yours. I caught him snooping through
your dirty magazines. I wish you wouldn't keep that trash in the
house."

Weezal and Marty were sweating, deep in a drunken sleep. The smell
of Marty's meatballs was thick. Italian dreams.

A storm was approaching, preceded by a humid calm that spooked
the pets. The three lonely wind chimes in the trailer court were silent.
Occasionally, you could hear the rumble of distant thunder. Occasionally, you could see a silver sliver of lightning. The storm was moving
fast.

It would only be minutes before the tin roofs would be beating med-
itative rhythms, hypnotizing, soothing everyone to sleep.

Big Bass Lake and its accompanying creek were lying naked, legs
spread wide, waiting for the storm. Fuck me. Flood me.

It came. And when it came, it came hard. Big Bass Lake let out a
great big moan.

Marty and Weezal felt the first blow of thunder like a punch in the
face. Four wide open eyes staring into the darkness. Neither set of lips
spoke a word.

Another crack of thunder, another bolt of lightning and the show
began.

In the Big Tent

Ladies and gentlemen, boys and girls and all of those with a soft heart and a curious mind: Welcome to the greatest show on earth!

You'll be dazed and amazed! Dazzled and frazzled! Filled with lust and disgust! As we take you on a terrifying journey through the shit holes of the modern world!

Step right up, get your tickets. Don't dilly. Don't dally. Don't delay. This is one night and one night only! Get your tickets and keep the line moving.

Take a look around you, folks, we've got freak shows and acrobats. We've got dangerous feats of impossibility, tough man competitions and animals that do tricks that will amaze. We got clowns. We got chills and thrills. So step right up and let the Circus begin!

Tough Man Competition

The storm lingered over the trailer court. A long cool August shower. The repetitive patter of rain drops on Weezal's tin roof turning into a continuous battery of assaults. Neither Weezal nor Marty could remember the sounds of the earlier calm—a memory fading, like all memories do, with the liquor. The trailer lights were off. Weezal and Marty were trying to catch glimpses of each other's expressions with every flash of lightning.

Weezal thought that Marty looked scared. He had the eyes of a dog that'd been beat too much, caught shitting on the carpet. He wondered if Marty looked that way when Darlene threatened to take Rose and leave him. He tried to imagine Marty doing anything but farming and he couldn't. The next flicker of lightning caught Marty with his lips puckered, as if he was about to give someone a kiss.

Marty hated the thunder. It reminded him of how small he was, how afraid. And how fat. He was staring out the window watching Polk

Mountain light up with each spray of electricity. He thought about how small and round the mountain looked. A brother in this lonely world. He puckered his lips trying to pick what felt like a piece of Pop-Tart from his teeth.

"I'm the toughest man in this trailer," Weezal thought.

Weezal had the face of a fighter. A broad flat nose and red puffy eyes. But he had only ever been in two fights. One fight justified, one a mistake. The mistake costing him a night in the can. But he looked like he fought often and that was enough to keep most tough guys at bay.

"I could kick your ass," Weezal said in a moment of alcoholic bravado.

"That's only because I'm in love," Marty faintly replied.

And Weezal knew he was right. But, still, that made him the toughest man in the trailer and he took a moment to bask in the glory. The next bolt of lightning caught Weezal with his arms raised in triumph, fists pumping violently above his head. A glorious symphony blasting in his head.

"Don't be so proud of yourself," Marty said.

In the darkness Weezal lowered his hands. He leaned forward and grabbed the bottle of Beam. He took a big swallow and gave the bottle a shake. There wasn't much left. He didn't feel like getting up for another just yet. He waited for a flash then passed the bottle to Marty.

Marty continued to think about how weak he had become over the years. He remembered challenging his friends to wrestling matches when he was younger. Testing his masculinity. His reflexes. His strength. And these games had always made him feel like a man. Bloody noses and beer. Sweat and dirt. But now he had grown weak. Even farming, which at one time made him feel strong, had become nothing more than a chore. An escape. From Darlene. From Rose. From responsibility. "Escape isn't particularly masculine," he thought, "unless it's a matter of life and death." But his escapes of late—the farming, the running to Weezal's, the drinking—they required nothing more than sitting on his ass.

His fading masculinity bothered Marty. It bothered him more than ruining the sunflower fields for Darlene. It particularly bothered him when he was drunk. Marty took a swig from the bottle and handed it back to Weezal. Weezal couldn't see it so Marty waited, arm stretched, for another bolt of lightning.

Weezal grabbed the bottle. He looked at his hand wrapped around the label. It looked like his father's hand. Weezal's father was a fighter. He'd smack some guy around, spend the night in jail and then usually get a pat on the back from Sheriff Fendenbacher on his way out the door. Weezal's father only smacked around guys who needed to be smacked around and it made the Sheriff's job easier. His father laid brick, built and rebuilt cars, mowed lawns, fixed dishwashers—just about anything that needed to be done, his father did it. And that included smacking around people who needed to be smacked around.

Weezal wasn't nearly as strong as his father but had inherited his reputation as a fighter. A loose cannon. It ran in the blood, some would say. He thanked his father for the hand-me-down once and his father smacked him in the mouth. Broke his lip. He wanted his son to earn the reputation for himself. So he smacked him good and hard and when Weezal didn't shed a tear his father said, "You're welcome." Weezal took another sip, saving the last swallow for Marty. He had inherited his father's drinking etiquette as well.

The rain on the roof had returned to a gentle pitter-patter of spit and the lightning so infrequent Weezal had to tap Marty on the shoulder with the bottle. Marty snatched it and took the last swallow.

He was angry. He didn't know why. But he held onto the emotion because it made him feel strong. He held onto it and got angrier.

"You're nothing but a drunk," Marty said, challenging the toughest man in the trailer.

"And you're a coward," Weezal said, accepting the challenge.

"You're rotting from the inside out. I can smell you starting to spoil."

"And that stink is going to haunt you, Marty. That stink, known as me, is going to stick to your clothes like the inks they were dyed with. You're going to be thinking about me tomorrow, when you leave. But me? I'll forget about you before you get to the end of my driveway. And why? Because you mean nothing to me, Marty. And that's the truth."

"You lonely bastard. I feel sorry for you."

"Don't give up so easily."

"At least my existence has meaning. I have a family," Marty said, weakly, not really believing what he said. Weezal, seeing his guard down, attacked ferociously.

"That which you call 'a family', I call a mistake. And under your breath, while you're gardening, or while you're taking a shit, you call it a mistake, too. Don't you, Marty? Your life. Your family. Big Mistakes. You married a girl you didn't love."

"I love her now," Marty said, knees buckling.

"But you didn't love her when you married her and now it's too late," and Weezal landed hard into Marty's chest. Marty felt it cave in. He excused himself and went into the bathroom. Weezal Peterson, no doubt about it, was the toughest man in the trailer. He went to the refrigerator and grabbed another bottle of Jim Beam. He could hear Marty puking in the bathroom. He walked down the hall and knocked on the door.

"You okay?"

"Fine."

He heard Marty wretch again.

Weezal broke the seal on the new bottle of Beam and took a long drink. A victory drink. He raised the bottle and toasted the imaginary crowd.

Jim Beam was his courage
  his family
  his lover
  his coach
Jim Beam was his doctor
  his dentist
  his cover
  his reproach
Jim Beam was his faith
  his body
  his mind
Jim Beam was his answer
  his confessor
  his kind

Amazing Feats of Impossibility

Marty came out of the bathroom and returned to the couch. He grabbed the whiskey bottle and took a swig. He swirled the juice around, rinsing away the remaining bits of puke. Then he swallowed.

"If Our Ink is Good Enough for Freedom, It Ought to be Good Enough for You"

It came to her in the bathtub. She was running a sponge down her long, muscular leg and:

"Boom! just like that, I thought of it. Jumped right out of the tub, went running through the house, naked, got a pencil and wrote it down. I spent two hours reading that slogan, over and over again. Just standing there naked, for two hours. If it's good enough for freedom..."

Penn Ink, under the strong and forceful hand (and wonderfully wet and naked body) of Harriet Bayles-Penn, was a growing business.

Three Years, Three Months and Three Days Ago,

down to the hour was when she killed her second husband. She was twenty-one. She was sitting, parked in her Valiant waiting for him to walk out of his girlfriend's house. She didn't intend to kill him, just confront him. And she was curious. Wanted to catch a glimpse of his lover. See her breast size. Color of her hair.

Maisey thought about that woman, that lover, as she drove down Muddy Valley Road through Monkey's Paw, on her way to Joe's and the supermarket. Oh, the look of embarrassment on that woman's face when she spotted Maisey in the car across the street. She thought about that pink cotton bathrobe. That red hair.

And after she had run over her second husband with the '69 Valiant, killing him, she remembers this:

That pink robe shaking in pain. That red hair dipping in the blood. How terrified. The Lover. Waiting for the sheriff to arrive. She knew it wasn't going to be easy to explain and she was hoping the lover, who had seen everything, would tell the truth.

The truth was:

Maisey was trying to drive away. And Nick (car salesman—a job he said would kill him) chased her down. Begging her to understand. How he jumped in front of the car and how she had no time to react. Nick, up and over the hood, slamming into the windshield, cracking it. His neck snapping, just so. A fluke, really. Only a small gash on his head, but it bled like a faucet. She wasn't even driving that fast.

"More shit luck." She lit another cigarette.

The lover initially claimed that Maisey had deliberately run Nick down. She was all red hair and pink bathrobe hysterical. The lover loved Nick. She was a single woman working at a sewing factory in Dunkleville. Nick was the sweetest person she'd ever met.

Maisey thought Nick weak. He was always decent enough but he had no backbone. No balls. His smile was a mask, hiding his fear. Fear of offending, fear of an opinion, fear of making false moves. He was passionless. And Maisey fell in love with that simpleton because after the first marriage, simple seemed better. It wasn't.

But she never wanted to kill him. She wanted to face him. Smile at him. Wink and wave. That was all she wanted to do. He may have been a shitty husband but he was harmless. She was going to file for a divorce that following Monday.

"And you can have him," she said sitting in her car, watching their shadows through the bedroom window. Shadows created by flickering lights. The work of candles. Nick had never made love to her with candles. Still, she never wanted to kill him.

Eventually the lover admitted the whole run-down was an accident. Nick's fault. She apologized for overreacting and asked Maisey if she could attend the funeral. The lover and Nick had been lovers since long before he married Maisey. "Sure," Maisey said, "someone should be there."

The lover and Nick's father were the only two who attended the funeral. The sheriff rounded up a few men from the prison to carry the casket. They were happy to get outdoors. Father O'Something held a brief service. Maisey stayed home and washed her clothes.

Maisey went to the gravesite once and there was a fresh bucket of flowers near the headstone. Maisey figured the lover had left them.

That lover loved Nick.

And as she drove past the lover's house she saw that same pink bathrobe drying on the clothesline. Maybe it had been drying there since the lover washed the bloodstains from its sleeves. That poor woman. The lover. How she tried to put his head back where it belonged. How she held it together like his neck hadn't snapped. Like he might just start talking to her, whispering loving words. Gentle words.

How we never get what we want.

The marriage lasted only two months so as far as Maisey was concerned, it never really counted.

Maisey looked down at her gas gauge. She pulled into the Texaco. Full service island. Clyde Parker, a guy she'd gone to high school with, came out of the garage. He looked cute in his overalls. Covered in grease.

"Maisey fucking Walker! How the hell are you?"

Clyde had been away. "Tried California, too freakin' weird. Moved to New Orleans then headed up to Alaska. Eventually crawled my sorry ass back to these parts. Now I'm thinking about Florida. I hate the cold."

"I'm good. Just give me five." Clyde put the nozzle into the tank.

"Still driving this beast?"

"Still runs."

"These things never die. So what have you been up to? Heard some stories." He said with a smile.

"Don't believe everything you read, Clyde."

"Aw, shit, I don't read. People talk."

"The stories are true. Two husbands. Two deaths. I'm twenty-four and I feel like I'm ninety."

"I hear that."

The gas handle clicked and he removed it, putting it back in the pump. Maisey handed him a five spot.

"This one's on me," he said. "Listen, you know where I am, so stop by some time. We'll go get a beer after work or something."

"Sure," said Maisey. "And thanks for the gas."

"No sweat."

Maisey pulled back out onto the highway and Clyde watched her drive away as he wiped his hands on the grease rag.

"Goddamn beautiful," he groaned, watching her Valiant putter down the road.

Maisey picked up the speed, thinking about Clyde. Sexy. He looked like a man now. Probably a decent man, too. Make somebody a good husband. But she wasn't interested in a good husband anymore. She had been through enough shit. Her mind was made up. The next fellow she got serious with would have to have money. Lots of money. Enough money to make her happy. Clyde Parker and his greasy overalls didn't have enough money for her. But he sure looked cute.

Maisey pulled into the A&P parking lot. She made a quick note of the things she needed: shampoo, soap, tampons, butter, milk and eggs. Maybe a can of olives. She loved olives. Pitted black olives. She could eat three or four cans in one sitting.

The supermarket wasn't crowded and she was able to get in and out without a hassle. She headed for home. Her father's home. She did the cooking and he paid the rent. He knew what Maisey was up to down at the courthouse and he didn't like it. Everybody knew what she was up to. It was a small town and everybody knew everything. Maisey didn't care if he or anybody else liked what she was doing.

Maisey pulled into her father's driveway. It was a long circular driveway laid with stone. The house was a torn up farmhouse that her father had been "fixing-up" for ten years. It had no siding and the windows were replaced with plywood that had to be removed to get sunlight. Fresh air.

Her father owned seventy-five acres that included a twelve-acre pond and a horse barn. No more horses. Not since Crooked Knee. The barn would eventually become the guesthouse.

The mailbox was stuffed with bills.

She took the groceries from the car and headed for the side door. They didn't keep it locked. No one in Monkey's Paw locked their doors.

Maisey dropped the groceries on the table and ran into the bathroom. A few moments later:

"Damn it!"

She'd forgotten to bring the tampons.

Animal Tricks and Taming

The trailer was dark but Marty's eyes had adjusted. He could see shadows. Weezal wasn't in the living room. Marty could smell something. It was a familiar smell but he couldn't place it. His mind had slowed with the alcohol and he was having trouble connecting smells and sounds with their origins. He'd smell a Pop-Tart and think it was a cigarette. He'd taste the whiskey and think he was drinking cider. But this smell was strong and he thought for a moment, then he remembered what it was.

"I smell gas," he said.

"I'm cooking the steaks," Weezal called back from the kitchen.

But the smell of gas was strong, too strong.

"Is that stove working right? You smell that?"

"I haven't smelled anything in six years," Weezal said, trying to remember what was the last thing he did remember smelling. It was perfume. A perfume he had smelled on Darlene. She had come to bring Marty a change of clothes. (A particularly long stay of Marty's—depressed as all get-up because he had forgotten to attend his father's funeral). The scent was so delicious and Darlene had looked so clean and fresh that day Weezal immediately got a hard-on. Darlene was wearing a tight, faded white T-shirt. Her hair pulled back into a French braid. Weezal tried to steal glimpses of her breasts when she wasn't looking. He had been successful enough to recall the image for use while masturbating. He could no longer remember what Darlene's breasts looked like. But he remembered the smell and the faded T-shirt and he remembered wanting to touch her and put his lips upon her chest, to try to taste the perfume. To lick a nipple.

Darlene had caught him looking. She looked at Weezal, then down to her chest, then back to Weezal. Smiling.

She waited for Marty to come out of the bathroom so she could talk to him. And while she waited she looked out the window, giving Weezal privacy for his inspection. She liked the way it felt and it reminded her of the first time Marty had touched her naked body. When Marty entered the room Weezal went into the bathroom. He couldn't hear what they were talking about but hoped it wasn't him.

"Weezal, you better not light a cigarette because that gas smells pretty strong," Marty said, worried the whole trailer might blow.

This made no sense to Weezal. After all, the flames were already pouring from the burner, but Weezal figured he would take Marty's advice anyway. Besides, he was the kind of hungry a cigarette only makes worse. So he just stood, listening to the grease crackle, waiting for it to get hot enough for the steaks. He pushed his finger into the center of one of the pieces of meat and licked his lips. He lifted the meat and put it against his face, inhaling deeply, searching for a trace of perfume, imagining the steak to be Darlene's breast. He was drunk. No perfume. No nipple. No nothing. Nothing except a bloody, wet meat stain on his face. He put it back down on the counter.

Marty was sitting on the couch. He never thought of Darlene's breasts as meat. He heard the grease sizzle. It sounded like the rain on the trailer's tin roof. Marty took another swallow. He pinched his belly.

"I did love her," he said softly, to himself, "I just love her more, now." But he never loved her the way he had loved Daisy. Never held her hand the way he had held Daisy's hand on a snowy night at Big State University.

Daisy was a strong jawed girl with big ideas. And she was passionate. And she was beautiful. Not plain like Darlene. Her beauty was sharp. A beauty that jumped out and screamed obscenities at you. Shoulder length blond hair—frizzy in the humidity, dirty in the winter. Sometimes Marty would forget what he was saying to her, mid-sentence, because her violet eyes would spring forward and bite him on the neck. He gave himself to Daisy in ways he had never given himself to Darlene. He let Daisy put her fingers up his ass.

Daisy didn't love Marty. No one would ever love Marty the way Darlene loved him. Daisy loved his company. She loved his sense of humor. But Daisy never loved Marty. Darlene was the only person who ever loved him, and he rejected her. Rejected her until he had no choice but to accept that Daisy was never going to love him.

He used to sing to Daisy:

Daisy, Daisy, give me your answer do,
for I'm half crazy
all for the love of you.
It won't be a stylish marriage,
we can't afford a carriage.
But you'll look sweet, upon the seat
of a bicycle built for two.

"Come again," Weezal called from the kitchen, having only heard a whisper of the song. Marty sang it again. He sang it the way he used to sing it to Daisy, on one knee and from the bottom of his belly.

"That's a nice song," Weezal said, "I could fall in love to a song like that. As a matter of fact, if I ever fall in love I'm going it to sing it to my lover."

"What if her name's not Daisy?" Marty asked.

"That would be my shit luck, wouldn't it?"

Weezal threw the steaks into the frying pan. They screamed. Smoke poured. He flicked on the fan. The steaks smelled good. A little salt, a little pepper. A little Jim Beam. Nothing fancy.

"I'm leaving farming, Weezal."

"Take another drink."

Marty didn't want another drink but he took one anyway.

"I mean it," he said and thought about his pet, Rose. A pet he was trying like hell to tame. She was obedient.

"How's Rose?" Weezal asked, still thinking about Darlene's breasts.

He wanted to stand outside their window at night and watch her prepare for bed, the way he used to watch his sister/lover. He wanted to watch Darlene take off her summer dress, remove her bra and put up her hair. He wanted her to know that he was watching and he wanted her to like it. Then she would take her time. She would caress herself, rubbing away the day's tension while Weezal was rubbing away his own.

"Rose is good. No longer wets the bed. Learning new tricks all the time. I suppose someday I'll have a relationship with her."

"I'd like to meet her."

"Maybe when you're sober and I'm not depressed."

Weezal turned the steaks over. Both he and Marty liked them rare because that's how often they had them.

"Darlene says I should invite you over for dinner but I always figure you'd be too uncomfortable."

"That'd be real nice."

"Really? You'd like that? Well, I'll be damned. Maybe in a couple of weeks then."

"Sure," Weezal said. He didn't want to touch them, just look at them. He hoped Darlene would wear something a bit revealing when he went to dinner. Not so much so that he couldn't eat. Just a bit. A tit. A nipple here. A nipple there.

"The steaks are done."

A couple of dirty plates in the sink. He cleaned them with a dish towel. He put a fork in the steak and the juice leaked out, making another hiss in the frying pan.

"Smells great, but you should really get that gas checked. You probably have a leak."

Weezal cut into his steak and watched the blood run to the rim of the plate. He picked a chunk up with his knife. It was a good steak, no fat. He hadn't realized how hungry he was. He took another chunk, this one bigger. Marty was eating his steak with his fingers. He wiped the grease off on his pants.

"What will you do?"

"When?"

"When you quit farming."

"Maybe go back to college, pick up those three credits and get my degree. So damn close for so many years. Seems silly not to finish it out. I don't know, maybe I'll teach."

"Will you stay at the house? Still live in Goddfree?"

"I don't know. Darlene keeps talking about New Mexico like it's some sort of paradise."

"Why New Mexico?"

"Some book she read or something. But she won't want to leave. She hates to be far away from her family. She's a dreamer but reality never lives up to her dreams."

When they first got married, they lived in New York for six months. Darlene got homesick and it was soon back to the farm. Darlene had been born and reared in Goddfree and relied on her family for support, both emotional and financial. And when they moved back from New York and were flat broke it was that financial support that got them on their feet. That's when Marty started to love Darlene. It was a decision. To love her. He simply weighed the options.

Weezal took a gulp of Jim Beam, washing down his last piece of meat. He handed the bottle to Marty who did the same. The rain was beginning to pick up and the thunder and lightning were once again making their way over the mountain. They listened to the music.

"I can't wait until Rose can talk," Marty said, breaking the silence.

"Why's that?"

"So I'll have something to say to her. It's overwhelming to think that for the next however many years I'm just going to be teaching her new tricks. As if I'm some kind of expert. Ain't that the fucking joke of it?" Marty laughed, "Ain't that the fucking joke?"

They both took another swallow.

"I am drunk!"

"Me, too"

And they listened to the rain.

Elephant Shit

Weezal spilled the Jim Beam bottle and Marty spilled the grease. A sock soaked up the Jim Beam. A sock soaked up the grease. They left the socks, wet and stinky, sitting in clumps on the floor. Clumps that, in their drunken state, resembled giant piles of elephant shit.

Bigger, Better

By 1823 rumors of a "secret ingredient" lacing the inkwells at Penn Ink had begun to cause much excitement in the market place. Whether or not there really was a secret ingredient was unimportant. The public liked secret ingredients. The marketing sperm was jet skiing its way into the capitalist cunt and Penn Ink was erecting a twelve-story phallus in downtown Philadelphia in preparation for the All-American fuck.

During her reign as Chairman (and in between the birth of her seven sons), Harriet single-handedly turned Penn Ink into America's leading seller of, well, pens and inks. Donald continued to fish.

Their oldest son, Eugene, was groomed to take over the family business and after four years at Such and Such Prestigious and Expensive University, Eugene moved in and Harriet moved out. She joined Donny on the Delaware.

And the business prospered.

And Eugene begot George.

And the business prospered.

And George begot Edward.

And the business prospered.

And Edward begot Thomas.

In 1954, a scientific dissection of the curious Penn Ink ink began. And guess what folks? There weren't no secret ingredient! Thomas Penn (then commander-in-chief) simply sent out a press release stating that "the secret ingredient in Penn ink wasn't something that could be detected with science. The secret ingredient was, in fact, the company's commitment to produce the finest ink in the world." A public cheered. A stock quote jumped.

And Thomas begot Jacob.

And the business prospered.

And Jacob begot Millard.

And the fun began.

By the mid-1970s Penn Ink had established itself in the top five of the Fortune 500.

Jacob Penn loved to work and his love of work was infectious. The company was proud of its many charitable contributions to various ecological, educational and, of course, artistic organizations. Penn Ink was earning a fine American reputation. An example other major corporations could follow. Elsewhere, for instance:

"Why, Jimmy, if Penn Ink can do it, by golly, so can we. Let's give back some of those profits to the people."

"But who are the people, Mr. So-and-So?"

"Well, Jimmy, the people are the people who buy our products, of course. They're the hardworking folks who make this country strong. The men and women who get up everyday and punch the clock, mend the gasket, milk the gosh-dang cow!"

"You mean the Poor People, Mr. So-and-So?"

"Now, Jimmy—we call them hardworking. We call them the face of the nation. We call them (sometimes) the silent majority. But never— NEVER—do we call them poor. Understand? Poor is a state of mind, Jimmy. This is an important lesson, so listen carefully: If you start calling them poor, they think they have less. Tell them that they are the backbone of what made this country great, tell them they are why this country is one of the greatest, most prosperous countries in the world, tell them that if they just keep working harder, well, then, they too can have whatever they want. And those motherfuckers will keep zinging away. Day after day, night after night, midnight shift after midnight shift. Tell them they are poor and they will spit in your face. After all, what is poor, Jimmy? I repeat—it's a state of mind."

"I think being poor is having no money to get the things you need, Mr. So-and-So, and I don't think the state of one's mind has much to do with that. I think being poor means that people don't get the opportunity, no matter how hard they work, to get ahead financially. I grew up poor, sir, and I have to tell you, when you are poor there is no time to get ahead. There isn't a spare moment for you to make a better situation for yourself. Every moment is about survival—making the rent, getting some food, doctor bills, electric bills, phone bills, etcetera, etcetera, on and on ad infinitum."

"You are cute, Jimmy. You are taking "poor" at face value. I don't think I need to tell you that's not the American way. Are you a Communist, Jimmy?"

"What?"

"Are you anti-American?"

"Not at all I was just trying to point out..."

"You're fired, Jimmy. Good day."

"But..."

"I said good day. Oh, and, good luck."

Yes, Penn Ink was a fine example. And Jacob Penn was leading the way. A way that he hoped was heading straight into political office. Jacob's fatal heart attack in 1976 abruptly brought his political aspirations to a halt.

Penn Ink mourned.

After two weeks of memorials and tributes and legal mumbo jumbo-ing, the 22-year-old Millard Winston Penn took over the throne. Skeptics and cynics in the market place, fearing that Millard was too inexperienced, forced Penn Ink's stock to drop a few points.

Those who knew Millard were less concerned. They knew that he had studied hard and that his father had groomed him well. And, most importantly, Penn Ink had a Board of Directors that consisted of some of the finest business and scientific minds in America. They surely wouldn't let the company stumble.

Millard took his seat and the company continued on its steady, conservative path. Within two months stock value returned to normal and Penn Ink was again enjoying its position as the biggest, richest ink manufacturer in the world.

Millard Penn was someone you wanted to hate. His handsome, masculine face, perfect smile, curly blond hair (shoulder length, ponytailed during business hours), pale blue eyes (yes, they lingered on), and infectious, youthful behavior (frequenting dance clubs, racing stock cars), made him an international celebrity. The fucker was a privileged rock star. And he knew it. He wore the latest fashions, partied with Van Halen, was invited by President Carter for tea and a game of nine-ball (Carter won), owned houses in seven countries, spoke three languages (French, German, English), was a member of the Screen Actors Guild and he had a notoriously large dick.

Articles appeared in GQ: "Big Nib, Big Nub." Vogue: "Millard's Pen. My Inkwell." Hawaiian Daily: "The Biggest Kahuna."

Worse for those who wanted to hate him for his money: he was a very charming, smart, charitable and compassionate man. Most of the time.

But something was always slightly amiss. Unfortunate Coincidences. Like the time a feisty young actress, hurt by the break-up of their relationship, gave a scathing interview. Called Millard a liar and a cheat. The actress was found dead a week later. Just another Hollywood drug overdose. Millard was not suspected. He cried at the funeral.

And some argue that it was the celebrity status that eventually got the best of him. Others thought it was the drugs. Really, though, it was loneliness. Millard Penn had no friends. The parties, the nightclubs, the cocaine, the starlets—it was all beginning to sour.

By 1983, at the age of twenty-nine, Millard had become a recluse. He had an apartment built on the roof of the Penn Ink building and there he stayed. He'd attend meetings when necessary. He watched a lot of television. He was depressed.

And it was in the middle of a long hot bath (just like his great-great-great-etcetera grandmother) when it hit him. A secret ingredient. Why not? Bring back the damn secret ingredient. Only this time (he was feeling particularly frisky) there really will be a secret ingredient. The thought aroused him. He played with himself. He came.

Six and a half million dollars and one year later Penn Ink produced an ink like the world had never seen.

In November of 1984 Penn Ink unveiled its newest product. The secret ingredient was back. Sales were up. And for the first time in two years Millard seemed out of his funk. He cut his hair. He grew a thin mustache. He rejoined the public and was again making headlines.

Soon after the unveiling of its new product a group identified only as DDS began tearing away at the chemical make-up of Penn ink, trying to expose the secret ingredient. No one knew exactly who DDS was or what it stood for (though it was known to be a German based organization) or why they were trying to figure out the hidden mysteries behind the ink. Certain Wall Street analysts thought the DDS were wasting their time, suspecting that Penn Ink's secret ingredient was, yet again, a whimsical sentiment. Just a silly (but smart) advertising campaign. They, of course, were wrong.

Millard had a suspicion that his oldest rival, BIC, was behind the DDS. This, however, was never proven.

But why all the fuss over ink? Because Penn Ink had developed an ink so creamy in texture, so rich in color, so fun to write with, people were calling in sick to work so they could stay home and write letters. No shit. These inks gave a spark of life to every page they squirted on. And they had an odor. An odor that mystified. That goose bumped. Each pen had a distinct and, well, funky smell. Sometimes the smell would make you feel nostalgic—like, maybe running a seventy-yard touchdown on a broken play. Other times it would soothe, maybe make you want a cigarette. Sometimes you couldn't write fast enough, you'd break out in a sweat.

The U.S. Postal Service claimed a 72% increase in revenues a month after this new ink was introduced. Penn Ink had created a freaking letter writing frenzy.

Tunnel of Love

Weezal believed in love once and it let him down.

Marty married a girl that he didn't love and maybe that was the secret. Love that hurts in muscles that you've never exercised or stretched, that kind of love might be impossible, unbearable. But a passionless love, a love decided on out of discontent, maybe that could last for years.

Weezal wanted to think about love. He wanted to think about sex. But he didn't want to participate. Sex never lived up to his expectations. He got more pleasure from watching sex. Hearing sex. Naked bodies from a distance. All tangled up in sweat and skin.

He had stumbled into his first sexual experience. It felt like this: thoughts crashing down like books on a weak bookshelf. He laid on top of the girl with images swirling around his brain of street lights and wet roads and swimming holes and high school cafeteria laughter. His childhood. A knee scrape. A belly laugh. Sarah. Everything except the woman who was lying with him. He forced an erection. The hard was on. Embarrassed when the woman reached down between his asshole and scrotum, scratching small circles with her long nails. The hard was off. He buried his head in the pillow, breathing heavily into her ear. She pushed him away. She felt inadequate. Unattractive. Unwanted. She was none of that. He couldn't escape his thoughts. He tried letting himself just feel but there was no feeling. Rubbing at a wet melon. Smaller and smaller. Roll away. And sleep. Wet roads. Street lights. A knee scrape.

While thinking about Darlene's breasts he got an erection that could last for hours. But lying naked in the middle of a sexual act, he went soft.

"Marty, do you find sex pleasurable?"

"Extremely."

"Where do you feel it?"

"All over." And people had been saying that to Weezal for years.

"I could fuck Darlene. She has beautiful breasts. I could fuck her breasts," Weezal said.

"I won't be offended because I know you're drunk. But please don't say things like that." Marty was hurt. He didn't want to picture Darlene with Weezal, and now here he was, picturing it.

"I'm sorry."

Marty had often fantasized about Darlene taking another man's cock in her mouth. But it wasn't real. It was Darlene. But it was fantasy. It was another man's cock. But it was fantasy. She was an actress in a movie. A stranger. And it excited him. But it was fantasy. His fantasy.

"Why you gotta go and say something like that? Now I have to think about it."

"Sorry."

"I don't think she'd fuck you anyway."

"Why not?"

"She doesn't love you."

That was okay with Weezal. He could see that Marty was tense—taking one, then another, then a third shot of whiskey. He handed the bottle to Weezal and reached into his shirt pocket, pulling out a pack of Pall-Malls. He struck his match, lighting up the trailer. He let the match burn, staring at Weezal, who was staring back at him.

"Did you really mean that or are you just drunk," Marty asked.

"Just drunk." Weezal put out his hand and Marty shook it. Then Marty lit his cigarette and blew out the match.

It had been years since Marty and Darlene had slept together. Once he tried masturbating while she was in bed with him and she got angry and slept on the couch for a week.

"Weezal, does your dick work?"

"How do you mean?"

"I mean does it work? Does it stand at attention? Does it salute a pretty lady? Does it please her? Does it do things she says have never been done to her before? Does it make her cry? You know, does it work?"

"No," said Weezal. "No one ever cried."

"And how do you live with that?"

"I like to watch."

"Other people," Marty asked, smiling.

"Yeah. Sometimes I watch the Wilson's."

"Used to be, when I made love to Darlene, I'd watch, too. I'd separate from myself, like I was standing outside our window, and watch. She has such long legs. They'd wrap around my back a mile or so."

Weezal didn't want to watch Marty and Darlene making love. He wanted to see Darlene alone.

"And, sometimes..." Marty continued but then finished by taking another drink. Finally: "I'm not that fat, am I?"

"No, just a little chunky."

"It's a healthy chunky, though, right?"

"Yeah."

"She can kiss my ass."

Marty reached into his pocket and pulled out his wedding ring. He put it in his mouth, like a pill, took a swig of whiskey and swallowed the ring.

"I have a headache," he said.

The rain started harder now. It was late. Weezal and Marty sat in silence, listening to the storm. Marty's eyes fluttered. He was tired. Weezal gave him a shove and he fell over. Passed out. Weezal took a blanket from the back of a chair and put it over him.

"Hey, Marty"

"Mm?"

"If I find a letter tomorrow—and you've seen me the whole time, I haven't written anything—if I find a letter tomorrow will you believe me that I'm not writing these damn things?"

"Mm."

Weezal pulled the blanket up underneath Marty's chin. He kissed him on the cheek. Family.

Forgive Me Father,
For I Have Sinned Four Times

"It's my daughter. Then I drink. Drink away the electric bill. The phone bill. Drink away the car insurance on occasion. Then I lie. I say it's an oversight. The check is on the way. Then I drink some more. I'll send the money. Eventually. It's my daughter. Then I drink.

"She's a good hearted girl, my Lord. Dealt a sour hand. She tries, you know, my Lord, but may not be the most faithful. I set an example as best I can. It's my daughter. She scares me. Why is it so hard to understand her? Why does she ignore me? Then I drink. I must learn to trust in you, oh God, and I must learn to be your servant. I'm listening.

"I have taken your name in vain. Jesus Christ where is the butter. Goddamn it stop calling my house. Disturbing my peace. I am a sinner and forgive me.

"It's my daughter, my Lord. She comes home late. She never tells me where she's going or where she's been. But I can smell it on her—the sin. I can smell the desperation and the pain. She hides things from me, Lord. She talks quietly on the phone so that I will not hear her conversations. She receives mail and burns the envelopes before I can see what was sent. She doesn't trust me and she does nothing to hide the fact that she despises me. I set an example as best I can. I walk softly and remain humble. But she refuses me and she refuses you. And I drink.

"She is a child of sin, but it was my sin, father, and she should not be punished for it. My passionate ways are long behind me. I have been righteous. Except for the drink. I have swayed but have remained faithful. These days I sway less. I still drink. But you knew that I would. I am praying to you, oh Lord, now for my sweet Mary, because she is my child. Sin as she might, she is my daughter and I love her. I know you love her, too, oh Lord, so please forgive her of her trespasses.

"I have been lead by the very Devil himself to the bottle. Have mercy on me. I am but a humble servant and your hand I kiss a thousand times. Would that I never drink again. Have mercy on me. I beg for forgiveness for my daughter and me. Have mercy on us. Show her the light. Let her breathe the breath of Jesus Christ, Amen."

Gripping the rosary beads, he began, one bead at a time, the Hail Mary. He would continue this for three hours if necessary. It was time for Maisey to be saved.

"Dad?"

Maisey walked into the living room and saw him kneeling in front of the candles and a statue of the Virgin Mary, head bowed and hands clasped around the rosary. He was mumbling.

"Oh, Christ," she muttered and walked back into the kitchen. She unloaded the groceries and put them away. She left the box of microwaveable macaroni and cheese on the table. Her father liked macaroni and cheese and when she cooked something he liked, he talked less. Tonight she wasn't in the mood to hear a word.

Maisey finished setting the table as the macaroni swirled in the microwave. She made a fresh pot of coffee. She smoked a cigarette while trying to make as much noise as possible to drown out her father's mumbling.

"Dinner's ready."

Her father walked into the kitchen and kissed her on the top of her head.

"Any luck?"

"No. Just the usual run-of-the-mill dirt bags and scam artists. Nothing I want to get involved with."

"I really do wish you'd…"

"Dad, please, not tonight. I'm tired and hungry. Let's just eat."

And they did. In silence, just the way Maisey liked it.

Who was this man, her father? All this pleasure in guilt. All this pleasure in pain and poverty. Why? She never understood any of it.

"Did mom leave you because you were so weak?"

She didn't mean it to sound so cruel. Mr. Walker gently placed his fork at the side of his plate and finished chewing. His eyes tearing.

"I suppose that had something to do with it. But I'm getting stronger, Maisey. I'm getting stronger with the Lord. Your mother wouldn't recognize me now."

"I suppose not."

"It's not good to think of humility as a weakness."

"Humility, my ass. You're afraid."

"Only of the Lord."

"Sucker."

Mr. Walker swallowed some coffee, "Your mother and I are still married. I want you to know that."

"Some marriage. Sixteen years is a long time to go without seeing your wife."

"God sees her and he shows me."

"Well I wish the son-of-a-bitch would show me."

Mr. Walker slammed his coffee mug down on the table.

"Don't you ever and I mean ever call our Lord and Savior a son-of-a-bitch again! Do you understand? Not in my house! He died for our sins! You are an ungrateful little shit!"

He was shaking. He didn't know what to do. He went into the living room. He grabbed the rosary and started to pray. Maisey followed him.

"You bastard, don't you run away from me! Don't start that bullshit praying and crying and begging! I can't fucking stand it! I can't stand to hear it! Goddamn it, look at me when I'm talking to you!"

But Mr. Walker kept his head bowed, squeezing harder at the rosary. Maisey went back into the kitchen and stripped the table. She threw the plates into the sink, breaking one. She didn't care. She went upstairs into her room and slammed the door. She could hear her father mumbling through the ventilation slats in the floor. She turned the stereo on. She turned it up.

She needed to get out of this house. She needed a husband with money. And come Monday morning she was going back into that courthouse, pulling every fucking file and wasn't leaving until she had at least two or three prospects. All these low life schemers awarded big insurance claims. There had to be a couple of honest Joe's in that pile. She wanted some of that money.

Fuck her mother. Just like her mother fucked her.

Why couldn't the old man just come out and say the truth? Why couldn't he just say your mother was a whore? That she'd run off with a truck driver. She wanted to travel. And before the truck driver there were plenty of other truck drivers and schoolboys and on and on.

She was tired of her father's excuses.

"Excuses," she said out loud looking at her wind chime hanging in the window. A present from her second husband, Nick.

"Your old lady's a whore," to her dresser full of make-up.

"Your father's weak," to the teenage swimming trophies on her shelf.

"You're tired," she whispered to the gun shell hanging around her neck.

"Just a bunch of fucking excuses."

And just then she felt like talking to Clyde. Did he really want to have a beer? Maybe she'd let him kiss her and hold her. She thought she might like to feel his big hands rubbing down the back of her neck. Over her ass. Between her legs. Taking his time in the middle. Where it counts. Those big fingers.

She reached over to her nightstand and grabbed the phone. She called information and got the number. She dialed. She felt foolish and flustered. She blushed when he said:

"It's me and I'm bored so let's go do something before I get the notion to raise Cain my own self."

"Maybe what I have in mind, you don't want to do."

"Oh, shit. Who is this? Patty?" Clyde stammered.

"Patty who?"

"Come on. Who is this?"

"A lonely young lady wanting to go somewhere and have a good time. Interested?"

"Sold. But is that lonely and pretty or just lonely? And how young is young?

"Very pretty and very young. But legal."

"Who is this? Sally?" Clyde was confused.

"Sally who? My, my, so many women to choose from? If you have any balls you'll meet me at the Foxxxy Lady in an hour."

"Like hell I will. Who is this?"

"See you soon." And she hung up the phone hoping that he'd show. She was pretty sure he would.

Maisey sprung off her bed.

"You little slut. What are you going to wear?"

She gave a quick smell under her arms while contemplating a shower. She didn't need one.

Standing in front of a mirror.

"You still look pretty good."

Admiring the curves that still curved where a lady wanted curves, she picked up the brush from her dresser and started pulling it through her hair, which became brighter and more golden with each stroke. She went into her closet and rummaged through her dresses. Several seemed right but the summer had fully turned and they were too light for this October air. She finally landed on a pair of blue jeans and a tight fitting black shirt that highlighted her shapely breasts. Her father hated this shirt. She pulled on a pair of black work boots that had been her mother's long ago. They were comfortable.

One more check in the mirror. A smile.

She gave herself a quick spray of some dime store perfume. Lilac. She grabbed her leather jacket (Christmas present from Air Force brother) and headed down the stairs. She saw her father kneeling in the living room.

"I'm going out," she said, "I'll be back late and probably a little drunk. So don't wait up for me."

And when she said this his hands moved a little faster along the rosary. She saw this and smiled.

The back door opened. The back door closed.

Local Boy Punches Teacher, Lands Good Job

Jedidiah Peterson was an example employee for Penn Ink and had worked at the Hazleton factory since he was seventeen years old. A high school dropout done good.

He quit high school in late May of his Senior year after a scuffle with an English teacher. (Jed found his sister in her room packing. She had been crying. Her face bruised and swollen. "Something terrible, Jed. I can't talk about it." "Who?" "Mr. Vanderwolfe. After volleyball practice. Something terrible.")

Mr. Vanderwolfe was the girls' volleyball coach as well as Anywhere High School's Shakespeare teacher. The next morning Jed's sister was gone. Has been gone ever since. Jedidiah confronted Vanderwolfe. The old fart called his sister a liar. Jedidiah punched him in the nose. One punch. Hard. Broke it. Head slamming against a chair on the way down, splitting his skull. He survived.

The incident was reported on page fourteen of the local newspaper. Jedidiah was, of course, expelled, but other young students came forward. It seemed that Vanderwolfe had been preying on his students for years. No evidence, of course, and the school board, in an effort to save face and pretend that they would never let a treacherous lech teach on their watch, kept Vanderwolfe employed and backed him whole-heartedly, stating that, "rumors generated by infatuated teenagers should NOT be the criteria by which good educators be judged."

Point taken. BUT. What about all those other girls who came forward? And this gem by one of the board members after listening to the testimony of a woman who had been molested by this scumbag: "The past is the past. If you had something to say, why didn't you say it then?"

I don't know—because I was fifteen? Lost? Confused? Hungry?

Meeting adjourned.

The local paper didn't take the same conservative, hush-hush view that the school board took. They made Jedidiah out to be some sort of local hero. A boy standing up for his sister in the face of, at the very least sexual harassment from a teacher, and quite possibly rape which, of course, they couldn't say (nothing was proven) but about which they could hint. And hint they did.

Jedidiah also grabbed the attention of Millard Penn. And when Jedidiah applied for a janitorial position at the Hazleton Penn Ink plant, Millard interviewed him personally. Shaking his hand. A boy standing up for his family. He promised Jedidiah that he would not only give him the job, but that he would help him get his GED and personally groom him for better positions at Penn Ink.

Millard set Jedidiah up with a basement apartment in Hazleton at the home of Mr. and Mrs. Kashener, a nice, hard-working couple, both with twenty-years of dedicated service to Penn Ink.

And three times a week (after work) and every weekend, Jedidiah was tutored. Dr. John C. Smills, scholar and poet, (and former Super-intendent of Wrastleass High School, Home of the Wrastleass Rattlers) was chosen for the job. Dr. Smills was well versed in German and ex-perimental literature, so these became the primary focus of Jedidiah's studies.

Upon his retirement from secondary education, Dr. Smills began writ-ing a book (by hand and on long rolls of perfumed paper), a book that would explain, quite thoroughly, The Universe. All of it. A book, like so many, that never got finished.

Various chapters of the book appeared regularly in the Wrastleass Weekly, sandwiched between the wedding announcements and "Bertha's Coffee Klatch." And on a weekly basis the Universe was exposed. All of it.

When Jedidiah arrived for his first lesson, he found a note posted on Dr. Smills' door. It said, "Don't Rap On The Door! I'm downstairs. Working. Just come in and holler. I'll hear ya!"

Their first lesson began immediately (Dr. Smills teaching German vocabulary, the entire lesson spoken in French) and ended exactly three hours later, with an abrupt, "That's all for today, take this assignment list and I'll see you on Wednesday."

Jedidiah's head was in a spin. Dr. Smills seemed pleased for no apparent reason and told the boy, "We are on a search, you and I, for a better understanding of mankind. I hope you're not afraid."

"No, sir," was all Jed could think to say. He went home and got to work.

After a week in Hazleton, Jed called his parents and told them he was learning a lot and making good money. He asked if they needed anything. His mother assured him they were fine and wanted to know, for sure, if Millard wasn't just some kind of pervert who liked seventeen-year-old boys. Jed assured her everything was okay. His folks were proud.

Millard's grooming of Jedidiah momentarily took his mind off the pressures of Penn Ink. He liked having the boy around. To teach. To amuse.

They'd go bowling.

They'd go to the movies.

They'd talk about women.

Jed was a breast man. "I like breasts."

Millard went for ass. "Ass, ass, ass."

But Jedidiah was proving more than a pet. He took Millard's offerings with a seriousness and commitment that impressed even the most doubtful old fogies in upper management. After only a month of studies he received his GED. He began to think about taking some Lit. courses at the nearby community college.

Jedidiah's first job at the factory was cleaning toilets but within three months he was transferred to the mailroom. The mailroom job allowed Jed to get to know everyone at the Hazleton plant. 'Tis true, with every passing week it was taking him longer to get through the mail route (perhaps conversing too long with this secretary or that) but no one seemed to mind. Everyone liked Jed. Hell, he was a likeable guy. He'd listen to your complaints. He'd listen to your ideas. And that's what gave Jed the notion to start a newsletter.

The monthly newsletter became a forum for employee complaints and ideas. Upper management responded positively to the newsletter, sharing their thoughts with the Hazleton factory workers. The popularity of the newsletter grew. The monthly became a weekly.

Jed was taken out of the mailroom and given his own little office. He worked full-time as Editor-in-Chief of what he titled, *The PIP* (Penn Ink Paper).

And through these early years at Penn Ink, Jed continued his studies with Dr. Smills. He also began to help Dr. Smills (who was having trouble walking following a minor stroke) with house and yard work.

Two years of producing *The PIP* brought Jed his final promotion (a job created specifically for him): Employee Coordinator. His primary responsibility was to keep the Philadelphia headquarters informed with what was happening in the blue-collar world of the Hazleton factory. "A liaison," he told his mother, who had never heard of such a thing.

Jed continued to produce the newsletter (with the help of an assistant —usually a college student interning at Penn Ink) and would take bi-weekly trips to the Philadelphia headquarters to meet with the executives. He stayed with Millard while in Philly and those weekends were always more play than work.

Bowling.

Movies.

Boobs.

Asses.

It was in his fifth year of study (his German pretty good, his understanding of experimental literature still a bit shaky) that Dr. Smills announced that the lessons must end.

"I'm nearing death, Jed, and I simply have to devote all of my energy to finishing this book. I'm not as chipper as I used to be and this damn Universe is turning out to be a bit more complicated than I had originally calculated."

Jed understood. And though the lessons ended, he still stopped by on a weekly basis to help with the yard work.

Six months later, Dr. Smills died. Pen in hand. Jed helped the family pack the house up and found an envelope addressed: "To Jed When I'm Dead." He opened it. He read:

"Finally figured it out. It's Dust. Ash. Blown Sky-High. Floating down and landing by chance in your hand. And that's it. Not enough to fill a book. Who would have thought, Jed, that the universe was not enough to fill a book? Fuck. Tschuss."

The Universe. Dust. Chance. Fuck. Tschuss.

It was a tough year for Jed. The death of Dr. Smills was followed by the death of his parents. Both from cancer. Both under sixty.

His mother, Sarah, had breast cancer. She was a lesbian. She was a lesbian when, in small town America, it was not ok to be a lesbian. And Jed loved her. She was not a kind woman and she was not an extraordinary woman. She was mean. But he loved her. She was tough. She was strong. And one of the most disturbing things he remembers seeing is her, post-op, tubes running this way and that, teeth out, sunken cheeks, a corpse, essentially. Kept alive by science. He wanted her dead at that moment. It would have been better than seeing this. But it broke him. It changed him. She was frail—and somehow that meant that he could also be frail. He could be soft. Once this woman started dying off, he could live.

His father had brain cancer and was dead within a week of diagnosis. Luckily, he didn't have to see the tubes and fear in his father's eyes. That would have been the end of him. He worked through it all, taking an occasional day off for funeral arrangements or burials or...

And it was hard on him. You could see it in his tired eyes and thinning hair. You could hear it in the laughter that he forced. You could smell it in his dirty clothes. Jed was depressed. And Millard knew it.

"Why don't you take a month off and travel?"

"Where to? And I don't have the money."

"Nonsense. The money is taken care of, Jed. I'll see to that. And what about Germany? Put those years of tutoring to use. Ever been to Europe?"

"I've never been out of Pennsylvania. Well, one bad trip to New York. When I was a teenager."

"I know this painter, Charles Michel—heavy drinker, gambler, filthy mouth. You'll love him. He has plenty of space in his studio in Berlin. I'm sure he'd welcome you. And I'm sure he'd show you a good time. Maybe find you a Fräulein or two. Ever felt a German tit, Jed?"

Millard said this while poking Jed in the ribs, trying to get a smile out of him.

"A month? That's a long time, Millard."

"It's a fart in the wind. Take it Jed. It'll do you good. Besides, you can do me a little favor while you're there."

"What's that?"

"I've arranged a business luncheon for you and several members of the DDS."

"The DDS?"

"You bet. Called them last week. Disguised as you. Hope your German is better than mine. I love this spy shit."

"Haven't the DDS been working on trying to figure out the secret ingredient?"

"They have. And so I thought I'd make it easy on them by revealing what it is."

"I don't get it."

"You reading anything good lately?"

"Excuse me?"

"Reading anything good?"

"Not really. Trying to read Pound but he's nuts."

"Loony."

"A little Miller. He's good. Funny."

"Filthy old fart."

"For sure."

"Fuck Pound—stick with Miller."

"Millard, why are you going to give away the secret ingredient?"

"Because if they find out what it really is, I'm screwed."

"Why's that?"

"Because it's sperm."

"Excuse me?"

"Sperm. The goddamn secret ingredient is sperm, Jed. I'm telling you this in absolute confidence, of course. No shit. This is top-secret stuff. You can see the complications that could arise if this ever gets out."

Jedidiah just stared at Millard, unsure of how to react. He scratched his chin with a pen.

"You mean, what? Like whale sperm or..."

"Jism, Jed. Spunk. 100 percent human. The secret ingredient that laces every Penn Ink ink, in every stationery store in every country that sells Penn Ink ink, is sperm."

Jed couldn't help it. He tried. He tried turning away so Millard wouldn't see him. He tried squeezing his lips together tightly. But he couldn't hold it in. He laughed.

"So you see the problem."

"I see about a thousand problems."

"That's about a million less than I see."

"Who knows about this?"

"Me, you and Dr. James. That's it."

"And you want me to waltz into some fancy business luncheon and say what? Hello Dieter, Hello Franz, guess what: it's sperm. The secret ingredient is sperm."

"Of course not. I'd be ruined. Imagine the parental commotion. The idea that every day-dreaming-staring-off-into-space-pen-sucking kid is essentially giving someone a blow-job. That could upset a few people."

"You're nuts."

"My nuts. Yes, it was my nuts that produced the first bit of magic. Then we tested other nuts. I didn't realize how easy it would be to buy sperm. Never really thought I'd have to, actually. College boys all over the globe willing to sell. Beer money, I suppose. Then we began to buy and build sperm donation centers. But who cares about that. Listen, Jed, there's some money in this for you. Good money."

"What does the sperm actually do to the ink?"

"Who the hell knows? Nothing, probably. But maybe—just maybe—there is a bit of inexplicable magic in that squirrelly little seed. Who am I to question? Sales have been through the roof."

"But if I'm not telling them the secret ingredient, what am I telling them?"

"The other ingredient: Syntac X-423. It's a synthetic chemical compound Dr. James created to dissolve the traces of sperm in the ink. It basically, from what little I understand of it, renders the sperm untraceable. Something about X canceling out Y. I'm not a science man, Jed, no interest in it. We are going to sell them the ingredients to Syntac X-423. Then whoever is working for them can begin putting this useless chemical into their ink. Their products will be essentially the same. In any event, DDS gets the credit for solving the mystery, whoever-the-fuck hired them gets their secret ingredient and we continue to produce the funky, spunky ink that's driving the world crazy. Not to mention a few bucks in our pockets—to the tune of nine million dollars split three ways, equally, betwixt you, Dr. James and myself. Because when I called them, disguised as you, nine million was your price to squeal. Understand? We'll go over the details soon. But most importantly, Jed—and I mean this—you get a much needed vacation."

"Can I think about it? I'm going to do it. I just want to get better at saying things like, *can I think about*."

"You've got three days to decide. In the meantime, here's a file that's been prepared by Dr. James and myself concerning the meeting—what to expect, what to say, details, details, details. Study it. The meeting will take place a week from Friday."

"Okay."

"Two things, Jed. One, I wouldn't ask you if I didn't think you could do it. Two, sincerely—if you don't want to get involved, tell me."

"Okay."

"Goddamn this is fun!"

And they shook hands. A long handshake. A firm handshake.

"No one, Jed," Millard said, looking hard into Jedidiah's eyes, "this is not a fucking game."

"Of course."

Send in the Clowns

Weezal lit a candle and sat in his rocking chair. Marty had fallen into a deep sleep.

Thunder clapping. Rain beating.

Shadows dancing against the walls of the trailer.

Lightning slivers.

Shadows crawling into Weezal's living room. He didn't trust them. The shadows. They looked like faces. Faces of freaks. They grew and shrunk. Exploding cigars. Pies in the face. Oversized shoes that reminded Weezal of his missing toe. Every explosion an enormous black blanket across the wall, slowly sliding over Weezal.

Clowns.

Just shadows, he reminded himself. But they multiplied. Laughing and laughing. Popping out from behind the refrigerator, from under the stove, dancing across his thighs. Fiddling the hair on the back of his neck.

The carnival music. Seashell wind chimes.

With the next explosion of thunder, the next bolt of lightning, Weezal shit his pants. The clowns circled him pointing at the puddle of piss forming at his feet. Weezal sat wide-eyed and still. The clowns moved the circle. Set it in motion. With every flash of lightning they'd appear, lurching at Weezal. Taunting him.

Weezal was grabbing hard at the wooden armrests of his rocking chair. He didn't rock. He wanted to wake Marty up but couldn't speak. One clown leaned forward and stuck his tongue down Weezal's throat, choking him. Before Weezal could turn away another clown's finger forced its way into his eyes. Weezal gripped harder at the armrests.

The rain continued to fall. The ceiling began to leak.

Weezal was the...

In this...

Crying clown...

Couldn't breathe...

In this...

One tear spilled from his left eye and crawled down his cheek where it stopped. Weezal wanted to wipe it away. But he didn't move. The tear began to burn.

Weezal closed his eyes. The clowns were gone. The rain continued but the clowns were gone. He heard another crack of thunder but it sounded far away. The storm was rolling past, taking the circus with it. The smell of his shit and urine could barely be made out through the smell of Marty's meatballs. He had never tasted Marty's meatballs.

The rain was again a soothing dribble on the tin roof. Weezal lifted his eyelids slowly, carefully. Gone.

It was dark. The candle had been blown out. Or melted down. Or just plain stolen. Gypsies. Clowns.

The muscles in his back relaxed and his grip loosened on the armrests. His knuckles were sore. The puddle of urine at his feet was soaking through his socks. He wanted to reach down and take them off but when he attempted this, he lost his balance and fell forward into the coffee table, his forehead hitting an ashtray. He slowly sat back in the chair and rocked...

Rock-a-bye Weezal,
On the hilltop.
When the wind blows,
The trailer will rock.
When the mud slides,
The trailer will fall.
And down will come Weezal,
Trailer and all.

The room started to spin so he stopped rocking. He had gotten good at controlling the swirling. His gut was turning sour. The steak felt heavy in his belly, the digested parts creeping up his gut and into his throat. With great effort he was able to force it back down. He gagged only twice. Gagging clown.

The storm was gone. Weezal stared at the walls where the clowns had been. Weezal (sad clown, gagging clown), a tear still balancing on his cheek, rose from the chair and stumbled toward the bathroom. It was time to take his make-up off.

Weezal dropped to his knees and crawled over to the toilet. He lifted the lid and rested his head on the cool porcelain. He wanted to sleep. The toilet gurgled, singing him a lullaby. He wrapped his arms around the bowl and enjoyed its cold. Its dampness. He felt an eruption on the make. He didn't fight it. He had no fight left. He kept his eyes closed and let it pour into the bowl, grunting as his guts were squeezed into something smaller and tighter than a golf ball. Weezal wanted it all out. He squeezed hard. The filth. The poison. Then he flushed. The spray from the flush misted his face and felt good.

And then he cried. He cried because he knew he would never eat one of Marty's meatballs. He cried because he would never see Darlene's breasts. He cried because this was what had become of him. This life. This circus.

Drunk again. And drunk again. Always, always drunk again.

Weezal fell asleep with his head resting on the rim, his tears dripping into the toilet. It was a sleep so welcome by his body, that the very first words of his very first dream were, "Thank you."

Somewhere in Germany

Upon his arrival, Jedidiah's German was mediocre at best but by the end of his month-long stay (with the terribly wicked sculptor, Charles Michel—Kaiser of Cunt, Earl of Alcohol, Prince of Poontang) he found himself understanding and speaking with ease.

Beer and schnitzel.

And the deal went down.

Dancing in lederhosen at the Ballhaus Mitte.

And the money was exchanged for a detailed chemical breakdown of Syntac X-423.

A piss on the Berlin Wall.

He was a millionaire. Three times a millionaire.

And beautiful Francesca. An Italian, living in Berlin. But she was otherwise engaged. To an Italian, living in Rome. The affair was sweet. And sad. Like all the good ones are.

Jedidiah flew home. A party thrown by Millard. The high hog squealing with glee.

Five More Minutes, Maisey,
Give Him Five More Minutes

It had already been an hour.

"Five more minutes. This is ridiculous," she said, blowing out smoke. And then she saw him. Still dressed in overalls but now with a fresh white T-shirt and no grease. He stood in the doorway scanning the room. He looked embarrassed. She watched him saunter up to the bar and sit on a stool, searching. She thought about waving but wanted him to find her.

The bartender brought him a beer. He was in the middle of his first swallow when he noticed her sitting in a booth under the neon Miller sign. He smiled and shook his head. He wiped his mouth and walked over to her.

"Maisey fucking Walker."

"That surprised?"

"Yeah, I am."

"Well…"

And he smiled again, swigging his beer. He wiped his mouth with the back of his hand. He looked away. He looked back. He looked all cowboy.

"Maisey fucking Walker."

"Clyde fucking Parker," she said, feeling a little awkward. Maybe there was a reason she had stopped doing this years ago. They stayed that way for a few moments, neither of them really knowing what to say. Maisey laughed, pulling her hair behind her ear.

"You better have a lot of good conversation and plenty of drinking money. I'm in a mood," she said.

"I got stories, alright, but I'm just a garage boy. We don't use the words plenty and money in the same sentence. Maybe plenty and shit. Maybe money and none. But never plenty and money."

"Well, here's some money. Now go over there and get me a drink."

Clyde did what he was told. Good cowboy.

He came back and sat in the booth. He was still a little surprised. Maisey looked good. He felt a little sloppy in his overalls. He pulled at the straps.

"Did you have other plans tonight?"

"Me? No. I was just sitting around waiting for Frank, you remember Frank Dyer, curly hair, always coming to school with army fatigues?" Maisey nodded. "I was just waiting for him to call. But then this offer from a mysterious woman came through and I couldn't pass it up."

"It's good to see you, Clyde," Maisey said, grabbing his hand. They were both painfully aware of the touch and she pulled back. Again, she pushed her hair behind an ear.

It was good to see him. Like the first sweater in autumn.

"I can't believe I'm in this place."

"It ain't so bad." Clyde said, nodding his head to someone off behind Maisey.

Maisey looked around and saw many familiar faces. Some were looking at her and talking. She knew what they were talking about. She didn't care. She never imagined she'd be coming to the Foxxxy Lady. It was a dive. Full of underage girls and tired old drunks.

"I just wanted some company, Clyde."

"Did I say anything?"

"Just to tell you."

"It's cool."

They got to talking about where they'd been and how they got there. Maisey separated the truths from the rumors about her husbands and Clyde laughed a lot, making her feel comfortable.

Maisey kept noting to herself that it felt good to be spending time with someone her own age. She had forgotten how easy that could be. Clyde was a pretty smart guy. He learned about engines in the Air Force. Engines and computers. He had only been out for a year. Got kicked out for smoking weed. Never finished the computer training.

"You wanna dance?"

"Shit, Maisey. I don't dance."

"I could teach you."

"I'm too embarrassed. You see that? It's this goddamn town. I might dance if I didn't know everybody in this place."

"What are they going to say about you sitting here with me?"

"Oh, they'll get their tongues a-waggin' about it, for sure. They'll probably say I'm nuts. That's okay. They can think I'm nuts. I don't care about that. But I don't want them thinking I can't dance. I couldn't live with that."

And another round of beers. This one on Clyde.

"You've got nice hands, Clyde."

"My father's."

And another round. This one on Maisey.

"You remember Denise and Dawn? I hear their playing in some rock and roll band in New York City. That must be something."

"It's not that far away, Clyde—you could drive in and see them."

"I hate that city. No way I'm taking my truck into that town."

"Take the bus."

"Yeah, maybe some day. You keep in touch with anybody?"

"No. It's hard with work and everything."

"I know what you mean."

"And with all the bullshit that's happened—it's not like people go out of their way to spend time with me. I don't blame them."

"Do you go out of your way to see them?"

"I called you, didn't I?"

"Indeed you did."

And another round. Clyde. And another round. Maisey.

And they kept drinking until Maisey felt like she had had enough. The barroom was packed and the music was loud. It was Friday night and one of only three places in the Lowlands to hang out. Maisey needed some air. They went out into the parking lot.

Clyde walked over to his truck and jumped in the back. Maisey followed him and they both leaned back against the cab, looking up at the stars. A Pennsylvania early autumn sky. Deep black. Spangled to the nines. Clyde saw a shooting star. He made a wish.

"Any luck," he asked.

"With what?"

"Finding a husband?" Everybody knew.

"Oh, that. Nope."

The cool breeze sent a chill through them both. Maisey moved closer to Clyde and leaned against his chest. He lifted his arm and put it around her.

She didn't want Clyde. She was sure of that. But it felt nice to be held. She let him squeeze her a few times and his hand drifted toward her breasts. She let his fingers crawl under her jacket and caress her nipple, which became hard with his touch. To be touched, and so softly. It had been a long time.

Clyde pulled his hand away and rested it on her shoulder.

Maisey pushed herself harder against his chest. She wanted him to know that it was okay (touch me, please). He responded with a push of his chest against hers. They looked at each other and smiled.

"Jesus Christ, Maisey."

"It feels good."

"Yeah," Clyde said and drifted off into a thought of Patty. "But I ain't no rich man."

"Come on, Clyde. Don't ruin this for me. I'm not thinking about that right now."

"Me either," he said, "but I am thinking about something."

"Well, don't," Maisey said and leaned up, offering Clyde her lips. He bent his head forward and they kissed. They pulled away and Clyde put his arm down alongside of Maisey's and began to caress her hand. She lifted her head again. Another kiss. She let his tongue find its way into her mouth and she gripped it with her lips. He tasted like beer. And smelled like Old Spice. She laughed.

"What?"

"You're delicious," Maisey said.

"You're a freaky chick. You know that."

"Shut up and kiss me."

Maisey reached into the side of his overalls, rubbing just above his crotch. Clyde let his legs widen. Maisey reached in further and pulled his cock up toward his belly button. She tickled the tip of it with her fingers and felt Clyde stiffen. She slowly let her fingertips trace over its length. Then two of her fingers began to trace its outline, its stiffness, pushing hard against his underwear. She gently pulled back the waistband and reached in, grabbing him firmly around his shaft. She gripped him firmly for a few moments, could feel the blood pulsing, and slowly began to stroke him.

Clyde let out a growl and pulled away. She wasn't startled. She'd had this happen before. She simply leaned back against the cab, looking at the sky. They sat in silence for a few moments, Maisey listening to Clyde's breathing.

"Sorry," he said.

"It's okay."

"It's not you. It's me. I shouldn't."

And she had heard this before, too. The guys throughout the Lowlands had become afraid of her.

Maisey looked back at the bar and stared at the cars in the parking lot. Everything was still and quiet. Lots of lonely hearts she was thinking. Ford Hearts, Chevy Hearts, Dodge Hearts. Looking for love. All these lonely hearts. Not her. Not love.

"Listen, Clyde. You don't have to say anything. I liked being with you tonight."

"You don't understand, Maisey."

"Let me finish. I wasn't planning on anything happening. I wanted to talk to someone. A familiar face. And this is nice."

"Sure. It's nice. I just. I'm drunk. It's just that," he felt like an ass, "I was supposed to be somewhere tonight."

Maisey smiled, rolled over into his arms, looked right into his eyes and said, "What's her name?"

"Patty."

"Not Patty Kleinburger?" Clyde looked away. "You and Patty?" Maisey let out a roar. Clyde started to giggle, too. He tried telling her to stop, but the words didn't come. And soon they were both laughing so hard that tears were streaming.

Nothing was really funny. It was just that Patty Kleinburger hated Maisey. Everyone knew that. One of those silly things involving homecoming queen nominations, or cheerleader tryouts or was it the prom queen debacle? Maisey couldn't remember. But somehow it seemed funny. And the laughing was infectious. Neither could stop. They were laughing so hard that they didn't hear the footsteps. But the voice cut through their laughter like a machete through the jugular:

"Clyde!"

They froze.

"Patty?"

There was an awkward silence as Patty stood, hair so high and stiff the wind couldn't budge it, staring at Clyde. Her arms crossed. Her eyes squinting mad. Tapping her foot. The whole bit. Then she looked at Maisey.

"You remember Maisey? Maisey Walker? We were..." but he couldn't finish and he didn't want to. "Shit, we were just making out," he finally said and Maisey had to bow her head to hide the laughter.

"We were just making out?" Patty screamed. "Are you out of your fucking mind? We were just making out? You suck, you know that, Clyde!"

And she ran to her GTO, jumped in and peeled out of the parking lot. Both Maisey and Clyde watched as she fishtailed onto the road, arm sticking out the window, her middle finger as high and hard as her hair.

They sat for a moment in silence and Maisey finally burst. Clyde laughed with her.

"I'm so sorry," she finally said, wiping a laugh tear.

"Hey, I fucked up. What's new? Besides, it was going to happen sooner or later."

"Being that you're a man, thus a pig, yeah I guess it was going to happen sooner or later."

"And what about you?"

"I am quite single, mister. No attachments. No hearts to break. No one to hide from." She looked to the stars. Nothing falling. "No one to wish was dead."

And she knew she probably shouldn't have said that. Clyde looked away.

"It was a joke, Clyde. Lighten up."

But he couldn't. There were just too many damn stories. He wiggled gently away from her. This hurt Maisey.

"It's late," she said.

"Yeah."

"Hey, Clyde. I mean it. It was just a joke."

"Oh, no. Nothing about that. Just thinking about Patty, that's all. I don't want to be that way. Like you said, a pig."

"Well, listen, I don't hang out much but I'd like to see you again. And that's that."

"Yeah, that's that," he said.

She leaned over and kissed him on the lips. He kissed her back.

Maisey climbed out of the truck and started to walk to her car. She was very drunk. She weaved. Clyde watched her weave. That was one sexy weave.

"Hey," he called out, "you look beautiful tonight!" She blew him a kiss and mouthed the words, "thank you." She stuck the key in her car door.

"Hey," he called out again, "drive safe and don't you dare try to run me over."

Maisey lifted her hand like she was holding a pistol and shot Clyde. He caught the bullet in his chest and fell backwards, collapsing into the bed of his truck, disappearing from her sight. She laughed and stepped into her car. She wondered if he'd pass out and end up sleeping there. She honked the horn thinking it might wake him as she pulled onto the road.

Maisey lit another cigarette and rolled down her window. The cold air felt good on her swollen barroom eyes.

"Mom," she said, "tonight I want you to crawl inside Clyde Parker's ear and make him dream about me."

And her mother said, "Now, that's mommy's little girl."

Somewhere in France and Somewhere in New York, They Were Sleeping

In France, Dijon probably, Marty snored. Sunflowers standing twelve and fourteen feet tall. Miles to the left. Miles to the right. Tall green stalks with yellow dials the size of Cadillac tires. Young lovers walking hand in hand. No one was angry yet. No one was jealous or bitter.

There was a bottle of red wine. And, yes, there was bread. The sky was blue and only a few thin wisps of clouds were lazily floating by. There was a crow. Then there were two crows. But they flew away. There weren't any children, yet. There weren't any ultimatums.

Of course the cafes and the pastries.

Nothing was ruined. Nothing at all.

This is the most important fact: that whenever this is in France, nothing had been ruined yet.

Marty didn't love her. But they both agreed he would learn to.

In New York:

The streets were now empty because even though they say New York never sleeps, it does, at 5:30 in the morning. It's only for an hour, but the entire city is asleep. And they were walking around looking to buy a pack of cigarettes. So they walk up to this deli that calls itself "24 Hour Deli" and there's a "Sorry, We're Closed" sign hanging on the door. Finally, they find a place that's open but when they walk up to the counter the owner is fast asleep. He's chained to the register. But that's silly. Because even the thieves are asleep at this hour.

And she misses her home. She misses her mother and father. She misses Thanksgiving and Christmas. She misses everything that used to be simple in her life. Back home, she says, they would never even want a pack of cigarettes at 5:30 in the morning. Back home they would have been asleep by now.

So he starts thinking that maybe he can't learn to love her. Stop. Have faith. Too many times he had begun things and quit. He wasn't going to let that happen with her.

It was exactly 5:46 am when they started packing their bags. He wasn't concerned about the security deposit on their apartment. It was only a couple hundred dollars. He just wanted to get her home, where she wanted to be. They tried to sneak out of New York before it woke up. You can't sneak out of New York. It sticks to your skin. In between your teeth.

At least he'd have stories for the future, he thought. And that was the last time he ever thought about the future. Because it depressed the hell out of him. Thinking about the future.

Back in France, Paris probably:

Weezal snorted.

There were only skinny men wearing black berets and sporting narrow mustaches. Poodle shit lined the sidewalks. There was cheese that smelled worse than his father's feet. He noticed a French woman riding a bike with a skirt. A blue skirt. A blue bike. With a basket and baguette. He peeked at her panties. Blue. She didn't notice him.

He had never been to a museum. His world was all velvet Elvis and shopping mall landscapes. Deer Drinking from a Lake. Sunset in The Valley. Paintings never moved him. Sometimes a photograph would grab his attention but never a painting. He preferred a good book. And in this France, where he'd never been, he could still read.

He couldn't speak French. Never thought he'd need to. France was just a dream. But he liked the way Marty's farm looked during the sunflower years and if he could go somewhere and see miles of that, he wouldn't mind.

In his New York:

Where he'd been once, he bought a hooker. She was a baby, maybe fifteen, and was only wearing a dirty negligee on a brisk December morning. She grabbed his crotch and asked if he wanted a date. He was with friends. He couldn't remember who they were. He said no. His friends paid for it and before he could protest she had him unzipped and swallowed. He leaned against a building. It was on 25th Street and Ninth Avenue. He remembered that because he stared at the street sign while she did her job. She did a good job. She was a professional and there was a difference. He told her that and she said he was sweet. He wanted to buy her flowers but couldn't find anyplace that was selling them. It was 5:30 in the morning.

He didn't feel ashamed as he was told he would. He liked it. He wanted more. He wanted her name and number but she said she couldn't do that and asked if he was a cop. He thought that was a funny question and said no. She took the money from his friends and got into car that had stopped on the corner. She never even looked back at him.

His friends were laughing, yelling things like, "fucking whore!" and "scum bag!" He just wanted to sneak away and get out of New York. You can't sneak out of New York. It sticks to your crotch.

Again in France, Paris most likely:

Marty rolled over.

They made love outside. They'd seen a French movie, once, where a couple made love outside in a park and wanted to try it. They wanted to be French.

He was surprised that Darlene would do it. It was in a dark empty circular park. It resembled a coliseum made to feed Christians to lions. And it was a struggle. A struggle to get his penis through his fly, a struggle for her to get her underwear around her ankle, set her skirt to hide their bodies, as they sat on the bench. A struggle to mount him and find a comfortable place for her knees. A struggle every time they heard a noise and would stop and peer around, looking for voyeurs or cops. But they did it. It wasn't romantic. It wasn't sexy. It was awkward and clumsy and embarrassing. But they did it. They had a story for the future.

She left her underwear underneath the bench where they had made love. She did this because she had seen a pair of underwear under another park bench earlier and thought it was a custom. She wanted to be as French as possible. They were only going to be there for a month.

He smiled thinking about someone finding the underwear. He wanted to leave a picture of Darlene and himself so that the person who found the underwear could better imagine the goings-on. But he didn't have a picture. Just another memory that would haunt him. He knew this before he even zipped up his pants. He knew it would be their last adventure. He really didn't love her. She knew he'd learn to.

So they go to New York:

And they never made love outside in New York. They rarely held each other's hands. All she did was take the subway to Times Square to buy the Goddfree Record, her hometown paper. She didn't want to know what was happening in New York.

Marty liked New York. But he couldn't stay there with her. He thought, "Someday, she will no longer love you, and then how will you feel?"

"Relieved," he said out loud, stepping off the bus.

"Me too," she said, "it's nice to be back home."

France, one last time, Paris:

Weezal's Paris wasn't real. It was what he imagined all European cities looked like: Berlin. It was the only place he had ever been in Europe. And the only difference between that city and

New York:

Was that in New York, people spoke English and in Paris they spoke, what sounded like, German.

In Goddfree:

Both were still asleep. Marty was snoring louder than Weezal was grunting. But both were into it. Deeply.

Burger vs. Vanderwolfe

1988. Anywhere, Pennsylvania. A rape case.

A schoolgirl's pair of pink and white undies. They were your basic pink and white undies, no high-cut, no lace, no skinny strap riding up that hypothetical seventeen-year-old crack of ass. Just pink with white trim. One hundred percent cotton. No rips. No tears. And, most importantly—no cum stains.

But this ordinary pair of pink and white panties was about to change Millard Penn's life forever.

Unbeknownst to Millard, Dr. James (the genius behind Penn Ink's other secret ingredient, Syntac X-423) had been moonlighting. Imagine everyone's surprise, including Dr. James' when he was summonsed to appear before the Anywhere Court to testify in what had become the most popular case in the nation: Burger vs. Vanderwolfe.

The case was making tabloid headlines because the girl, Diane Burger, was a seventeen-year-old beauty. An American wet dream.

And she wasn't afraid of the press. She'd talk to anyone who'd listen (well, anyone who'd pay to listen—she was trying to get enough money together to pay for her education at Stanford University where she had recently been accepted. Six interviews later, her education was paid for. Now she was working on a new house for her parents).

She had an Ivy League tongue and a Playboy Bunny figure. Her rural Pennsylvania Dutch accent coupled with a slight lisp (Oh! that innocent lisp, that quirky accent!) helped to make her America's sweetheart.

Movie deals were sure to follow. A Sports Illustrated offer to appear in the swimsuit issue. (In a pink and white bikini fashioned after her underwear. In bad taste. She turned it down.)

The alleged rapist was Willem Vanderwolfe, a balding middle-aged, high school English teacher—always sweating and hiding his devilishly beady eyes behind a dark pair of Ray-Ban sunglasses.

America couldn't trust him. No way, no how. He was the pedophile nightmare dancing in every father's sleep. Those long, strong fingers. That sharp wit. Those hip Salvation Army suits. Those Shakespeare quotes. A dangerous man.

The arguments were familiar:

She was wearing provocative clothing during a particular volleyball practice. (Mr. Vanderwolfe was the girls volleyball coach, Diane Burger the team's star player. The uniform she was wearing was a school issued skintight short short. Yes, she had taken the liberty that day of tying the shirt in a small knot around her midriff, exposing her navel. It was hot.)

Diane came from a very poor family and that same week her father lost his job and as fate would have it (and it always does in families like this) his car broke down on the way to the unemployment office. She needed a ride home and Vanderwolfe, the big bad Vander-wolf, was more than willing to help.

In the car (his big red muscle car) their stories differ.

Her story starts with him pulling off Millhouse Road. A pull-off used by local teenagers for making out and smoking dope. She was scared. She didn't know what to think as he slowly slipped it out of his pants. Just unzipped and slipped. Then he began to grease his...

"Well, you know, his..."

"Please, Miss Burger, you can say it."

"Okay, his peter."

"Peter, Miss Burger?"

"Penis. He greased his penis with something, well, something like Vaseline. But it came in a tube."

It embarrassed her to see it. It was the first she'd seen so close.

"You know, I'd seen pictures, of course, but never a real, live one."

Right there. Shiny and wet and growing.

"He was stroking it." The jury gasped.

And then he attacked. She didn't struggle. She was scared.

"He's my teacher." And the jury gasped again.

His story was different. He drove her home. He pulled over on the side of the road because she was crying about her home life. About her father losing his job. About not being able to afford college. He realized he may be overstepping his bounds as a teacher, but:

"Dammit, the girl was in need of help. And I wasn't just her teacher. I was her coach. She needed attention, someone to hear her out. I heard her out."

"And did you touch her?"

"I may have placed my hand on her shoulder, I really don't remember. I touch a hundred students a day in school. Male and female alike."

"But this wasn't in school, was it Mr. Vanderwolfe, it was in your car. Your big red muscle car. The backseat of your big red muscle car." The jury gasped and shifted uncomfortably in their seats.

"Like I said, she needed time to gather herself before going home. She didn't want her father or mother to see her like that. Crying. Swollen eyes. It was more comfortable to sit in the backseat."

"And certainly easier to get your hands all over her"

"Objection!"

"And certainly easier to force your way inside of her."

"Objection!"

"I talked to a student. I gave an ear. That's all."

"She is just a little girl, Mr. Vanderwolfe, if anyone should be consoling her it should be her parents." And the lawyer said this while pointing a stiff and dramatic finger at the beady-eyed little monster. And the courtroom sketch artists captured it perfectly—Vanderwolfe was actually licking his chops!

But the evidence was inconclusive. There WAS a shadow of a doubt. A long noontime shadow that fell over the pair of pink and white panties. There was no semen to be found. (Even Diane said there was no condom. "Just the greasy Vaseline looking stuff.")

"So, then, ladies and gentlemen of the jury, where was the semen? Did it vanish?"

There were no pubic hairs. Not one. (She said he was shaved, bald. He said that was a lie. No one could be brought forth to say one way or the other.) There were no scratches or signs of struggle. ("He's my teacher. I trusted him." Gasp.)

And what could the jury do? Really? What could they do? They believed her. Sure. But that wasn't enough. America groaned. He was actually going to get away with this. Maybe a slap on the wrist for sitting in the backseat along a deserted road with a student. But rape? That couldn't be proven.

And Jedidiah had been following the case closely. That animal, that wolf, had struck again. He wanted to talk to his sister. Had he raped her, too? It was a long shot, but worth a try. He called Diane's lawyers. He didn't say anything too revealing. Just asked them to check the pink and white panties for traces of a chemical. He hung up the phone. No name. No number. An anonymous tip. They didn't believe him. Vanishing potion? Disappearing cream? Syntac X what? But the paperwork for Syntac X-423 appeared at the office and they went to work.

And day fifteen of the trial began like this:

"Ladies and gentlemen of the jury, the reason we can not let this case rest is because the sperm in question, the sperm that *didn't* appear on the undergarment was, and yes, this is going to sound like science fiction—the sperm was chemically covered-up!"

"OBJECTION!"

The plane ride from Philadelphia to Anywhere was brief but filled with anxiety for Dr. Wilbur James. And in that brief flight, he drank six martinis. So he was drunk and a little nauseous when he exited the plane and headed toward the gentleman holding a sign that said, "MR. JONES". It was Millard's idea to have that name used when he landed so as not to alert the press who were eagerly awaiting his arrival.

The jury and press settled into the courtroom on day sixteen while Dr. James was brought up to date.

In Philadelphia, Jedidiah Peterson was moving quickly through his office, packing his belongings into a large gym bag. He knew he'd soon be out of a job. He didn't want to be around when the fan started spitting the shit.

A team of Penn Ink trouble-shooters and attorneys arrived in Anywhere, turning their hotel room into a showroom of technology.

Jedidiah was casually walking to his car with the gym bag when he was suddenly grabbed by the arm and dragged back into the building. The shit was about to hit the fan from every possible direction.

From the East it looked something like this:

Jedidiah stepping through large oak doors that were the entrance to Millard's office and before a squeak could come from his throat Millard was on it and squeezing. Jedidiah was fighting for air. Millard let him turn blue before releasing the grasp and smacking him backhand, twice, across the mouth. Jedidiah's top lip broke and started to bleed. A tooth felt loose.

"You little motherfucker."

Jed was shaking his head as the oxygen was rushing back into his brain.

"Talk to me, Jed. Because I can't figure it out. I've been thinking and thinking and I just can't fucking figure it out. You understand my confusion?"

"Excuse me?"

"Excuse me? You know goddamn well what I am talking about and I want an explanation within the next two and a half seconds or I begin ravishing your teeth!"

"I'm sorry. But I…"

"Fuck sorry." Another backhand. A lip split wider. "I want explanations. I want you to talk to me Jed. Me, Millard. Talk to me."

Jedidiah looked out the window and could see the Philadelphia skyline glowing gold with the setting sun. He thought about how he had never imagined having the life he'd had so far. He thought he was probably going to die. Would it be a gun shot, a stabbing or an accidental suicide from the top floor of the twenty-seven story Penn Ink

Philadelphia Headquarters.

Millard punched him hard in the face. Jed almost blacked out. He fell to the floor. He felt nauseous. He started to cry. Quietly. Another tooth was loose.

Millard was now staring at the same skyline and was silent. His silence scared Jedidiah. Millard sucked on a knuckle, a bruised knuckle from the punch. He asked quietly: "Why did you do it?"

"I knew someone like her once. I thought I could help. It was just a guess. I figured if I was wrong no big deal. I didn't say much. But if I was right, then—I don't know. She reminded me of someone."

"You have to tell me something else. You absolutely have to. Make something up, I don't care, but don't tell me it's because she reminded you of someone. Don't tell me you decided to turn on me, to ruin my life, and the life of thirty-five thousand employees because some fucking little teenage cunt gave you a woody—reminding you of someone." The words spit out across the room and fingered Jed like a date rape.

"I didn't turn on you. I never said anything about you."

Millard turned to Jedidiah and offered him a hand to get him off the floor. Jedidiah accepted and Millard pulled him up. It was hard for Jedidiah to look him in the eye.

"I don't think you fully understand the magnitude of your current situation. We have two things, Jed. Money and loyalty. Of course, knowing now what Dr. James has been up to, I don't have much hope concerning his loyalty. But they're all we have, Jed. Money and loyalty. They're all we ever have. And we make decisions based on them. We gamble on them. I fucked up thinking someone as dumb and fucking ass-backward as you could understand. You better pray that Dr. James remembers how good we've been to him. For your sake, he needs to remember that."

Dr. James was going to have to do time. There seemed little doubt about that. He'd sold the Syntac (black market, of course) to help many prominent politicians and wealthy movie stars get out of sticky situations. By getting rid of the sticky. From the situation. (Needless to say, these former clients were now staining their own little undies.)

What Dr. James hadn't counted on was that when you sell a product like this, a loathsome product like this, it eventually leaks further into the underground market. It becomes available. It was now easy to get Syntac X-423 in most sex clubs in Philadelphia. Which is where Mr. Vanderwolfe purchased his.

So the buyout idea was simple. Set up an account for Dr. James worth x amount of dollars for him to retrieve upon release from prison in exchange for silence. No one had to know his dealings with Penn Ink. And even if they did, there certainly was no connection between sperm vanishing potion and ink. Just a mad scientist done bad. No big deal. The world would forget.

Millard looked at his watch and knocked on his glass desk three times. A security guard entered the room. "You better hurry Jed, your plane leaves in half an hour. I want you nearby until this thing is over. Oh, and Jed, of course you're fired."

The security guard grabbed Jed by the arm and escorted him to the door.

"You know, Jed. I hope that little whore finds out exactly who her hero is. You deserve at least a little piece of that ass for throwing away everything you had."

Jed left. The big oak doors closing with a slam.

The following day in court was when the shit flew in from the West. Looking something like this:

A long night of talk with Dr. James produced little results. He was scared. He nodded yes and yes and yes to the Penn Ink team (Operation Whiteout) and thought no and no and no. He seemed confused by Jedidiah's involvement. His mind was elsewhere.

He wanted out. He knew his only way out was to point his scientific finger at Penn Ink. He didn't want money. He wanted out of the whole business. And so he swore (under oath) that his only connection to Syntac X-423 was its use in Penn Ink products for the purpose of removing traces of sperm—their ink's secret ingredient. He had to have a reason for creating the chemical. A reason that satisfied the court. A reason that turned the attention away from his black market dealings. (And who was going to come forward about those?) He guessed (it was a professional guess) that someone from inside Penn Ink must have stolen some of the chemical. How they knew what it was or how it ever left the plant was a mystery to him. But yes, he was the creator of the chemical, "and by God, had he realized it would have been used for such preposterous purposes, he would never had created it!"

Those beady little Vanderwolfe eyes bugged-out. Those pearly whites of Diane Burger blinded the jury, judge and cameras.

The story unfolded. The chemical demonstrated. Yes, the chemical was found on the pink and white panties. Yes, the "Vaseline like tube" was found, half empty, in the glove compartment of Vanderwolfe's car. Yes, the backseat was smothered in Syntac.

And, yes, a giant turd came tumbling in from the North smacking right into the fan. Looking like this:

Heads spinning.

Stocks falling.

Papers printing.

News reeling.

And finally, a Southern shit hit. The fan grinding to a halt. One can only take so much shit, after all.

Millard demanded that his security guard retrieve Jedidiah Peterson. But Jedidiah Peterson was nowhere to be found.

And Millard suffered the first of his thirteen nervous breakdowns.

America's sweetheart was booked on a national tour that would include high school lectures on warning signs of sexual abuse by your teachers. And an Emmy Award-winning TV Movie of the Week was already in production: *Little Red Ride Home: The Diane Burger Story.*

Chapter 11

Millard Penn and Penn Ink went bust.

Sick, Sicker, Sickest

Sick because that is how she felt after she drank.

Sicker than she ever remembered being, including the time when she was four, had pneumonia and had to be put into an air quality controlled tent.

Sickest words ever spoken to her: If you loved me, you'd do it.

But right now, lying on her bed, still in her clothes, all she wanted was for the room to stop spinning. She'd close her eyes and feel her body sway. It would go up and down, tilt sideways, come back. She'd open her eyes and objects in the room would split into separate images of themselves. Then the room would take off. It would take off and she would swallow hard, trying to attach herself to some physical feeling that was real. The bed. The shoes on her feet.

She was so damn tired. She felt like she might be sick. Sick all over her bedroom carpet or maybe the pillow. But she was too damn tired to be sick. So she fell asleep. And she lay there snoring.

The Abortion Room Floor

The following weeks were a whirlwind of lawsuits, sales declines and cancelled contracts. Penn Ink employees who had learned of the secret ingredient and falling stock value became nervous about losing their jobs and started suing the company for any bump or scrape they could muster. Ninety-eight percent of suing employees were victorious.

Millard was losing funds faster than he could keep track, if he were keeping track, which he wasn't. He was trying to find that weasel, Jedidiah Peterson. He wanted him killed. But he was losing power and many of his "friends" were looking in other directions, trying to stay as far away from the Penn Ink stink as possible.

And Jedidiah was gone. Long Gone.

Millard, who paid absolutely no attention to his lawsuits, was convicted of fraud and negligence. He was sent to a low security prison. Five years. Twelve more nervous breakdowns. He lost a lot of weight.

Penn Ink was gone. Most of Millard's estate was gone. He had some money that was untouchable by the lawsuits (a couple million) and a blue Rolls Royce. That was all.

And now, ten years and seven months since his incarceration, that blue Rolls Royce was his mobile home. He shared that home with his roommate, Teenage Jesus. His one and only mission had become to find and kill Jedidiah Peterson. He was on the verge of his fourteenth nervous breakdown, in the middle of his fifth year of searching for Jed, as Teenage Jesus drove the Rolls Royce down a poorly paved road in the middle of Goddfree, Pennsylvania. The two men drove from town to town, taking odd jobs (mowing lawns, painting houses, cleaning barns, whatever) to make money for gas and food. Millard's money was still in the bank and earning interest. But in order to retrieve it, he'd have to resurface. He feared that might ruin his chances of finding Jedidiah. He wanted to surprise him. So he stayed underground. A millionaire drifter and his ex-junkie sidekick.

Right now they needed money. Goddfree looked like as good a place as any to make a buck. So when they passed two men walking on the side of the road they honked, smiled and waved to let them know they were friendly strangers. Teenage Jesus and Millard had learned that when driving through small towns it was best to make peace quickly. And waiving at the strangers on the side of the road was just a small but important step in making that peace.

The End of Book I

Marty woke with the first ray of sun, anxious to get back home. He left a note sitting on Weezal's coffee table.

Marty was sure to sign and date the note so Weezal wouldn't think some stranger had left it. He thanked Weezal for his hospitality and said that he was feeling much thinner and was heading home to finish his 364 days of farming. The note also mentioned that Weezal should drop by for some meatballs. The note concluded with a P.S. that said, "I hope I see you soon." Marty slipped out the door and headed home.

It was another hot August morning, but the storm had dragged the humidity with it somewhere farther north and farther east. Summer was coming to a close.

Weezal tried to roll over and fell on the floor. This woke him up. He looked at the bottom of the toilet. He remembered. He remembered falling asleep on the toilet but didn't remember how he got there.

He picked himself up, using the toilet as leverage. His head hurt. It wasn't a pounding headache, just a constant reminder. Weezal walked over to the sink, stepping lightly on his sore foot and looked in the mirror. His hair was matted down and little specks of vomit were sprinkled on his face and chest. He splashed some cold water on his face and reached for the towel that was hanging behind the door. He hobbled out into the kitchen. He looked over to the couch and could see that Marty was gone.

Christ! A note. Sitting on the coffee table. He picked up the letter and read it. He was relieved. It was from Marty.

Walking, yawning back into the kitchen. Wednesday morning. He spotted the three remaining bottles of Jim Beam and thought about maybe hiking into town, to the Effen State Store to pick up another case. First he'd have to have some coffee. Then he'd have to remember where he'd hid his money. He kept it in a safe spot. Always the same spot. And he always forgot where that spot was. He would spend a good portion of the morning retracing his steps since he last took money out. Eventually he'd remember and he'd pat himself on the back for having such a good hiding spot.

Weezal opened the fridge so he could make a mental list of some necessities. He wasn't expecting to find a pile of paper at the bottom of the fridge. But wouldn't you know it—a goddamn poem!

And to top it off, this motherfucker was typed!

Weezal didn't own a typewriter, he was sure, and it made him nervous.

He ran to the front door and called out Marty's name but Marty was long gone.

He went into the living room and opened the only book he hadn't buried, the dictionary. It would be hard work but he was going to read this note. Enough was enough. He was tired of this person, this thing, whatever it was, that was teasing him with these poems, these notes, these letters.

Weezal began the morning with a shot of Jim Beam as he read the first words, sounding them out very carefully:

O my l u v ...

The Sonnets

I

Oh my love, the bottle, wash over me
And disinfect my soul with your sweet sting.
Handle me like prayers in a nunnery
And songs of devotion to you, I'll sing.
Wet my chapped lips, soothe my blistered tongue,
Be still my chattering teeth with one sip.
When your journey to my soul has begun,
Setting sail to this alcoholic ship,
I'll travel the lands, unknown to all men
I'll be first mate to your Captain, at sea.
We'll battle the storms, as only we can
Sailing right through the pain and misery.
Sailing, sailing o'er the land of the brave
Weezal, Weezal you good for nothing, knave.

II

Beer is too bitter, the wine is too sweet
Therefore Jim Beam is my poison of choice.
Drink it with fish or the reddest of meats
Or when you're alone and want to rejoice.
A glass with some Coke, or straight up with ice
Is a perfect way to start the new day.
No rot is more appropriately priced,
Or goes down in such a glorious way.
Songs have been written and stories been told
About this drink that can wash away pain.
"Careful", they say, "it will make you look old,"
Like skin that's been sitting out in the rain.
Drink it in swallows, set fire to your throat
Then hiss out a sigh of heart broken notes.

III

Oh vile and wicked juice thou infect me.
With Godspeed travel through this mortal coil.
Spin my yin, yank my yang, delicately
Stir me until my blood begins to boil.
I'll cat to your mouse. I'll dog to your bone.
I will sit here like a lump on a log.
You must promise not to leave me alone
But to glaze over me with your dense fog.
Like the dying pins on a Christmas wreath
I want to fall apart slowly each day.
Shedding my skin, you'll find underneath
Nothing but dreams that have melted away.
Into a dull funk I want to be sent
Hoping tomorrow I can pay the rent.

IV

Slip further into a drunken braggart
As my bravado gets swollen and mean.
And with every note sung by Merle Haggard

My killer instincts become very keen.
I'll fight for the woman I never had
When the man I never knew calls her name.
I'll fight for my children, though I'm no dad
I'll bark. I'll bite. I'll viciously maim.
Every foolish man, I'll play like a pawn
If he's not gentle with my psychosis.
I'll be known for a temper, red as dawn
I'll split men like the sea à la Moses.
This rage will subside, this fantasy end
Whilst the sorrow and heartache begin.

V

Littered with dull moments, me in this house
I sit waiting for something to happen.
But nothing does stir, not even a mouse
I get antsy and fingers start tapping
I look at the cupboard, spot the moonshine
And I tell myself, "just one little sip."
Before I burp out the first taste of wine
The liquor is gone and Lordy I'm ripped.
Once again, me all alone on this couch
No, not much further along than before.
Pinch myself hard, just to hear me say "ouch"
These are the things I do when I am bored.
Me and this sofa have come a long way,
Sharing each moment of every dull day.

VI

Aging in this room like stinking French cheese
Or like fine wine in a dark, musty room.
Pull all the shutters, keep the sun out please
I've come to favor the light of the moon.
Just me and the darkness, wrestling sins
Only the strongest of men can survive.
I'll make them beg mercy, then I'll give in

Because the sinning it keeps me alive.
Pull up the covers, underneath my chin
Sweating like a blade of grass in the dew.
Swearing at Jesus and all of his kin
For not helping me give Satan his due.
To sleep perchance to dream, aye, there's the rub,
For in that drunken sleep what dreams may come?

VII

Squeezing and gagging the back of my throat
Oh! It's a chore to keep everything down.
Burping an opera of out of tune notes
They say if you puke in your sleep, you'll drown.
My stomach is heaving and cramping up
I'm doubled over, not really in pain.
Just waiting for everything to erupt
So I can flush this disgust down the drain.
A brief moment of pause gives me false hope
I pull away from the toilet with care.
Immediately, I shake my head, "nope"
And I fall hard to my knees to prepare.
My insides explode and tear me to bits
Now I'm inside out and staring at shit.

VIII

My body is empty, must give me time
For some rest on this porcelain pillow.
I'm languid and loose and feeling sublime
Whilst I'm draped on this john like a willow.
I hear a faint buzzing inside my head
Ah, that sweet gurgling of toilet bowl sounds.
There is not one thing I can think to be said
Just listening to my heart as it pounds.
This cool, slick bowl I hug like a lover
Cheek to rim I profess love until death.
It will not, I'm sure, hog all the covers

Or turn away from my puke tarnished breath.
A porcelain God? Nay, say I, not quite.
Just an old friend I can hold through the night.

IX

Queer and morbid droning is in my ears,
Just one constant unharmonious tone.
Bringing to rise my most ambitious fears
That trick me into thinking I'm alone.
Back you cunts or I'll slit your fucking throats
I'll watch the blood pour down over your chests
Go ahead, keep laughing, this ain't no joke,
I'll come out slashing if I don't get rest.
I'll start from your ear and drag it across
Not flinching at the ripping of your skin.
I'm already empty, I won't feel loss
For kicks I'll make your wound fizzle with gin.
The droning goes on until I'm asleep.
This is my drunken way of counting sheep.

X

Depends on how much I drink, that I'm drunk
(And I suspect that I had quite a few)
For nothing can throw me into this funk
Quite like a big bottle of Jim Beam do.
My stomach's on fire, my heads in a vice
I'm shaky and tired and want one more beer.
Demons are laughing, I'm paying the price
For that one too many swallows of cheer.
I raise my head slowly, pull it back down
The pain more intense than my will to rise.
I think I once had my feet on the ground
But today I'm not even gonna try.
To sleep on this bed gives rest to my head.
Jesus fucking Christ I wish I were dead.

XI

Remember that willow, just off the road
Blooming purple in the middle of May?
I'd go there to think and lighten my load
And quite often I'd go there to pray.
I'd sit underneath and lean on the trunk
Close my eyes and, mm, feel the springtime breeze
I'd empty my head of all of its junk
And whisper my troubles to the new leaves.
I'd always depart calm and relaxed
Feeling ready to begin all anew.
My ego and spirit would be quite intact
My worries shrunk to sizes I could chew.
Well, that willow is dead, it's been cut down
And nothing remains, save the cold, cold ground.

Weezal folded the letter and put it on the bookshelf. "I'm glad I'm forgetting how to read," he said. And when he said this he said it with the conviction of a man who could see the future.

Weezal knew that he'd never eat Marty's meatballs. He knew he'd never be able to read again. He knew his life had begun to spin into a cycle of destruction. He knew he was dying. He knew all of this for certain.

But he was wrong.

December seventh was coming. And then all of his luck would change.

The Second Book of Weezal, called
Genesis II, or
Beginning Again

Marty was zeroing in on a subject matter and Weezal didn't like it.

"What the hell do you know about chickens," Weezal asked.

"Nothing. Absolutely nothing. Not a goddamn thing, really."

"So why are you going to write a book about them?"

"Because I think there's a market for that sort of thing. I've only ever seen one book about raising chickens and it was poorly written and too technical. No soul."

"And just how, knowing nothing about chickens, do you intend to improve upon that?"

"I'm thinking in more literary terms. I want to write a chicken-raising book that is more poetic. Lyrical. I'm looking to appeal to the educated farmer. Agriculture is a blossoming field of study at the universities and this new farmer, Dr. Farmer, if you will, needs material that will rise to his level of poetic appreciation."

"I guess I can see your point."

"More importantly, Darlene approves of the idea. And although she's not happy about the immediate financial prospects she said it would be nice to here my typewriter clucking again."

"Clucking?"

"Clicking, I mean. Ha! You see, it was meant to be!"

Now Weezal understood why he hadn't smelled Marty's meatballs and why Marty had waved off the bottle of Jim Beam that was offered.

It was early December and the winter chill was settling into Effen. Weezal's trailer was trapping the cold air like only a tin can can. The whiskey was his blanket. He tried to appeal to Marty from this angle. Nothing doing. Marty was on the wagon. A book brewing in his mind. It was going to be the best damn book about raising chickens ever written. He was trying to think of an opening quote. Weezal was feeling lonely.

"Have you written anything yet," Weezal asked.

"In just three days time I have come up with a title and the dedication page. It will be called, "A Poet's Guide to Poultry," and the dedication will read:

"For Darlene, to replace the sunflowers.
For Weezal, to replace the circus."

Weezal was moved by the dedication and said that it sounded nice. Marty sat smiling, staring at his three lines of text. It was the first thing he'd written since burning his copycat version of *The Sun Also Rises*.

He liked the way the words looked typed out from his Underwood. Thick, black and bold. The little e's tearing through the paper. Passionately. (The paper was an ordinary twenty-pound stock. He couldn't afford a heavier grade. Actually, he couldn't afford any grade. Darlene was stealing reams from the high school supply room.)

Weezal noted that Marty's page didn't look like the notes he found in the trailer. Marty's words looked permanent. The words on his found notes always had an air of mistake and uncertainty. There were no mistakes on Marty's page. Not one.

It was true. Marty was a writer.

"Congratulations," Weezal finally said.

"Thank you, but don't say it with a tone that suggests I will never see you again." Weezal had used that tone.

"I'm just hungry, that's all," Weezal lied.

"Oh, shoot, I forgot the groceries. Sorry Weez. I tell you what. Why don't we walk into town and go to the Effen diner? My treat. We'll have a little celebration on account of the fact that when this book gets published, I'll have lots of money. Famous writers from the past were always doing that—spending the money that would eventually come their way. I want to try it."

"Okay," Weezal said, again using a tone that suggested he would never see Marty again. This time Marty let it slide. But Weezal knew that his relationship with Marty was coming to a close. He was going to miss smelling the meatballs. He was going to miss thinking about fucking Darlene's breasts.

"And I'll tell you another thing," Marty continued, "next week you're going to come down to my place. Meet my kid. We'll eat chicken. Lots of chicken. I need to do research and taste all kinds of chicken. Darlene and I can only eat so much. So that's that."

"That's that."

"Grab a coat. We'll go to the diner and get some Chinese food."

"Chinese food?"

"Yeah, beats the hell out of me. They started a Chinese menu though the sign still says, 'Pennsylvania Dutch Home Cookin'."

"I don't think I've ever eaten Chinese food," Weezal said.

"That's all I ate when I lived in New York. It was cheap." And suddenly Marty didn't feel so good.

Goddamn New York. How he'd run out of there with Darlene before he was ready to leave. He liked New York most in autumn. A clear sky. A river breeze. The blast of heat rising up from a subway grate, catching you by surprise, just as you were getting a bit too cold. New York like the best Christmas surprise. New York like a sexy flirtation when you least expected it. New York like that "bad" friend who was always the most fun. New York, New York. A hell of a town.

But Darlene was right. New York was no place to start a family. Not even in autumn.

In his college years he thought he'd never start a family. He wasn't sure that he could finish one. He hated to start things and not finish.

And Darlene made it easy. She paid the bills while he played the farmer. One day while standing in the middle of his field he saw those thirteen years whiz over his head. He ducked. But when he stood up he noticed he was fatter and Darlene was telling him it was time to stop fooling around.

Now he had started a book. He wasn't going to think about New York anymore. He wasn't going to think about sunflower fields or foreign movies or baby girls or vanilla ice cream. He was going to think about nothing but chickens and Chinese food. Maybe he'd get some General Tso's chicken. He hoped they'd have that on the menu.

It was a long walk into Effen, about four miles, but the weather was cool and Marty and Weezal were looking forward to it.

They walked along the shoulder of old Route 209, Marty leading Weezal.

Marty, was distracted by thoughts of:

* Raising chickens
* Cleaning chicken shit
* His father's toothless smile
* Various breeds of chickens

and women. One woman. Darlene. Providing. Someday. That's right. PROVIDING.

And this would have gone on the entire four mile walk into Effen if Weezal hadn't said, "Hey, Marty, tell me a poem."

Marty cleared his throat and scratched the back of his head.

He recited:

the carrots simmered too long
and mashed like a
sweet potato
I ate them all and
complimented your dexterity
in the kitchen

you tickled me
on the mouth and you
tasted like carrots
that had simmered too long

A car drove by. A horn blew. A smile. A wink and wave. A baby blue Rolls Royce. They waved back and kept walking, without distractions, into Effen.

With only a mile to go, Marty began practicing what sounded to Weezal to be Chinese. It made Weezal nervous.

"They don't speak English anymore at the diner?"

"Of course, they do," Marty said.

"So why are you practicing Chinese?"

"I wasn't. I was practicing chicken."

"Oh," Weezal said, "sounded Chinese."

"I guess I better work on it."

"I guess."

They both thought it odd when the same blue Rolls Royce passed them again. Another honk. Another smile. Another wink. Another wave.

"Friend of yours," Marty asked.

"Nope," said Weezal.

And they stepped into the diner.

Moo Shoo Scrapple

Weezal didn't like the looks of his Chinese food. Marty didn't realize that the New York memory would be so hard to shake. Both sat quietly staring at their plates.

"You can't escape New York," Marty said. Weezal didn't respond. "That's going to be the first sentence of my chicken book."

"What does New York have to do with raising chickens?"

"They hang them in windows tied to strings from the ceiling. Sometimes, if you pass by while they're hanging them you can watch the blood drip into puddles on the floor."

"That's a morbid way to start a book."

"Raising chickens to slaughter them is a morbid profession," Marty calmly pointed out. "I'm sure there will be chicken farmers who will find truth in this. I gotta tell the truth, Weez."

"Have you always had this dark side?"

"Everyone has a dark side, Weezal. Sure. The truth is dark. But mine's never been so close to the surface."

"I think it's a beautiful opening sentence," Weezal said.

The Effen Diner began to swell with a supper rush. Lots of tired housewives, happy to have a day off from cooking. Lots of men happy to have a day off from the wife's cooking. Lots of kids just plain happy. Lots of flannel.

First thing Weezal was going to do when he got back to the trailer was unpack his winter quilt.

And just at that moment he wanted a swig of Jim Beam.

"No more Beam," Weezal asked.

"Not another swallow. I'm sorry Weezal."

"That's okay, I understand."

And maybe he understood, maybe he didn't. It didn't matter. The setting sun was an invitation for Weezal. An invitation for a drink. He found it very difficult to not respondez-vous.

"I better get going. It's getting late"

"You hardly touched your Moo Shoo Scrapple."

"Looks like too many bad mornings."

"You want me to go with," Marty asked.

"No, go ahead and finish eating. I know the way."

Weezal stood up and reached into his pocket, scratching for some loose change. Marty reached out his hand and said, "On me." Weezal smiled and thanked him. He turned and walked out without saying goodbye.

Marty watched Weezal as he crossed the road and headed back into Goddfree. He admired Weezal's independence and lack of direction. But he felt bad that Weezal was a drunk. He realized he'd never asked Weezal how he got started drinking. Maybe next time he'd ask that. But that would probably be a long time from now. Marty had a book to write.

Marty sipped his coffee and watched until Weezal was out of sight. Then he noticed how lonely the road into Goddfree looked. The trees were balding, the soil dry and dusty. It had been a long hot summer. Autumn brief and to the point. The road connecting Effen and Goddfree, like a severed umbilical cord, served no purpose. The road was originally cut (way back when with machetes and tomahawks) to shorten the trip from New York to Philadelphia. There were other roads for that now. Better roads. Wider roads. Less lonely roads. Marty was glad that writing would keep him off this road for a while. No one needs that kind of loneliness.

Weezal was kicking some stones. His hands buried deep in his pockets. His tongue aching for some whiskey.

"99 bottles of beer on the wall, 99 bottles of beer—if three of those bottles should happen to fall, 96 bottles of beer on the wall."

It used to take a lot of energy for Weezal to not think about his past. These days he could barely remember the day before. Somehow, everything seemed so long ago. But he was only thirty-two. Nothing was that long ago.

As he was kicking the stone a sound brought him into a memory and he stopped. He glanced toward Blue Mountain for a clue. A black crow was circling a dying something or other. The shedding trees were shimmying away their last leaves. Maybe a deer was rustling about, working itself higher into the mountains, fearing the first shot of hunting season. But the sound wasn't coming from the mountain. It was coming from the Effen Firehouse. It was the five o'clock whistle. Something about that sound made Weezal feel strong but he didn't know why. It was a soothing sound and brought a smile to his face. He didn't move again until the whistle had run out of breath.

Weezal could see the trailer court planted in its ridges. The trees, now mostly bare, were no longer hiding the more embarrassing elements of the court and it made Weezal want to turn around and run like hell in the other direction. Just run until he was somewhere that wasn't so lonely. He couldn't even imagine where that might be. He kept walking.

"96 bottles of beer on the wall, 96 bottles of beer—if three of those bottles to the third power should happen to fall, 69 bottles of beer on the wall."

Marty stood up from the table and unbuttoned his pants. He had eaten too much. Chinese food always played funky games with his intestines. He wanted to hurry up and pay the bill so he could step outside and fart. On his way out the door he grabbed a sugary pink mint and a toothpick.

Once outside Marty gave a long look at Route 209 and decided he'd hitchhike. Marty hitchhiked with the patience of a fisherman. He was the kind of hitchhiker who stood in one spot and waited for someone to stop. If he had wanted to walk, he'd walk. He waited for a ride. Twenty-five minutes he waited for a ride. Thumb stretched out like bait. Nobody biting.

Tired of waiting, he stepped back into the diner. He called Darlene from the pay phone. She wasn't home. Probably at her mother's. He didn't want to call over there. Marty didn't like Darlene's mother. He decided he'd get a cup of coffee and try again in an hour. He hung up the phone without leaving a message.

Marty sat at the counter. He ordered his coffee sweet, no milk, and smiled at the tired waitress who didn't smile back. She'd been there since five a.m. and her warm and friendly demeanor had turned sour with the milk around three. Marty took a napkin and sopped up the spilled coffee on his saucer. He threw the napkin into an ashtray. The waitress let out a sigh and emptied the ashtray, slamming it back on the counter, just out of Marty's reach.

"Sorry," he said. But there was no response as she slipped through a pair of saloon style doors, wiping her hands on a rag that swung from her hip, disappearing into the kitchen.

Marty had lied. He told Weezal he didn't want to have a drink and right now, more than anything in the universe, (except maybe for Darlene to pick him up) he wanted to have a solid swig of whiskey. And a good laugh. He sipped his coffee and it momentarily filled the void. He smothered the whiskey temptation altogether with the thought of the second sentence for his book: "I'd rather be a chicken in Chinatown than a small-town farmer in Middle America."

He scribbled it down on a napkin so he wouldn't forget. The tired waitress caught sight of this and sighed again, slamming a new napkin down to replace the one Marty had taken.

"Sorry," he said again. And once again she busted through the saloon doors, this time without wiping her hands, disappearing into the kitchen.

Joker! Joker! Joker!

Maisey loved classical music but she didn't own any classical records because she couldn't remember the names of the classical artists that she liked.

The classical radio station was perfect. Perfect because they kept the disc jockey talk to a minimum. She hated that deep soothing voice. It reminded her of her first husband. It was also the newly adopted voice of her father.

Her father used to have a tough voice. Sandpaper rubbing on rocks. It was the voice of experience and maturity. The voice of fearlessness.

Mrs. Furlong, the courthouse secretary, had a voice like a faulty bladder, weak and wet. It surprised Maisey when she walked through the door.

"Oh, my God, where have you been!"

Mrs. Furlong rushed into the back room returning with a file.

"Number 777, can you believe that? It's like hitting the jackpot on one of them slot machines in Atlantic City!" She handed Maisey the file.

Maisey took the file into the basement, which had become her office. It was quiet in the basement. No interruptions. Especially on Saturday. Saturdays were Maisey's favorite because she didn't have to rush through the files before heading to The Polk Mountain Love Palace to clean bathrooms and change soiled sheets, to pick up used condoms left strewn about the floor. It was her day off.

She opened her McDonald's coffee container and stirred in some milk and sugar. She looked at her watch. 12:40. A late start. A long morning fighting a hangover. Burying herself deep in the comforter. Snooze button after snooze button after snooze button. Her eyes still burned. Her head was still tight. But the shakes were gone. She looked at the file. Then she pushed it away. Let me have my coffee first. A sip, at least. Coffee before disappointment. That was a Maisey rule.

Why was it that one night with a boy and it was so easy to forget the misery? Was she that hard up for affection? Nonsense. It was moments like this when she missed or hated her mother most. Maybe both. Either way, the old lady wasn't around to help. Wasn't around to give her strength. What kind of strength? What kind of help? Who knew? Where the fuck was that woman? And didn't she care, at all, about who Maisey was? Had become? It was hate, for sure.

Her period was starting and her belly was cramped in knots. Sometimes they'd get so tight she'd double over, forearms resting on thighs. Her period came in like a lion, a wild hungry lion, and left like a lamb, a tortured slaughtered lamb. And this month she had the added annoyance of bloating. That was new. This menstruating shit was for the birds.

Fuck her mother.

Her coffee was too strong.

Fuck McDonald's.

And just as she was about to take her second sip, a cramp took hold of her tummy and yanked her, belly over thighs, toward the floor.

"Goddamn it!"

Fuck being a woman!

She reached into her purse and pulled out two Advil. She swallowed them dry. She remained doubled over waiting for the pills to take effect.

If she could trade it all in she'd trade it all in for a dance in the desert. A pink sunset floating down. Twirling in the summer sand. Feet bare. Hot on her toes. Until she exhausted herself and collapsed. Not tired. Exhausted. Empty and breathing heavy. Listening to that breathing. The pink floating.

Down.

Turning blue.

Turning black.

A long sleep.

She caught her breath and slowly sat up. The knot loosened. Another sip of coffee.

Fuck the desert.

"You know what, Maisey Walker? You should get up from this chair, walk out of this room and never come back."

She looked at the folder. It was thin. It was old.

Fuck the folder.

"Okay, 777, come to mommy." She picked the file up and read the name.

"Peterson. Jedidiah."

A biblical name.

Fuck Jedidiah.

Teenage Jesus

Teenage Jesus was a badass motherfucker with a picture of himself being crucified tattooed across his chest. He believed in his father. He believed, somewhere, he probably had a son. And he believed in the Holy Spirit, or heroin, which he called "medication." "I need my medication" or "Let's go get so and so on the health plan." He was clean now, at twenty-four, but Teenage Jesus was a junkie and a drunk.

There were stories. The night he turned a fifth of Old Overhalt whiskey into a wide assortment of liquors and wines, forty bottles deep. Enough for his crew. This miracle was easy. A sawed-off twelve gauge poking at the temple of a State Store clerk in Bethlehem, Pennsylvania. Clerk didn't move a hair. Raided the place. Threw a party and everyone got high.

The miracles kept coming. Blind man story was an exaggeration. Blind kid. Wasn't really blind. Just high. Kid was taking his medication. Kept shooting. Veins were collapsing. Face covered in boils, all bursting. Started to sweat and shake. Got scared, panicked. Lost his sight. Couldn't see a fucking thing. Black. Heard his buddies run off. Alone on the curb at the 7-11. Right out in the open. Shaking, scared, blind.

Teenage Jesus was driving by, but that was no miracle. He was always driving by. Drove a dark green Gran Torino. Windows rolled down because it was summer. Spied the kid stumbling through the parking lot.

"Fuck. What the piss are you doing?"

But the kid was crying and scared. Trying to run away from Jesus. Couldn't see who it was or he wouldn't have tried to run. You just didn't do that. Jesus had sympathy. Didn't get mad. Just grabbed the kid by the shirt collar, smacked him hard in the face and dragged him into the car.

"It's going to be alright, kid. Hold on."

"I can't fucking see. Fucking blind."

Jesus smacked him again and told him to shut up.

They drove out by the old train station. Run down now. No street lamps. Jesus pulled up along a rusty old freight train, opened his glove compartment and took out some dope.

"Gimme your arm."

Jesus, shaking his head at the track marks. Bruised and swollen. Nothing left. Dried blood.

"This ain't no good, Cuz."

Jesus reached down and took off the kid's sneakers, held his foot in his lap. He grabbed hard around the kid's ankle, forcing a vein to pop on the bottom of the kid's foot. Jesus jabbed the needle in. The kid winced. Jesus pushed the medication in. Slowly. Then he withdrew the needle and threw it out the window. He put the kid's sneaker back on. The kid started to calm. Jesus pulled him to his chest and stroked the kid's hair. He didn't look at the kid. Kept staring out the window, looking at the freight train, thought he heard a whistle, a train whistle, blow. Thought about Huck Finn. Trains and Huck Finn. Rivers. Veins.

The kid wasn't moving now and Jesus could hear him sucking snot up through his nose and down his throat.

"I can see," the kid finally said. Said it sleepily. He was high.

"Yeah, I'm a fuckin' angel," Jesus said.

"I know."

"Do what I tell ya."

"Sure."

"Get some new friends. Those fuckers left you to die, brother. A bunch of lousy shits."

"They were scared."

"And they fucked you."

"Yeah, I guess."

"Now get outta here."

And the kid got out of the car and Jesus drove away. He didn't know where he was going. He rarely did. Just driving. Listen to the radio and drive. Spent a lot of time these days trying to make his mind go blank. It was hard. To blank his mind.

He had saved many lives with those magical injections. Made believers of them all. And those who hadn't befriended him because they believed, befriended him because they were scared.

His twelve apostles helped spread the word. Helped spread the junk. They spread it through schoolyard's and supermarket parking lots, bowling alleys and shopping malls. That's where they'd run mostly. Rent-a-cops on patrol. Middle-aged, overweight, none too bright. Could practically deal out in the open. Rent-a-cops none the wiser.

And yes, he was a carpenter, but not a very good one. Lazy and late for work. He didn't show up one too many times and was fired. Now he was his own boss. Kept his own hours. When Teenage Jesus spoke, they listened. The apostles held court in the welfare complexes throughout Bethlehem and Nazareth. Their services were brief and communion was a needle.

It was TJ's stuff.

And TJ's stuff was good stuff.

Rushing through your veins it felt cold like ice. In your body. In your blood. Made your teeth feel loose.

Teenage Jesus slept with his whores. A stable of riffraff and runaways. The meek and the mild. The scared shitless. And they flocked. Giving their body. Their blood.

Teenage Jesus bought his mother a house in the suburbs of Philadelphia. She didn't care that it came from junk money. She loved that house in the suburbs. And things were going well until that son-of-a-bitch rat-mother-fucking-fink bastard, Judas Iscariot (Jeeter Kreger), blew the whole door wide open and TJ got nailed.

Jeeter was sloppy. He got busted selling to an undercover cop in broad daylight. Fourteen hours in lockup, heavy DT's, and he talked. "Loquacious," said the Sergeant. Jeeter was willing to pull a job, wear a wire—whatever—just get him some fucking dope! And they got him some dope. Cops have good dope.

Teenage Jesus was caught with his pants down. Busted him on route 611, out toward Easton. A basement apartment. A ten-year-old runaway tied naked to the bedpost. Laughing. High. She was laughing when the cops came in. She said, "You wanna suck my titties? Tell them TJ! Tell them what you'll do to them if they try to suck my titties!"

She was ten. She didn't have titties.

They stripped him down and threw him in a cell. They smacked him around. A nightstick across his teeth and up his ass. A boot in the gut. His body spilling blood.

Judas put a revolver in his mouth and sprayed a fresh coat of brain onto a bathroom wall. The suicide note said he was sorry.

Teenage Jesus told the press (immediately after his arraignment, and through an attorney) that he would be out in three days. The news broke first on the AP wire: "Teenage Jesus Busts from State Pen in Penn State."

This Day

This day, like all days, began at the beginning of time. A slow and dusty tumble through the heavens. The beginning of the end. But every beginning is the beginning of the end.

No feet were wet.

This day, without pause, tumbling over itself on perfect route to its final destination: This day.

No cards turned.

This day never drawing attention to itself before its time. Its perfect time: This day.

No blacks. No blues.

It wasn't anybody's day. It wasn't a day that took place anywhere. It wasn't a day yet known. But here it was, tumbling down, through the millennia, the centuries, the decades, tumbling into the previous night gently and innocently. Entering the previous night where it would rest, preparing for its dawn. Its day. This day.

Optimism is what this day looks like from the beginning of time. Idealism is what this day looks like from another day. Shit Luck is what this day looks like from a trailer court, a failing farm, a county courthouse and the back seat of a baby blue Rolls Royce.

So these souls, the sad ones like Maisey, Marty, Weezal and Millard, had given up on this day. Thinking, "just a day like all the others."

But this was a different day.

And soon it would arrive.

They suspected nothing.

December 6th

Weezal was about to put his key into the door when he noticed a note taped to the storm glass window. It was written on a torn piece of paper bag. It said: "Tomorrow is December 7th, get a good night's sleep. Forget it. Forget it not."

Weezal pulled the note off the glass, crumpled it into a small ball and ate it.

Maisey Get Your Suitcase

Maisey's cramps were frequent now. Maybe it was time to stop all the nonsense. Maybe it was time to realize that Dunkletown, Joe's and Monkey's Paw were all she'd ever have. Her cramps always made her want to quit.

Fuck quitting.

And she was scared. What if this really was the one? What then? She had never given much thought to what she would do had she found someone who met her requirements. What she would really do. And what if the perfect man had a hitch? Let's say—he was married? She couldn't bear that and, with murder being no stranger to her past, she was afraid of what she might do.

"I am such a pussy," she said taking a deep breath, opening the file.

Peterson, Jedidiah. High school dropout. The file was concerning a barroom brawl that he'd once gotten into at the American Hotel, a run-down drinking hole in Monkey's Paw. He was sentenced to three days in the can. "Enough time," the judge wrote, "to sober up and calm down. And maybe just enough time to pray."

"An ordinary drunk." Maisey laughed. Had Mrs. Furlong lost her marbles? She read on.

Buried in the last few pages (behind the fingerprints and photographs of the rapscallion's swollen face) was a small but intriguing article from the Monkey's Paw Press.

Local Philanthropist Jailed.

On Friday night State Police were called to the American Hotel to break up a brawl that erupted over a game of pool. Seventeen men were placed under arrest. Most notable of those charged with disorderly conduct was Jedidiah Peterson, a local eccentric best known for his one and a half million dollar donation that created the much needed John C. Smills Junior High School.

Mr. Peterson, who declined to comment, was taken into custody and brought to the Monkey's Paw Courthouse where he'll remain throughout the weekend.

Mr. Fred Hatchett, Principal of the John C. Smills Junior High School, said, "An unfortunate incident like this should do nothing to mar the reputation of one of our most outstanding citizens. His contributions and dedication to local education are unparalleled." When asked if he knew how the brawl broke out Mr. Hatchett replied, "Clearly the gentleman opposing Mr. Peterson scratched on the eight. And at the American Hotel it's plainly stated on the House Rules, posted directly above the jukebox, you scratch on the eight—you lose. The opponent, however, decided he'd rather play by his own rules. Words were exchanged. Fisticuffs ensued. The police were called."

The American Hotel is located on Kunkle Road in Monkey's Paw. Saturday Night is Ladies Night. Ladies drink for half price.

One and a half million dollars! Given away! To a school?! How much must you have to be able to GIVE AWAY one and a half million dollars? To a school? Twelve million? A hundred million? She didn't know. She didn't care. The son-of-a-bitch was loaded. But no other details. Was he married? Was he gay? Judging by the picture in the paper he was maybe early forties. But who knew when that picture was taken. The article itself was eight years old.

"Hello, baby, can I get you a beer? Need your slippers? Want some dinner? A back rub? Name it. I'm yours."

She looked at the picture. His thinning hair was a mess but he had just been in a fight. His face was square and his lips as fat as night crawlers. His eyes, too swollen to metaphor. She imagined he had a deep voice.

Maisey leaned back in her chair and pulled out a cigarette. She lit it staring at the "no smoking" sign. A smile started pulling at her mouth. She wanted to laugh out loud.

"One and a half million freakin' dollars. Given away. To a school."

When she finished her smoke, she ground it into the carpet. She wrote down the essentials:

Jedidiah Peterson

Big Bass Lake, Goddfree Pa, 18331.

No phone.

Big Bass Lake? She hadn't heard of that. Probably a private resort. But in Goddfree? No matter. She tucked the information into her shirt pocket. She felt a cramp coming on.

"Back off!" she growled and the cramp went away.

She headed up the stairs to the office.

"Well?" said Mrs. Furlong, bright red lipstick pulled back tight.

"The freakin' jackpot."

"Woo-Hoo!"

And they hugged, giggling like schoolgirls.

"I have to get going, Mrs. Furlong. I have a million things to do and a million dollars to bag."

"Good luck, Maisey."

But Maisey didn't hear her because she was already out the door making a mental list of everything she wanted to pack, quickly composing the letter she would leave for her father. A letter she'd tack to the forehead of his Virgin Mary Statuette.

Tumbling, This Day. Tumbling, Tumbling.

"Sir, you're going to have to leave, we're closing up. That's your tenth cup of coffee and the boss is getting pissed."

Marty spun around on his stool and looked out the diner window. It was dark. The waitress was removing her apron, her shift ending. Marty slipped into his jacket.

Weezal sat on the toilet with his feet propped up on the edge of the tub, cutting his toenails. His nails were hard and yellow. His feet stunk from the walk into Effen and the infection.

"This little piggy went to market," Weezal said, clipping his big toenail. "And this little piggy stayed home. This little piggy had roast beef," and Weezal's mouth watered, "and this little piggy had none. And this little piggy," he said, poking at the infected spot where his littlest toe used to be, "this little piggy packed up and split."

Weezal looked closely at the foot and could see a red line driving its way up his leg, momentarily pit-stopped at the truck-stop of his groin. The red line was sore. It was a curious matter so he took another swig of the Beam and tried to forget about it. He folded up his clippers and put them on the edge of the sink. Then he washed the feet stink off his hands.

Marty pushed himself off the stool and reached into his pocket, pulling out thirty-five cents for the ten cups of coffee (free refills) and six one dollar bills he intended to leave as a tip. He didn't want the waitress thinking she got the best of him by being rude. She was having a bad day and Marty understood that. He had bad days all the time. He put the tip on the counter and walked outside.

Marty looked down the road half expecting Darlene to drive by. She didn't. Which was the other half of what he expected. He decided to hitchhike again.

The waitress came out of the diner and spotted him at the edge of the road. She shouted, "You need a lift?"

"Spiritually?" Marty asked and before the waitress had a chance to respond he added, "Sure, if you're heading in my direction."

"Come on," is all she said and unlocked the doors to her rusty brown Buick Skylark.

Marty walked to the car and pulled on the handle. The door didn't open. From the inside the waitress leaned over and kicked it with her foot. "It's broken, you gotta give it some love," she said and Marty climbed in. He could smell the pine tree air freshener and imagined it dangling behind the dash. He could also smell, slightly, the waitress's perfume. He didn't know what flavor she was wearing but he liked it. Smelled like fresh produce.

The waitress turned the ignition and the Skylark coughed a bit but started. She flicked on her headlights and said, "Where to?"

"You know where the McGraw farm is? In Goddfree?"

The waitress smiled at Marty and said, "I didn't ask where you lived, I asked where to?"

Marty looked out into the field behind the diner. A pumpkin patch. Maybe he should have tried pumpkins. Big, fat pumpkins.

"The Foxxxy Lady," she asked. "I need a night cap."

"I don't drink anymore."

"Everybody drinks, honey. A little." And she pulled out of the parking lot onto Route 209 and headed south, toward the Foxxxy Lady. Marty started feeling guilty exactly two-tenths of a mile down the road. Exactly two-tenths. His eyes were fixed on the odometer.

Weezal let the hot water rush over his feet. It stung where his toe was missing. He dried his feet with a dirty towel and pulled on a fresh pair of tube socks. He put a second pair on for comfort and warmth. He poured himself a tall glass of whiskey and put the bottle back on top of the refrigerator.

He stood by his kitchen sink looking out his window towards Marty's farm. No porch light. This book was going to cut Weezal out of Marty's life forever. Weezal could just feel it.

"Here's to your goddamn chicken book, you fat bastard," Weezal said, holding his glass for a toast.

Weezal stepped into the living room and switched on his radio. He kept it tuned to 104.4 FM, his favorite country station. They played the old guys—Willie, Waylon, Merle. But tonight he didn't feel like country. So he tuned to the classical station. Mozart. A Requiem. He took another swallow of whiskey.

He walked in small circles around the living room in time with the music. He swirled his whiskey in its glass. Pretended he was high society. But his sore toe and the chill in the trailer kept him from feeling as rich as he wanted to feel. So he stopped swirling the whiskey and drank it as he always did, like a poor man, too fast and with the thought of pouring himself another.

The Foxxxy Lady parking lot was empty. Marty was relieved that the band, Muskrat Love, wouldn't be playing until later. He didn't want to hear it right now. All that noise. He didn't want to hear anything.

They walked into the bar and took a seat at the curve by the jukebox. The waitress threw her purse on the counter and said, "You drinking beer? Good. Charlie, bring us a couple of beers and a couple of shots of J.D. and mister watch my bag because I'm going to put a couple of quarters in the jukebox. Want to hear anything special? Do ya?"

"Do I what?"

"The jukebox. Want to hear anything special?"

"No." He didn't want to hear anything.

The waitress bent over, inspecting the jukebox, then gave up and blindly punched a few numbers. Marty glanced at her ass. It was a fat ass. A really fat ass. Disproportionate, actually, to the rest of her body. The kind of ass you would look at once, twice, maybe three times and then finally declare—Okay, now that's a fat ass. And he liked it. Had never considered himself an ass man, but, then again, had never seen such a fine, fat ass.

Charlie, the bartender, delivered the drinks and Marty felt his jaw tighten and mouth water. Before he had a chance to say no thank you, Charlie was taking five dollars from the waitress's stack of cash and she was holding her shot glass waiting for Marty to join her in a toast.

"It's not going to kill you."

"I'm writing a book."

"And, me, I'm in the movies."

"No, I'm really writing a book."

"Are you trying to pick me up? You don't have to…"

"Sincerely. I am writing a book. About chickens."

"That's nice. I mean, sure you are. Congratulations, then. Now, drink."

"You believe me?"

"Of course I do. Why the hell not? Drink."

"Okay," Marty said, and they clicked glasses.

"To chickens," the waitress said and Marty wanted to kiss her. The shot was quick and smooth. The waitress lifted her beer and Marty did the same.

"To tomatoes," he said.

"And carrots," she responded.

"And fat asses," he said, slapping it.

"And fat cocks," she said, grabbing to see if he had one.

Seven crumpled pages of paper were sitting on the kitchen table. False starts.

"Don't be mean. No reason to be mean," Maisey said, taking another sip of tea.

"Pop, don't cry." She crumpled the paper again.

"Oh, Christ—I can't do this."

A fresh sheet.

"Dad, I'll call you when I'm settled. Love Maisey."

What else did she need to say? Her suitcase was packed with a week's worth of clothes, an old photograph of her mother and some toiletries. She didn't want anything else. This was a fresh start.

She took one last look around the kitchen: the peeling linoleum floor, the table propped level with a matchbook under one of the legs, the refrigerator gurgling like it was being strangled. It was time to leave. She took a deep breath. It caught her off guard. The smell of this house. It still smelled like horses. Like her mother. Could she really do this? Before thinking too long on that, she turned out the light and slipped out the door.

Weezal was standing, motionless, listening to Mozart and it began to confuse him. He sipped his whiskey carefully, trying not to disturb his senses.

Marty looked at the waitress while she was looking toward the pool table pretending not to notice that Marty was looking at her. Marty watched her eyes. They were big and green. Silver dollars from a sunken treasure. Definitely distinguishing features. Darlene had no distinguishing features. Most people, he had noticed, perhaps even all people, had at least one distinguishing feature; a messy eyebrow, a crooked nose, a missing tooth, a high forehead—something—but Darlene was as plain as a blank page. Marty sipped his beer.

Without looking back at Marty the waitress exhaled smoke from her cigarette and said, "What are you staring at?"

"Excuse me?"

"You were just staring at me. What were you thinking about?"

"I'm a private man, I don't share that kind of thing with strangers."

"That's a shitty answer," said the waitress, turning now to look at Marty.

"I agree."

"Another beer?"

"I haven't finished this one yet."

"I know," said the waitress, "but when you're done, are you going to have another?"

"Maybe," Marty said, looking toward the jukebox wishing the damn song would end.

Goddfree was only a short drive from Monkey's Paw. She'd be there in less than an hour. She didn't think one damn thought the entire drive. Just listened to the dull hum of her '69 Valiant. Numb. Good numb.

Weezal had taken off all of his clothes, excepting his tube socks and was now conducting the orchestra in the nude. In between grand crescendos and delicate pizzicatos he'd swig from the bottle of Jim Beam. There was something glorious and nostalgic about prancing around his trailer with his dick slapping against his thigh in rhythm to the music. He didn't know why. Had he done this in the past? He couldn't remember. But just now, Weezal felt free, truly free. He marched. He waltzed. He sashayed. Mozart sounded better to Weezal in the nude and he was upset that it had taken him thirty-two years to figure that out.

The knock at the door didn't surprise him because he was nakedly conducting an orchestra, it surprised him because he wasn't expecting Marty, and Marty was his only guest.

The waitress leaned on the bar and yoo-hooed the bartender, placing her hand on Marty's thigh. Marty didn't move, giving her permission.

"Two more beers and two more shots, honey," she said moving her hand closer to Marty's hot spot.

"I'm married, you know," Marty said.

"So am I."

"I'm not that lonely."

"Neither am I."

"I don't cheat on my wife."

"I don't cheat on my husband." Her hand had crawled up his leg and was now cupping his swelling member.

"I have a daughter," Marty said.

"I have two boys. Monsters, really." She laughed.

"She's only two."

"Mine are six and ten."

"We shouldn't be doing this."

"Cliché."

"Excuse me."

"That's cliché."

"Okay," Marty said, "we should be doing this."

"Damn right we should. Now shut up and drink." They clinked their glasses and drank their shots.

Weezal paused for a moment, trying to remember why he was hesitant about answering the door. Was the music too loud? Was his place too dirty? "No," he thought, "I'm nude!"

Marty said, "Donnez moi ta langue," which was the only French he remembered from his trip to Paris. Unbeknownst to Marty, the waitress was fluent in French and responded by grabbing the back of his neck, pulling him close and running her tongue along his top lip. And then she slipped it into his mouth. She lingered there, swirling her tongue around his. When she exited a slight dribble of saliva slid down Marty's chin. She licked it off. Marty pulled her back and slipped his hand inside her blouse, fielding her breast. Fielding? It had been awhile. He fielded first, then he fondled. He was out of practice. Her breast was ample and Marty gave it a schoolboy squeeze. He pinched her nipple, which was swelling. She squeaked and pulled away.

Marty looked toward the jukebox (would that damn song ever end?) then to the end of the bar where two locals were smiling at him, raising their glasses in a "you lucky son-of-a-bitch" toast of approval—a boys will be boys approval.

And Marty, for the first time in five years, felt like a man. He raised his glass, giving the local boys a nod. They all drank, followed by a unison shift, making room for erections.

The waitress, noticing this, kneeled upon her stool and bowed. The local boys clapped. Marty was feeling more masculine by the second. He pinched her ass.

"I'm nude," Weezal called out from behind the door. But there was no answer and the knocks continued.

"I'm nude," he said again. Still no answer.

"If I open this door, I just want you to be prepared. Because I am nude." It never occurred to him to put on clothes. He was drunk.

"Another beer?" the waitress asked.

"It's my turn to ask," Marty said, wishing Weezal were there, too. "Another beer?"

"Sure." The waitress leaned in close to Marty's ear and whispered, "Are we going to fuck?"

"No."

"Then maybe I should go."

"Don't go," Marty said, "I'm sorry."

"You scared of it?"

"A little."

"You're afraid to fuck?"

"I think so."

Weezal tried peeking out the window but it was too dark, he couldn't see who was knocking. He tapped on the glass trying to get the stranger's attention, but whoever it was didn't look over, just kept knocking on the door. Weezal paced the room nervously, unsure of what to do. He took another drink.

Did it matter that the shag red carpet depressed the hell out of Marty? Nope. He wasn't in this motel room to feel better about himself. He was here to have an adventure. And so bodies in sweat roll about the mattress. And pricks engorged and gliding, slick and wet, find homes in holes inviting. Shh. Just the heavy breathing and the slapping of tummies. And asses. The banging of a headboard against marks on the wall where the headboard has banged before. And this muscle stiffens in his ass. And these muscles stiffen deep in her groin, in her thighs, in her gut. And he squeezes. Shh. Just now the heavy breathing, behind her neck, his head buried deep in a pillow. Her fingernails crawl up his back, lightly.

"Choke me," she says.

"What?"

"I want you to choke me."

Marty chokes her.

"Nobody's home!" Weezal shouted, then tiptoed to the window to see if the stranger would leave.

"What?" the voice called back.

"Nobody's home!" Wait a minute. That makes no sense. "I mean, I'm sleeping!" Shit.

The knocks came again. Weezal jumped on the couch and pulled the covers up over his head.

"Do you think your wife would leave you if she found out?"

"My wife would never leave me," Marty said.

"Never?"

"Maybe if I killed her parents."

"And you don't want to screw again?"

"I can't."

"Why not?"

"I feel guilty. Don't you feel guilty? What about your husband?"

"He left me three years ago."

"You tricked me."

"How do you mean?"

"You told me you were married and I..."

"I am married."

"... and I thought we were in the same situation."

"You thought wrong. But let me get this straight—as long as you thought we were in the same situation—you get to fuck around on your wife? That's fucked up."

"You told me you didn't cheat on your husband."

"And I don't. He left me."

"You tricked me."

"Like I said—that's fucked up."

Marty wanted to cry. But if he cried, he'd also want to curl up into a little ball and have the waitress hold him. And he didn't want the waitress to hold him so he didn't cry. He stared at the ceiling fan and thought about the motel clerk who had given him a knowing, snotty look. He wanted to punch that clerk in the nose but thought better of it because he was drunk. He was a lot less drunk now.

"You want to go home," the waitress asked, rubbing her hand through the hair on his chest.

"Nope."

He just wanted to stare at the ceiling fan and watch it blur until he fell asleep. He never wanted to go back home. How was he going to be able to look at Darlene? And she would never know, she'd never even suspect. It pissed him off that she would never suspect anything. She would continue to love him, without passion, without lust or desire, forever. He knew that. She loved him in a way that he had been trying to figure out for twelve years, and she would love him like that forever. And he hated it. He tried everything. He told himself he needed her love. He told himself that she was the best thing he would ever have. He told himself she needed it. But everything he had told himself was a lie. It was hard sometimes to wake up in the morning and see that lie looking back from the bathroom mirror. Or hear that lie in his head while he read the morning paper. So he had a kid, and that kid, his little baby Rose, was so distracting, that he forgot the lie and for a while everything seemed fine.

But he didn't love Darlene the way he wanted to love somebody. And right now he was lying in a hotel room lusting after a waitress in a way he never wanted to lust after anyone.

"You tricked me."

"Don't be such a baby. You came here and you fucked me and it was a good fuck. Period. You liked it and it was good. Goddamn it, admit that at least. At least you have to admit that."

"I admit it."

"So fuck you."

Marty hated her mouth. He wanted to wash it out with soap. He got off the bed and walked into the bathroom. He looked at his naked body in the mirror. It was hairy and fat and sagging and looked nothing like what he remembered it looking like. He was embarrassed so he turned on the hot water and let the steam rise until the mirror was fogged and he could only see his eyes. Nothing special, he thought. Nothing distinguishing. He wiped away the steam down to his nose. His nose had character. It was broad at the nostrils and thin at the bridge. It was an exact combination of his mother's and father's noses. 50-50.

He wiped away more steam, trimming his fat. He looked good. Athletic. It was a lie. He grabbed a bar of soap from the sink and unwrapped it.

Marty walked back into the room and the waitress was putting out a cigarette. She looked tired and old. Marty sat next to her, a breast smearing on his thigh.

"Let me see your tonsils," he said.

She smiled, thinking he was cute and said, "aaaahhhh."

And Marty stuck the bar of soap into her mouth and placed his hand over it. He grabbed the back of her neck and drove her face first into the mattress. He held her there as she was struggling to breathe. The soap was sliding down her throat and she began to gag. Marty held on tight. He could feel the spit begin to spill from the corner of her mouth. He could smell the soap. The waitress reached back with her hand and her middle finger caught the inside of Marty's eyelid, tearing it. He screamed, letting go of her, and ran back into the bathroom.

The waitress was gagging and spitting. She puked up soap and spit, her head hanging over the edge of the bed, trying to catch her breath in between gags. She wanted to scream, "You fucking animal!" but nothing came from her throat except the soap and the spit.

Marty was rinsing out his eye. It was a small cut but stung like hell and wouldn't stop bleeding.

The waitress was crying. She grabbed the blankets and pulled them up to her face, letting the saliva run onto the sheets.

Marty grabbed a towel and applied pressure to his cut and walked back into the room. He looked at the waitress and wondered what he'd do to her next. He half wanted to apologize and he half wanted to kill her. He stared at her naked back and ass. All that fat shaking with her sobs. Big. Fat. Ass. Shaking.

Marty checked the towel and refolded it to a clean section and again applied pressure. He cleared his throat trying to get her attention. The waitress didn't move. She took several deep breaths and became quiet.

Her body stopped shaking. Beautiful ass.

The fan was still turning and now Marty could hear it squeak. He checked his towel again and there was less blood. He refolded and applied again.

The waitress was empty. She hadn't been beaten up in a couple of years and had forgotten how empty it made her feel. But the dialogue was always the same. She said, "What did you do that for?"

And Marty offered no surprises because he responded the same way that her husband used to respond. He said nothing.

Marty checked the towel and the blood was only trickling. He took the towel into the bathroom and rinsed it out, watching the blood swirl down the drain. He went back into the room and started to get dressed.

"What did you do that for?"

But Marty just zipped his pants and buttoned his shirt. He flicked on the television because the waitress had begun crying again and he didn't want to hear it. As she cried louder he turned up the sound until someone knocked on the wall and screamed something about turn that down, which he did. But not all the way. He tied up his boots and walked toward the door. He reached around and felt his back pocket, his wallet was gone. He walked over to the bed, backwards, because he didn't want to have to see the waitress. He felt around on the nightstand but couldn't find his wallet. He turned slowly. The waitress was holding it. Her eyes were swollen and there was a cut on her bottom lip. Marty wanted to kiss it.

"I'll pay for the room on the way out."

And she dropped the wallet on the bed and laid down again turning away from Marty. Crying.

Marty put the wallet into his pants, turned off the TV, turned out the lights and walked out the door.

It was cold. This night. This day.

Weezal checked the clock and saw that it was 12:23 and thought that it was awfully late to be receiving guests. But the knocks continued.

Maisey set her suitcase down. She was appalled at the trailer's appearance and even more confused by the fact that a millionaire would live in a trailer court. In Goddfree of all places. But she checked the address several times and this was supposedly the home of Jedidiah Peterson. A sudden panic thinking maybe Jedidiah had moved. Maybe this was his home before the millions. She knocked harder and could hear someone yelling, but couldn't make out what was being said so she knocked again.

The December air was crawling down the back of her neck and she started to shiver. She thought about taking a sweater out of her suitcase but didn't want to go through the hassle. Finally a light came on above the door.

Weezal opened the door. He was nude. Maisey was going to say something but not a single word came to mind. Stunned by the frigid air, Weezal screamed and slammed the door again.

This day had finally tumbled down.

"Excuse me," Maisey finally called, knocking again, "I'm looking for Jedidiah Peterson."

Weezal furrowed his brow. Had he heard that name before? It rolled around with the whiskey in his brain and gave him a bad feeling. But from that voice it sounded so nice. What kind of voice was that? A woman's. A woman's voice indeed! He wanted to hear it again. He cracked open the door, just enough room to poke his head.

"Come again."

"Jedidiah Peterson?"

Yes, it was music, perfectly played on her big fat musical tongue. Oh, and the way she blew the P in Peterson.

"One more time."

"Excuse me."

"Say it again."

"Listen, mister, are you Jedidiah Peterson or not? I'm not playing around."

Never had he heard such a pretty melody. He wanted to dance. Jedidiah Peterson, what a silly name. "Could that be me?" he thought. Why the hell not. Someone at some time must have called him that.

"I might be. And who are you?"

"That's none of your goddamn business if you're not Jedidiah Peterson."

There it was again! Oh, she practically sang that name. "I suppose there's only one way to find out," he said.

"How's that?"

"A birth certificate, or driver's license or something."

"You don't know if you're Jedidiah Peterson? Is this some sort of joke?"

If she sings that name again, Weezal thought, I shall faint.

"No. No joke. Excuse me. I'm drunk."

"No shit."

"When I'm drunk, I forget."

"Your name?"

"What name would that be?" And Weezal tightened his butt cheeks in anticipation.

"Jedidiah Peterson."

And he fainted.

"Jesus Christ." Maisey bent down, trying hard not to stare at his private parts and smacked him lightly on the cheeks. Weezal's eyes opened.

"You okay?"

"I think so."

"Let me help you up. Get you on the couch."

"Yes. The couch." And again he was out.

Maisey lifted Weezal and brought him to the couch.

"Oh my fucking God!" The stench was unbearable.

Maisey was sure she had come to the wrong place, or at least, at the wrong time. She was sure Jedidiah Peterson was long gone, no doubt living somewhere exotic and dating models and such. The trailer was a pigsty. She had definitely made a mistake.

"Fucking great," Maisey said, dropping Weezal hard onto the couch. She called his name a few times but Weezal was out cold and didn't answer. Maisey took a deep breath, gagged, and walked into the kitchen. There was rotten food and wrappers thrown about, dishes broken and dirty, glasses brown with hardened whiskey.

She turned on several lights and seeing the trailer in all its glory, screeched. She fingered through some papers on a table hoping to find out where she was and who was passed out on the couch.

She found what she was looking for on the inside cover of a dictionary (which appeared to be the only book in the house), it was written: "Property of Jedidiah Peterson." "But, Maisey," she said to herself, "this could have been left behind from when the real Jedidiah lived here."

And then it hit her. Was she crazy? Was she out of her fucking mind?

She noticed a small box sitting on a filing cabinet near the kitchen table. She opened the box and found a yellowed newspaper clipping, with a picture of the drunken slob (looking much more handsome and healthy), standing next to Millard Penn, billionaire ink manufacturer. The goddamn *New York Times*. The picture was taken at a celebrity softball game. The name under the photo said, Jedidiah Peterson.

"Jesus Christ, what in the hell happened to you? Just my shit luck—I find a frigging rich boy who lives like a bum."

Maisey was tired but too disgusted to fall asleep. She sat down in the rocking chair to think.

Weezal was drooling on the couch. The radio was still playing and it helped calm Maisey down. She watched Weezal struggle to breathe in his sleep.

"Drunk," she said, hoping he'd hear and feel ashamed. Weezal just smacked his lips a few times and rolled over. A big smile stretched across his face.

Maisey lit a cigarette and started to laugh. Two years of research had come to this. It was funny, really, and appropriate.

"Hey, Mom," she said, "what do you think about this? I found a million dollars and there it is, passed out on the couch. I guess I expected it to be different."

And Maisey's mom said, "Honey, it's all the same. Everywhere."

Another Millionaire's Mobile Home

Pulling the Rolls Royce off the road near the fairgrounds and killing the engine. Drawing the curtains around the windows and setting up camp.

Reaching under the driver's seat, pulling out a Bunsen burner and a can of beans. Starving. Opening the can quietly so as not to wake the sleeping Jesus in the back seat. Not wanting to share. Lighting the burner. Placing the can over the small flame, occasionally stirring the beans.

Staring at his blistered hands. Blistered from the last driveway laid. Thinking about the baby grand piano he used to play. Following a melody forming in his memory. Stomach growling and so pulling a spoonful of beans from the can. Swallowing beans. Dry beans while wishing for some vegetables or fruit or anything.

Millard was getting tired of the manhunt. Wanted to call it quits but threats from Teenage Jesus and an occasional pep talk kept him going. Teenage Jesus wanted to adhere to the contract. TJ was a man of his word.

It was a contract that promised Teenage Jesus $200,000 for the head of Jedidiah Peterson. A contract that was signed with a handshake. A contract that was made in haste.

Millard had found Teenage Jesus hitchhiking on Route 80 heading east from the State Penitentiary, fresh from the jail break. He picked him up, heard his story and the adventure began. TJ dyed his hair blonde. He bought a compound bow at a flea market (for protection) and a partnership was formed. A partnership that was beginning to spoil.

Millard was aching for a home. A home and his money. A hot bath.

Teenage Jesus smelled the beans but thought they were in his dreams and kept sleeping. Millard rolled down the window and got rid of the evidence.

Maybe a few more weeks. Just a few more weeks.

Millard stretched out in the front seat. It was quiet and cold. Too cold to sleep. It wasn't until the sun began to wash away the dirty black night that his eyelids crashed upon their shelf and he slept, shivering with lips the same pale shade of blue as the Rolls Royce. As his eyes.

And this day, this tumbling day, finally landed. Prostrate in Goddfree, Pennsylvania.

Marty Hemingway Fitzgerald McGraw

was sneaking quietly through the back door. Darlene and Rose would probably be in the kitchen eating breakfast. His clothes still smelled like the waitress' produce perfume and he wanted to get up and into the shower.

He got inside without notice. The house was especially quiet. All of the lights were off. Marty got to the bottom of the stairs and poked his head around the door frame, looking into the kitchen. It was empty. He relaxed and walked to the sink for a glass of water.

There was a note hanging on the refrigerator:

Farty,

I took Rose and we went over to Mom's for the weekend. I thought you'd like two days of peace and quiet. Just you and the typewriter. I left some dinner in the oven (you're on your own Saturday night and Sunday morning). You'll also notice (surprise, surprise) that I got you a fresh ream of paper.

I do hope the writing goes well—can't wait to read some! If you need us you know the number. But I won't expect any calls. Get downstairs and WRITE WRITE WRITE!

Love,

Darlene & Rose

He tore the letter up and stuffed it in his back pocket. "Goddamn her!"

Marty stripped naked. He took his clothes and walked out the back door. It was freezing. He stepped quickly over to the burning barrel and dumped the clothes in. He used the letter to start the flame. He watched his shirt catch. A car drove by and honked. A flame jumped high and the fire caught his pants, singeing a few hairs above his left nipple.

Marty went back inside. He was going to shave off his beard and take a long hot bath. He let the water run in the tub while he took a pair of scissors to his beard. He watched the hair fall into the sink. Thick black hair, seventeen, eighteen, nineteen gray strands. He lathered up his face. Shaved. His bare skin felt like chicken skin. The second chapter of his chicken book was going to be about shaving. And fuck the farmer who didn't have the patience to get through the shaving chapter. He was writing it anyway.

He climbed in the tub and lay down. The water rushed up and over his chest and rested just under his chin. He closed his eyes and reached for the soap. The soap smelled like the waitress.

Chicken in the evenin'
Chicken in the morn'
Chicken sneakin' in his house
Chicken forlorn
Chicken likes a bubble bath
Chicken likes it hot
Chicken scared of everything
Chicken in the pot

Howdy Do Da Day

Weezal raised himself off the couch and was blinded by the light in the trailer. All of the curtains had been taken down and all of the ragged shades were sitting in a crumpled pile on the floor. This didn't look like the circus.

The windows were thrown wide open and the trailer was freezing. Why was he naked? Weezal shivered and looked for his winter coat. He found it sitting in another pile on the floor that contained all of his clothing. He put the parka on and headed for the bathroom.

In the kitchen he saw a note posted to the refrigerator. He snatched it and it looked like a list. A peculiar list. It said:
  * curtains, contact paper
  * Xmas card for Dad
  * Mop/broom/etc
  * plants, coffee mug
  * LYSOL!!!

* Market: Everything.

And then, at the very bottom, a frightening post script:

POUR JIM BEAM DOWN TOILET

Which is exactly what Weezal needed to do, so he hurried down the hall and relieved himself.

Curiously enough, the bathroom did smell like someone had spent the morning flushing his Jim Beam down the toilet and that's when he heard the humming coming from the kitchen. Weezal looked for the nearest weapon. He grabbed the plunger and tipped on his good toes toward the kitchen. He paused at the end of the hallway thinking of a plan. He slowly peered around the corner and saw a woman on her knees, her head buried under the kitchen sink. It was definitely a woman. She was pulling various objects—most of which Weezal didn't recognize—out from under the sink, dropping them in a large plastic bag. Weezal didn't recognize the tune she was humming, nor the shapely design of her ass.

He cleared his throat. Maisey turned and laughed.

"Morning, sunshine," she said staring at the hair that was jettisoning off his head, seemingly in a hurry. Weezal thrust the shopping list forward, shaking it twice for dramatic effect.

"You write this?"

"Yes."

"And the others?"

"What others," she asked, sticking her head back under the sink, removing more unmentionables.

"The other notes. The poems! The letters!"

Pulling out what appeared to be a six or seven-year-old cucumber Maisey said, "You're disgusting." Weezal noted the aggressive tone. Aggressive like the letters.

"Come again."

"Get cleaned up. We have a lot to do today."

Maisey looked familiar. Where had he met her? Couldn't place it. Mozart was involved. But where?

He fled to his room.

"Think, Weezal, think." But there was nothing to think about.

He peeked back into the kitchen and saw Maisey shaking her head, dumping a pile of elephant shit into the bag.

She looked a little retarded, the way her eyes were spread wide across her face. Weezal had a soft spot for retarded girls. Ever since he was five. His kindergarten girlfriend, his first, had also been retarded. Maisey looked younger than Weezal. It couldn't have been the same girl.

He didn't mind at all that she was rooting through his cabinets and opening his windows and throwing out his shades. No, that was fine. What he minded was the letters.

He stood in the middle of his room frustrated because he had no clean clothes. Nowadays he only washed his socks. Filled up the bathtub with hot water and bleach and let them soak. Sometimes he'd soak his sore foot in the bleach to fight the infection. He zipped up his winter jacket and went back into the kitchen. Maisey, hard at work, was emptying the contents of his refrigerator.

"Excuse me."

"Yes?"

"Where is my Jim Beam?" He needed a drink.

"I flushed it," she said dropping a fermenting green something into the bag, holding it with the very tips of her fingers.

"Flushed it?"

"It's poison."

Just like the letters! How dare she storm in here and spill his Beam down the drain. Letter writing is one thing—wasting whiskey another. Weezal grabbed a pen and piece of paper from the table and handed it to Maisey.

"Write something."

"I'm busy."

"Write something. Now."

Maisey took the pen and wrote, "Go take a shower and get dressed. NOW."

Weezal studied it. The handwriting was atrocious, willy-nilly letters strewn about. Definitely the boorish hand of someone at the lower end of her graduating class. C average at best. There was absolutely no discipline. Even if she tried, full concentration, slow and steady movement, there was no way this woman would have been able to duplicate

Weezal's fine and delicate strokes.

He was partially relieved.

But if not the letter writer then who the hell was she? And why was she throwing everything that he owned into that big green bag?

"It might be easier to just move," Weezal said.

"Oh, no you don't, mister. You think I'm stupid? I don't even know if I like the way you sound or smell. Actually, I don't like the way you smell and why are you limping? Don't tell me. But if you think for one minute that I'm moving anywhere with you, you're crazy. First, I have to see how tolerable you'll be. I have no interest in being your lover. Companion, yes, lover, no. Let's get that straight from the git-go. But I can't even begin to think about any of that until this place is clean."

Weezal was offended.

"Well Miss whoever you are, I don't know if I have any interest in a companion. Let's get that straight from the 'git-go'! And another thing —I'll shower when I'm goddamn good and ready." He stormed into his room, slamming the door.

That word "lover" made Weezal want to have a drink. Just a sip. Maybe brush his teeth with it. A gargle. Didn't even want to swallow. His tongue was swollen and needed soothing. He thought about lapping at the toilet bowl like a dog to catch whatever Beam remained. He lit a cigarette and it was stale.

A Poet's Guide to Poultry
by
Marty McGraw
(an excerpt for Darlene)

As if Chicken could be ridden through the midnight black thundering toward a violent death.

As if Chicken could be called a thing you love: a wife, a child.

As if Chicken could bake the finest bread you've ever tasted. (My friend Glenn Burney might say, "lightly toasted and smothered in butter.")

As if Chicken could be a tractor that tilled the field.

Roll that Chicken over and make it take a test, a bath, a shit.

Chicken, like The Lord of Water Bugs, rummaging through those sagging, moldy boxes in your basement, searching for pictures of you with a smile upon your face.

Chicken pulling you close to hear the sound of your child's sleeping breath.

Chicken when it's suppertime.

Chicken when it's time to do the dishes.

Chicken when it's time to make love or conversation.

A perfect vocal imitation of Darlene, as if Darlene was Chicken.

Chicken as an evening enjoyed at the opera:

How was Chicken?

Smothered in Italian.

Chicken as a long drawn out punch line:

Chiiiiiicken!

Ha. Ha. Ha.

Chicken raised, like Chicken fried:

He was a good boy.

We don't know what went wrong.

Here's the thing: Chickens come and Chickens go. But the question is—did the Chicken come first, or go?

As if your best friend was a Chicken who later dated your high school sweetheart and called you to say he was sorry but he hoped you understood.

As if Chicken was all the loud conversations that you wished were just a little bit quieter.

As if Chicken were the people who decided they had enough of you.

As if Chicken was the moment you said, "Okay. I get it."

As if Chicken was your last attempt to say I love you.

And Chicken failed.

Something for the Men

Teenage Jesus was shaving his chest hair. He did it once a month to better display his tattoo. Occasionally he made a fresh slice over the thorny crown. No cuts this morning. He only had one clean shirt and didn't want to stain it.

Millard watched him shave. A nice tight chest and flat stomach.

"I'm starving, man." TJ flicked some shaving cream out the window. Wiped the straight razor across his thigh.

"Probably a local diner with a breakfast special. We can afford a couple of dollars."

"Scrambled eggs and sausage. Coffee."

"Buttered toast. Hurry-up with that. Why are you using a straight razor?"

"It's more romantic than a cheap piece of plastic."

"So you're a romantic."

"Goddamn right. Who else kills for money?"

"Scoundrels. Dregs. Psychotics," Millard said, turning away from TJ.

"Nah, they kill for revenge. Or jealousy. Or to help a friend in need. Some emotional reason. I'm doing it for the money and the romance. Now you—you hiring me—no romance. Not a romantic bone in your body. All revenge. Little rich turd playing cowboy."

"Fuck you."

Jesus laughing, folding his razor, putting it in the glove compartment.

"Done yet?" Millard wanted to leave.

"Just about. Hey, I read somewhere that if you shave your balls your dick looks bigger. No shit. Heard that porn stars clip the hair down. You ever done that?"

"No."

"I shaved 'em once 'cuz of crabs. Didn't notice I looked any bigger. Ever have crabs?"

"No."

"You rich boys don't get crabs?"

"I'm sure us rich boys do get crabs, TJ. I'm sure we get crabs and venereal disease and herpes, even the goddamn common cold. But you know what we do? Us rich boys? We don't go around talking about it."

"Motherfuckers take forever to get rid of. Crabs. Chomped and chewed on my nuts for six months. Threw out the bed, the couch, all my clothes. Everything."

"Can we please go and get something to eat?"

TJ was slipping his clean shirt on.

"Sure, man."

"And you are not wearing the goddamn Robin Hood get-up into the diner."

"Robin Hood was a petty thief. Don't ever compare me to Robin Hood."

"I mean it, TJ, the bow and the arrows stay in the car."

"Alright. It's cool. Let's go, I'm starving. Had this dream last night that you were eating a big old can of beans. Holding out on me. I sliced your throat."

Millard pulled onto the road. Using his left foot to kick the Bunsen burner further under his seat.

"It was just a dream, man. Relax."

The crisp morning had gotten to Millard. His feet were cold. And once his feet were cold it was hard to shake the shiver. He blasted the heat trying to thaw.

They drove past the fairgrounds. The lonely winter fairgrounds. No Ferris wheels. No carnival games. Just a few shacks where maybe they judged the vegetables or pigs or arts and crafts. White buildings. Gray shingled roofs.

"You think it's true?" TJ asked, licking his fingers, pasting his blonde hair to his head.

"What's that?"

"That your dick looks bigger if you shave your nuts?"

"I don't know, TJ. I only went to Stanford. Maybe, had I gone to Princeton or Yale, I'd know something like that. At Stanford we were less progressive."

"Well, lah-dee-dah."

And the baby blue Rolls Royce turned right at the stop sign, heading past the dead cornfields, on route to the Effen diner.

Which Came First,
The Pickled Egg or The Chicken Pickled?

Peter Pepper Pickled Chickens.
She sells pickled chickens down by the chicken shack.
Rubber chicken, chicken chicken.

Marty stepped away from the typewriter, inspecting the page.

"Bawk! Bawk-Bawk-Bigawk!" he screamed.

"Marty," Darlene loudly whispered from the kitchen, "keep it down. Rose is asleep."

"Marty, BAWK, please keep it BAWK-BAWK. Little Chicken Flower is asleep, BAWK," he repeated quietly to himself in a perfect vocal imitation of Darlene. A perfect vocal imitation of Darlene as if Darlene was chicken.

"Fuck it," he said. Just like that. It was easy. Like striking a match. "Fuck it." He tore the page up and sent the pieces into the air. "Fuck it."

He wanted to say it again and again. He went into the kitchen where Darlene was grading papers and leaned in close to her and said, "Fuckit fuckit fuckit fuckit."

"Fuck what?"

"Just fuck it, Darlene. Fuck it."

She smiled. His artistic temperament. She had room for that.

"You big baby—get back down there and write."

Marty's eyes widened. The nerve. "Excuse me?"

"I said, stop being a baby and go write."

Marty's head shaking for no apparent reason. "Baby?"

"It's hard. You know that. I know that. Now get to work."

"Fuck it."

He turned from her and said fuck it six more times, counting each on a finger. He wanted to say it ten times but Darlene interrupted him.

"Please. Take it downstairs. Rose is asleep and I have a lot of work to do."

Marty stuck the sixth fuck it into a belt loop and headed to the basement.

"Ugliest goddamn typewriter in the world."

"Fuck you! You fat bastard."

And Marty smacked it hard across the side. Violently fingering a few keys. Like this:

Chapter Four

, cock said. Spit flying.

, hen said. Tears swelling.

, cock said.

, hen said.

, cock said. Looking out the kitchen window to the loneliness of his dying alfalfa field.

, hen said, pulling her sweater tight around her neck.

, cock said. She didn't answer.

, cock said again. Louder.

, hen said.

Little chick began to cry. Finally,

, cock said.

Hen walked out of the room. There was nothing left to say.

Goggling the Go-Getter

The banging and clanking went on for hours. The rustling of plastic bags. The grunts and groans. The occasional "gross." The frequent "disgusting." Breaking glass. Collapsing shelves. Weezal stayed still on his bed. Drifting in and out of sleep. Dreaming of his dad's big hands wrestling with a faulty starter. A Plymouth Duster. Mud brown and rusting in the wheel wells. Sheet metal riveted over a hole here or there. Just got to get it to pass inspection. If I can get the damn thing to start, it will pass. His thin hair dancing in the wind covered in grease and sweat.

"Disgusting."

The knuckles torn and black. The hammering of a wrench on a starter. The slow turnover, a coughing fit. A squirt of exhaust. Rich. It starts. Wash the windshield. Leaving streaks. Because the rag is dirty. Damn kid, don't you think? And that steering wheel, big and hard. How it would crush you in a head-on. The centerpiece of the horn tattooing

PLYMOUTH to your chest. Those knuckles bleeding.

"I'm gonna puke."

And how soft those hands could hold you. Careful not to squeeze and bruise the young fruit. Palm his little boy's ass. Palm his delicate skull. Stare at him as he scrunches and spits and twists and twirls. A plucky sumbitch. Squirrelly.

Asleep in those big hands. Where it's the safest place on earth. Those knuckles clean when they hold the baby. And let him chew on a finger. The teeth come in. The teeth go out. So chew baby blue baby chew baby blue! On daddy's big fingers.

"Jedidiah!"

The sun spilling into the bedroom. The winter air deep in the waking throat, scratching it.

"Jedidiah!"

The knock on a door. And the father disappears giving way to her hair, golden, tickling Weezal's nose as she leans over his face.

"Wake up."

That voice. Those chestnut blue eyes. Devilish, for sure. And searching. Don't look so closely at this dirty skin of mine. Don't look so closely at the hair that has been crawling out of my nose for several years now. Please take those eyes and put them in the other room.

"Come on get up. I made some breakfast."

And it was the smell of eggs. And toast. Perhaps the coffee was but fantasy.

"You hungry?"

Starving, sweet breath. Starving.

"This room stinks."

As do all the rooms.

"Now get up and get some breakfast."

And there it goes. That hair. Those eyes. That ass. That beautiful ass so round and perfect. Swinging this way, swinging that. Out the door.

Weezal sat up in his bed, poking a finger into the corner of his eye, digging at the crust. A cough. And another. So goddamn cold. He pulled the hood up over his head and walked into the kitchen.

Seventeen green plastic bags, bulging, sitting in the living room. The kitchen empty but a box and two chairs. Food on two plates. Eggs, for sure. And toast. And Holy Christ, it's true: Coffee! Steam rising from the cups. Maisey already with egg in mouth, writing while she chews.

"Hurry before it gets cold."

"Smells good."

"Just eggs and toast."

"Still."

Weezal takes a seat. Embarrassed. Perhaps forgot how to eat at a table. To use the silverware. A knife. Dunks a crusty corner of the toast into the yolk, which breaks and gushes to the edge of the plate. A swipe and brings it dripping to his mouth, which hasn't been treated so nicely in years. His mouth cries. Because it's delicious. This egg yolk and toast. Seems a bit decadent, but what the hell. He sips the coffee. This may be the last day of his life. Because he doesn't need more than this. This egg. This toast. This coffee. That ass.

"I've barged in. I know. I've been aggressive. But I'm after something."

"Have you found it?"

"I don't know."

"You're welcome to keep searching. I wouldn't want to stop that."

Fried in butter. These eggs. And you taste it best around the burnt brown edges.

"I will, thank you. But I've drawn up a contract. Because I think it's important we understand each other."

"I can't read. I've forgotten how."

"I'll read it to you. This is just a first draft, so changes can be made."

Coffee mug in one hand and a soggy piece of toast in the other. Bite, sip. Bite, sip. Read on, mistress mysterioso, read on.

"That I, Maisey Walker, hereinafter referred to as, Maisey, work in conjunction with, but not limited to, Jedidiah Peterson, hereinafter referred to as Jed."

"Weezal."

"Excuse me?"

"Hereinafter, refer to me as Weezal."

"Okay—Weezal."

She crosses out Jed and writes in Weezal.

"That Maisey agrees to water the plants, do the laundry, cook dinners three times a week—dinner being defined as one evening meal in a twenty-four-hour period."

Dinner. More eggs. Sunny side. Omelets. With onions raw not fried. Toast toasted and buttered with butter. Three times a week. There are no plants to water. But eggs. Yes, eggs would be very nice for dinner, thank you.

"And to keep orderly all household accounts, checking and otherwise, groceries, bills, etc, etc ad infinitum, and that Weezal agrees to agree with this and to share his fortune with Maisey."

Chew, sip. Sip, chew. Swallow. Wipe with a winter coat sleeve.

"Fortune?"

"Yes."

One last swipe of toast to soak up the remaining yolk. A swallow of the sweet coffee. Another wipe with a coat sleeve. A tongue pulling at a crumb lodged between two molars. A dainty burp.

"Deal."

"Sign."

"I've forgotten how to write."

"An X will do."

And Weezal x'd the paper. Maisey folded and tucked the contract into her pants. Next to that nice round ass. She collected the plates and brought them to the sink.

"Now get showered and dressed. We have to go to the mall. Supplies."

Weezal sat smiling at her. What adventure this?

"Hurry. Scoot."

With Their Bellies Full of Breakfast

Millard and TJ headed south on Route 209. Bound for nowhere. Fiddle-dee-dee.

"How much we got left?" TJ loosened his belt giving the sausage and eggs some room.

"Fifty-three dollars and change."

"Let's take a day off."

"I was thinking we might do that."

"Sure, find a nice spot, I could practice some archery and I don't give a rat's rectum what you do."

"I'll read."

"Read what?"

"I bought a few books in the last town."

"You bought books? Bought?"

"Yes."

"With fifty percent of my money? You bought books? I'm eating goddamn beans and you're buying books?"

"They were used. A dollar a piece."

"How many?"

"Six."

"Six freakin' books?"

"Relax, TJ, I'll give you an extra six bucks on the next job."

"Here we go."

"Here we go what?"

"Fifty-fifty. We had a deal. You broke the deal. We specifically said fifty-fifty and you specifically broke the deal. Deal breaker!"

"I said I'd settle up, next job."

"Ain't the point, Milly. We had a deal and you broke it. Now I have to kill ya."

"Will you stop it."

"No. I won't. You don't break deals with me."

"I said I'd settle up. Here, here," Millard reached over to the passenger side and pulled at the glove compartment door, "take your goddamn six dollars out of the fifty-three. Okay? Okay?"

"No, you shit. It ain't okay. We had a deal. Fifty-fifty."

"You stubborn little shit."

And Jesus punched Millard in the jaw. Knocking him out. Millard's head smacking against the window, shattering it. His hands falling from the steering wheel, his foot heavy on the gas. The car swerving into the oncoming lane. A truck oncoming. Horn whining as Jesus yanks the steering wheel to the right. But too hard. Jerks onto the shoulder, dirt kicks up, the car tilting. On two wheels. Slams back down spinning three hundred and sixty degrees. Skidding. TJ climbing over Millard, kicking at the breaks. Millard's mouth bleeding onto Jesus' only clean shirt.

"Goddamnit."

The car skidding to a stop. A cold morning. Clear sky. Naked trees notice nothing. Stiff and silent. In the cold. And the car. Idling in the road. A hundred yards ahead an ice cream parlor. Closed these winter days. Pulling slowly into the parking lot. Stretch these shaking legs.

Teenage Jesus getting out of the car. Sitting on the hood. Catching his breath. The blood over his cigarette pocket. Taking out a cigarette.

Lighting it with fingers tipped with blood. Knuckles on his left hand sore from the punch. A deep drag. A wet cough. Spitting. Walking around to the driver's side. Opening the door and pushing Millard to the passenger seat. Millard's head hitting the door. Hard.

"Sorry, brother."

Teenage Jesus spotting an outdoor spigot. Trying to clean the blood off his shirt. A car pulls into the parking lot. Radio playing loudly. TJ comes cautiously from the side of the building. Big fat man stepping from a station wagon. Dirty brown hair sticking out from under his John Deere ball cap. A gut busting through a flannel shirt. Fat man hurries near the car.

TJ quickly to meet him.

"Can I help you?"

"Rolls Royce?"

"Yep."

"Give you eight thousand for it. Cash. Right now. Been looking for one of these babies. My goddamn lucky day."

"No it ain't."

"Ain't what?"

"Your lucky day."

"I said eight thousand. Cash."

"I heard you. I said. No."

Big fat man laughing.

"Wow."

Big fat man takes his John Deere hat off and wipes his brow. Sweating in this frigid air. Fat man sweat.

"What? Nine thousand? Ten thousand? Can't go any higher'n that."

"She's not for sale."

Fat man peering in the driver's side window.

"What's with him?"

"Sleeping."

"His mouth always bleed when he's sleeping?"

"I punched him. Said something stupid."

Fat man smiling. Fat man laughing.

"Tell ya what. Ten thousand—cash mind ya—and I'll throw in the wagon. It's a good wagon. Only seventy thousand miles on her. Had the transmission rebuilt last month. New tires. You can see that. A baby seat."

"Mister, it's my day off. I don't do business on my day off. So, I guess that means you should get your fat ass turned around, march it over to that car of yours and drive away."

"You're terribly nasty."

"Yes, I am."

Teenage Jesus walking to the driver's side. Opens the door. The fat man follows, extending a hand. They shake.

"Sorry to trouble you. I don't really have ten thousand dollars. Not yet. Maybe someday. I'm writing a book. Chickens. BAWK! But saw this car and thought it would be fancy to have one. Wanted to sell the farm for it. Know what I mean? Just up and sell the farm for a nice fat car."

Fat man heads back to his wagon and pulls out of the lot. Honking a horn. Bawk-Bawking as he waves.

"Fucking hillbilly asshole town."

Teenage Jesus closes the door and starts the engine. A groan from Millard. A shake of his head. Reaches up to gingerly touch his jaw, stretching it open.

"What the fuck?"

"It was my turn to drive."

And Teenage Jesus pulls back onto the road, following a sign that says State Park Six Miles.

Marty thinking maybe it was time to leave Darlene. Up and leave her. Drive away in a nice blue car. A Rolls Royce. Stinky old station wagon, put-put-puttering up every hill, stut-stut-stuttering around every corner. Sure. If he had the money he would have bought that car and drove away. And Rose, your daddy loves you but he's got artistic intentions. And that's no good for a daddy. Artistic intentions. The road to the barn where you'll find me hanging from the rafters—paved with artistic intentions.

Walking in a Winter Wonderland

Main Street Stroudsburg dressed for Christmas. Tiny white lights twinkle, twinkle in the trees. Candy canes perch on lampposts. Nine red-robed children singing outside the Woolworth's. A junkie-thin Santa ho-ho-hoing. Bells ringing. Snow flaking.

The Valiant huffing and puffing it's way down the avenue. Maisey smoking. Humming a Christmas song. Roger Miller's "Little Toy Trains".

Weezal beaming.

"I hate the mall this time of year," Maisey saying.

She rolls down her window. The cold air swirls into the car and right up Weezal's nose.

"Never been to the mall."

At the stoplight a group of children, fat and stuffed into plastic coats, follow fat and stuffed parents into a church. Mechanical nativity scene. A Jesus jerking. Music coming from a speaker painted like a halo hanging on Mary's head.

What child is this?

The parking lot. Packed.

"Let's get this over with."

Weezal struggles to get out of the car. The Valiant's passenger door prone to sticking in the cold. He kicks it open, smarting his foot. He hobbles out. Limping.

"You okay?"

"Missing a toe."

"Christ."

"Yeah."

They make their way to the entrance. The cold stinging the foot, stiffening it.

The mall shoulder to shoulder.

Hot pretzels covered in mustard.

"You want to come with?" Maisey asks as Weezal turns slowly away from her.

"No. I think I'll walk around." His eyes fixed on a sexy Santa's helper, green leotards climbing up her ass. Children. This ain't no local firehouse Vietnam Vet Santa with a missing leg. This ain't no whiskey-soured, hard-on crawling up your ass while he's asking you questions Santa. And it sure as hell ain't no ninety-year-old saggy-titted grandma dishing out dime store goodies, pinching your cheek so hard you cried Santa's helper. No shit. These kids had it made.

"I'll be in Ryall's Hardware if you need me. And after that I want to go to Penney's. We need to get you a few things. I threw out most of your clothes this morning."

"I used to love Christmas."

"Everybody used to love Christmas, honey." And Maisey walks away leaving Weezal, hands in pocket, leaning on his good foot.

Perfume.

Sagging, tired eyes.

A collection of men sitting around an ashtray. Smoking. Looking at watches. Stretching necks. Occasionally following a teenage pair of legs up the runway.

A boy running.

Crying.

No more. Nor more money.

Just this.

No!

A toy store clerk, shirt hanging out of his pants, eyes cloudy. Nodding yes. Nodding no. Sorry Miss. Sorry so. Aisle three.

And a goddamn dancing plant. A flower wearing sunglasses. Dancing.

Weezal joins the smoking fathers on the bench.

Someone saying, "Budget Mart down in Bangor stays open on Christmas Day. You go down there at noon and everything is on sale. Wait till Christmas Day. Get up early. Saved a couple hundred bucks last year. Catch a little hell from the old lady on account of not being there when the kids wake up. But I don't hear them kids complaining when I walk through the door, couple of bags of Christmas cheer hanging from my hips."

Someone else saying, "My wife would kill me."

"Dead," says another.

"Shit, my wife!" one of them nearly shouts and takes off running. To the Piercing Pagoda. ("That's a real diamond, honey.")

Someone, in a quiet voice, saying, "Christmas. It's a ball-buster."

And everyone drags deeply from their cigarettes.

It is not daylight, I know it, I

Marty rolled the tent up under his arm and descended the attic stairs. He was moving into the woods. He couldn't gather the nerve to abandon Darlene entirely so he was going to slip quietly into the wooded area behind his dead field and see how he liked it.

Darlene was waiting for him at the bottom of the stairs.

"A divorce?"

"It's not a divorce, Darlene."

"Not yet."

"Not now, not tomorrow."

"What about next Wednesday?"

"You mean the future?"

"No, I mean next Wednesday. Huh? Divorce next Wednesday?"

"What's next Wednesday?"

"You know damn well it's my only evening free and I don't want to have to spend it at a lawyer's office."

"I will not divorce you next Wednesday, I promise."

"Marty, what about Rose?"

"I'll visit her on the weekends."

"Sounds like a divorce."

"Stop saying that."

Marty pushed passed her and walked to the closet at the end of the hall. He pulled out a Coleman camp stove and a lantern.

"Bawk! Bawk!" Darlene shouted. Marty dropped the lantern.

"What did you mean by that?"

"You're a big chicken."

"You wanted me to write this book, Darlene, remember? Quit farming."

Darlene turned, walked into her bedroom and locked the door. Marty followed her. He knocked but she didn't answer. He pinched his belly and said, "Fat." Then he turned, walked down the steps and out the door.

A thick crust of ice tore at Marty's ankles as he pushed on out to the woods. It was about a four hundred yard walk to the end of the field where he'd set up camp. He stepped with short hard steps, trying to cut a path. It was going to take several trips to get set up and by then he should have a nice smooth road to travel. He could take that road to visit Rose on the weekends or to head into town to buy groceries. Money was going to be a problem but he figured he'd sneak into the house while Darlene was at school and pinch a little from the coin jug. Darlene was going to have to hire a babysitter for Rose, maybe he'd apply for the job. He'd think about it.

Marty dropped his gear in a clearing in the woods and stood a moment, breathing in the wintry pines. He made a mental list of his next trip's bounty.

Maybe it was an emotional overload, maybe it was the need to feel wanted, or maybe she was just plain horny. But Darlene was looking at herself in the mirror and decided she was going to have a sexual tumble smack in the middle of the afternoon. She was tired of Marty. She was tired of pandering to his needs. This time she was going to fly solo.

"Strengthen my individuality," she thought.

Sexual passion? What was that anyway? Something she thought she should feel. She was uncertain and doubtful if she had ever experienced real sexual passion. That's what she wanted this afternoon and, Marty or no, that's what she was going to achieve.

She slipped out of her jeans and pulled off her shirt and bra. She jumped on the bed and furrowed deep into the comforter.

She laid back and spread her legs wide. She stayed that way for a long time, not thinking anything, but feeling very—invitational. She pulled the comforter down below her belly button, exposing her breast to the chilly air. Her nipples responded. She ran her fingers slowly over her breasts. That's when Marty knocked on the door.

"Yes?" she said softly.

"I need to get a few things."

"It'll have to wait. I'm in the very early stages of a sexual fantasy."

"What the hell is that supposed to mean?" Marty pressed his ear to the door.

"A trucker. Big hands. Strong jaw. Maybe a little rough."

She let her fingers slide down her stomach toward her groin. She gently stroked her pussy. She widened her legs. She spread herself, finding her clitoris, giving it a nudge. A soft squeak escaped her lips.

"Darlene, this is not funny."

"Marty, go fuck yourself." She laughed at the paradox.

Another whimper from behind the door.

"Darlene, in the middle of the afternoon?"

"His tongue is licking me, Marty. And his lips, every now and then, grab lightly at my clit and tug. You should have tried that."

Darlene rolled over onto her stomach. She pulled a pillow down between her legs and pressed against it. She rocked back and forth. She pushed her hips forward, hard into the pillow, rubbing. This trucker knew what he was doing. She squeaked.

"I'm sorry," Marty finally said, but not loudly.

She closed her eyes and pushed harder into the pillow. Her legs were tense and she gripped the edge of the bed. She squeezed with all of her might and gave one last long drag across the pillow and began to shake. She stopped breathing and her mouth opened wide, no sound coming out. She felt the muscles in her back spasm, then her belly quake. She released all tension and collapsed with a loud exhale. She took several deep breaths. Her belly continued to quiver. She could smell herself and smiled.

"I was with another woman, Darlene."

"I thought I told you to go fuck yourself."

Darlene reached over to the nightstand and grabbed a book of complete works by Shakespeare. She opened it and turned the pages quietly, she didn't want Marty to hear.

Marty heard the ripple of a page. "Slipping, huh?"

"It's just to get me started," she said.

"Oh, there was a day, Darlene, when someone else's words were crouched on your tongue waiting to dive off into the hearts of the unsuspecting. Poisoning them. You were well rehearsed. But look at you. Running to books to find the perfect nasty thing to say."

She tore through the book now, searching frantically.

Marty prepared for an attack. Name-calling, threats, flagrant jabs at her insecurities. He could have just as easily sent out a flare of kindness. But that made him feel soft. Pussy-whipped. Bawk-Bawk.

"I'm moving out of here and that's final." He waited for a response. There was nothing, not even the turning of pages.

"I won't accept this," Darlene finally said, "I love you." It made Marty weak in the shins, knees and feet when he heard this. He tumbled to the floor.

"The worst fault you have is to be in love," Marty began.

Darlene was prepared, "'Tis a fault I will not change for your best virtue. I am weary of you."

"By my troth, I was seeking for a fool when I found you."

"She is drowned in the brook: look but in and you shall see her."

"There shall I see mine own figure."

"Which I take to be either a fool or a cipher," Darlene said, getting louder now, more confident.

Maybe she was right. He thought about the waitress.

"I have to do this," he said, not quoting anybody.

"...what shall I do the while? Where bide? How love? Or in my life what comfort, when I am dead to my husband?"

"I must be gone and live, or stay and die. Thy beauty hath made me effeminate and in my temper softened valor's steel."

"Oh, I am fortune's fool!" Darlene buried her head in the pillow.

"Love goes from love, as schoolboys from their books, but love toward love, toward school with heavy looks." There was again no response. Marty pressed his ear to the door. He heard softly:

"That's backward."

"Excuse me?"

"It's—Love goes TOWARD love, as schoolboys from their books, but love FROM love toward school with heavy looks. You got it all mixed up."

"We always get them mixed up, Darlene. We always have. Wrong words at wrong times. Our words. Someone else's words. We're no good at this."

"You have to give me room to fail, Marty."

"And what about me?"

"I think thirteen years of a failing farm... Oh, who cares about the farm. I'm not talking about the farm, Marty. I'm talking about us. Do you still love me?"

"Yes."

"And I still love you."

"Man can not live on love alone," Marty said, pinching his belly.

"What?"

"Man can not live on love alone."

"Bread, Marty. It's bread."

He left quietly. As quietly as a fat man can. Tiptoeing like an escaping teenage runaway down the hall. Down the stairs. Out the door. A new life.

"Do you remember when Rose was first born, what you said? You remember that, Marty? Marty?"

A New Set of Clothes but Nothing to Drink

"You don't drink I suppose?" Weezal asked, pulling his tongue from the roof of his mouth.

"Sure I do," Maisey said, "but I'm not a drunk. It seems to me—and I've only known you a day—but it seems to me you have a drinking problem."

"I got more problems than that."

"Name one," Maisey said.

"I'm forgetting how to read."

"Drink less."

"I'm wasting time."

"Drink less."

"I'm not sure how old I am or where my family is."

"Drink less."

"My foot is missing a toe."

"Were you drunk when it happened?"

"Yes."

"Drink less."

"It's infected."

"Go to a doctor."

"I'm afraid."

And Weezal looked out the car window, ashamed that he was afraid of the doctor. He wasn't always afraid of things. He watched the hills, bare and angry this winter afternoon.

"I'm sorry," he finally said.

"For what?"

"For the times I can't remember."

Maisey couldn't help herself. She wanted to know exactly how much money Weezal had stashed away. She wanted a bank statement, a contract, anything with a big fat number on it.

"I'm sorry for flushing your liquor. That was wrong. I'll get you a new bottle."

"Turn left here," he said.

Weezal knew his way to the liquor store. Like a pig to mud. Like a fly to shit. Like a junkie to your VCR.

Maisey pulled into the parking lot of the Effen strip mall. The State Store was next to the K-Mart.

"Jim Beam, I suppose?" she asked.

"Perfect."

Weezal watched as she reached into her purse, pulling out I.D. and a ten-dollar bill. Maisey stepped out of the car and headed toward the store.

And then, without warning, without so much as a conscious sexual thought he said, out loud and to himself, "I'd love to lick you!"

His eyes popped opened wide with surprise and he threw his hands over his mouth, sealing it, to keep other such monstrosities from escaping. He was appalled with himself and wanted to say, "for shame," but didn't dare move his hands for fear of unleashing other unconscious motives. Motives that would escape his mouth in the form of vibrations, vibrations that Maisey would surely receive as sounds, sounds that would form words, words that Weezal was not at all interested in sharing with Maisey.

Maisey stepped out of the liquor store, pulling her jacket closed, battling the cold. She scooted quickly across the parking lot. Weezal lowered himself in the seat and fixed his eyes on the floor. He held his hands tightly over his mouth.

Maisey got in the car and handed the bottle over to Weezal, but he didn't take it.

"You okay," Maisey asked.

"Mm huh."

"You want this or not?" she said pushing the bottle into his chest.

"Mm huh." But he still didn't move his hands.

"Then take it."

"Mm huh," he said shaking his head.

"What are you doing?"

Weezal kept his focus on the floor. He carefully peeled away two fingers and said, "Holding it in." He quickly sealed back up.

"Oh," was all Maisey could say and let the bottle fall into his lap. "You're fucking nuts," she thought—none of it leaking out.

Sometimes a Broken Heart

Millard's head was pounding. He opened his eyes and felt his jaw. He pulled down the visor and looked in the mirror—his lip was swollen. It hurt like hell.

"Morning, sailor," TJ said, smiling.

"Pull over."

"What?"

"Pull the goddamn car over. I need some air!"

Millard frantically rolling down the window. TJ slowing onto the shoulder. Millard jumping out of the car and heading for the woods.

"Hey! Where ya going?"

Millard walking. TJ getting out of the car and shouting, "I said where the fuck are you going?" Millard hurrying back toward the car.

"None of your business," and again racing toward the woods.

"Calm down. It's a simple question."

Millard spinning back around and approaching TJ.

"You asked a simple question because that is the only kind of question you can muster. I'm not interested in your simple questions. Perhaps you can spend the next hour or so contemplating a more complex question. Then, when you're ready, when you're absolutely sure your question is complex, ask it, and—this is the exciting part: I'll THINK for a while and I'll try to answer your complex question. And maybe we'll go back and forth like that, sometimes me asking you, sometimes you asking me, sometimes debating the answers, sometimes debating the questions, the two of us back and forth like that, and we'll have— we'll participate in—what some ancient motherfucker once called a conversation! 'Holy Shit, Millard, a conversation? You mean we could actually TALK instead of using our fists to prove a point?' 'Yes, TJ we can.'"

Again, Millard turning toward the woods.

"Oh, you're pissed because I hit you. That's fine, but..."

"Observations of a genius!"

"...but I refuse to accept this abuse."

Millard spinning back.

"Abuse? Are you kidding me? YOU punched ME! Okay, you know what? You're right. I abuse you. Poor TJ. No more abuse for TJ. Okay? TJ leaves Millard alone, Millard leaves TJ alone."

And Millard spins again, this time moving quickly, making to just the edge of the woods when—

"It was just a simple fucking question!"

Millard charging back.

"So here's your simple fucking answer: I am going into the woods to BE ALONE. I want to be alone. I might think. I might not. I might play with myself. I might not. I might do nothing but stare blankly at a goddamn single dead branch for hours on end. It's irrelevant. I NEED. TO BE. ALONE. Simple, no?"

Millard turning. Millard stepping quickly. Millard reaching the edge of the woods.

"Alright! That's all you had to say, man!"

Millard screaming. Millard running into the woods. Millard not looking back. Teenage Jesus pulling his dick out. Teenage Jesus taking a piss on the rear tire of the baby blue Rolls Royce.

Maisey Joins the Circus

Maisey placed the paper bag on the coffee table.

"Open it."

Weezal reached with shaky fingers and grabbed the bag. He held it for a few moments trying to decide whether he should tear it open or peel the paper back slowly, surprising himself with its contents. He decided to surprise himself. He tore a long thin strip, it revealed:

Ji eam

and his mouth watered.

"I want to get drunk with you," is what Maisey said.

"I want to fuck you," is what Weezal heard.

"Excuse me," Weezal said, tearing at the wrapper now, opening the bottle, taking a long hard swallow.

"I want to get drunk with you."

Weezal handed her the bottle. She drank. Fat lips. Her tongue slightly poking into the bottle. A small swallow.

"Jesus Christ! It tastes like gasoline."

"Mmm," Weezal said, taking another family sized swallow.

"You don't like beer?"

"What's that," Weezal asked, mouth still aching for more.

"You always drink whiskey?"

"Mmm," was all he could get out. His mouth was full. And then Maisey grabbed the bottle from his mouth.

"Easy, mister. Share."

Fat Lips. Fat tongue. Caramel whiskey. Nice breasts. Fat Lips.

"What are you smiling at," Maisey asked, wiping a dribble from those fat lips.

"You're much better looking than Marty."

"You gonna tell me about your money?"

"Let's drink. We don't talk while we drink."

"We don't?"

"Never. We drink when we drink. We talk when we talk."

"Which I imagine is when we're done drinking."

"Right."

"And when are we done drinking?"

"When there's nothing left to drink."

"Then we talk?"

"Until there's nothing left to say."

Maisey grabbed the bottle. "Then we better get moving." This time she took a mouthful. Too much. It hurt.

Huddled with the Dead and Dying

Millard was propped up against a tree looking out into a field of snow that he guessed was smothering corn. Deer shit to the left of him. Rabbit to the right. Humility was his first thought. His second and third thoughts were interrupted by a stillness that crept over him and pulled him deeper to the ground.

I could use a bath, was the fourth thought.

Tired, the fifth.

The sixth thought didn't follow like you'd expect it to. It sneaked off leaving the seventh thought exposed and shivering.

"Shh," Millard said.

"Shh?" came back a reply.

"Yeah. Shh."

It went back and forth like this for quite some time. Broken, finally, by a horn blast. TJ had waited long enough. Millard rose, dusted off his pants and started back to the car. He had a change of plans.

Drunk, Weezal Spills the Beans

"And that's how I got all the money."
  "Hm," Maisey said and took another swallow.

Drunk, Maisey Spills the Beans

"And that's how I found you."

"Mm," Weezal said, taking another swallow.

Tiny Tabernacle of Freedom

Darlene was making it hard for Marty to stay away. Every morning he'd awake to find a thermos full of hot coffee sitting in the snow outside his tent. Always the same note attached: *"HOT COFFEE, LOVE DARLENE."*

Goddamn her and her hot coffee! Her temptation. Making him soft. Making him weak. Making him want to go home and sleep in his bed. His soft, comfortable bed.

Goddamn her and her soft skin!

Her soft voice and breasts!

Goddamn her soft bread, recently baked and smothered in hot butter.

Goddamn her hot coffee! (So good on a cold December morning.) Making him soft. Making him weak.

Marty's toes were cold. The snot in his nose was frozen and it hurt when he dug a finger into his nostril, trying to break it up.

Goddamn her hot coffee! Her goddamn delicious hot coffee.

The poetry of poultry was failing.

Fatherhood was failing.

His separation from Darlene was failing.

Ahh, Chicken! As if Chicken were Nietzsche saying something like: Life's the shits.

Just ask: Hemmingway, Virginia Woolf, Van Gogh, Brautigan, John Kennedy O'Toole, Jesus Christ.

It was cold. Cold pink sky. So pink. So cold. Marty's brain was frozen. The coffee sat, steaming, melting the snow. Tempting.

"Oh, fuck it." And he poured himself a cup. He lifted it to his lips and let the steam melt his snot. He wiped the snot with the cuff of his jacket. He took a sip of the coffee. It was hot.

"Oh, fuck it." And he took another sip. He looked out across his field. All his dreams buried beneath the snow. The cold snow. So many crops gone bad. So many useless sunflowers. So many extra ears of corn. Wide-open field. Exposed. Now buried and resting. Like his youth. Like his artistic intentions. All buried beneath the cold of winter and wives and daughters. And so fucking what?

Goddamn her and her hot coffee. Making him weak.

Marty could feel a pimple swelling on his ass.

"Oh, fuck it," he said, shifting from one cheek to the other.

Does Jesus Shit in the Woods?

Teenage Jesus was squatting down low, pants around his ankles, taking a shit behind a bush. Millard emerged from the woods, saw this and made a beeline for the Rolls.

"Hey! Hey!" Millard turned and could see Jesus' head popping up from behind the bush. "Give me a minute, Cuz—must have been some bad eggs."

Millard didn't say anything. He simply got in the car.

This day. It was time to end the nonsense. Time to part ways with his ruffian sidekick. He squeezed the keys that were dangling from the ignition. He glanced in the rearview mirror.

TJ was wincing in pain.

Millard turned the key. She fired up. He popped it into first. The tires spun, kicking up dirt. He pushed the accelerator as hard as he could, kicking it. The car jutted out across the double yellow lines. He swerved it back into his lane. He heard a pop. A loud pop. And then thump, thump, thump.

He pulled the car onto the shoulder. Defeated. Another glance in the rearview mirror and he saw TJ, pants still down around his ankles, standing tall, bow pulled taught with another arrow, ready for action. Millard's head fell against the steering wheel.

He wanted to cry. But he couldn't. He wanted to scream. Something profane. But nothing came to mind. He wanted, just then, to curl up and die. Or sleep. Or wake up from what must be a deep sleep. A nightmare. He wanted anything but to be where he was.

How do you outrun your past? How do you forget? A haircut? A new set of clothes? A wife? A family? What the fuck did it take to start over? To make a new life? To look at those fields and trees, maybe even city streets, and see beauty again? Why does the beauty fade? Why does the sadness linger? Why do we look, look, look but hardly ever find? Why do we find and then destroy?

Why can't I cry?

TJ tapped on the driver's side window. Millard rolled it down without lifting his head from the steering wheel.

"You little pussy."

Millard lifted his head. He looked at TJ: "What?"

"I said, you little pussy."

And Millard started to laugh. (He still wanted to cry.) Was this it? Years of education. Years of a successful business. Years of wandering aimlessly through the northeastern parts of Pennsylvania. A manhunt. Was it possible that he was nothing more than "a pussy"?

"Pop the trunk," TJ said, tightening his belt, making his way around to the back of the car. He pulled the spare tire out and went to work. Banging this. Banging that.

Millard looked ahead at the stretch of road. Tree-lined. Sad, dead trees. Skinny. A hundred knock-kneed amateur ballerinas swaying in the breeze. It had been a long time since Millard had been to the ballet.

The trunk slammed shut. TJ walked around the car and got in the passenger side.

"We have to talk."

"I'm sorry, TJ."

"Listen, asshole, sorry don't cut it. We had a deal."

"I can't anymore."

"We made a deal."

"We made a mistake."

"Don't give me that mistake bullshit. I mean it Milly—don't do that to me. Everybody and their fucking grandmother running around, fucking each other up the ass because they know that in the end they can say, 'sorry, made a mistake.' Well ol' TJ don't make mistakes. Ol' TJ makes deals."

"You know what, TJ? I'm not going to shout—though I want to. I'm going to stay calm. I'm going to try to explain something to you."

"I don't want your explanation. Now shut up and let's get a move on."

"No."

"What do you mean, no?"

"I mean we are going to sit right here and talk this through."

"I ain't talking shit. I'm pissed. So, if you know what's best for you, you'll start this car and get us moving. We've been here too long. It's going to start to look suspicious."

"TJ, I'm not moving. Understand? We're breaking up. This is it. It's over."

"You're starting to really piss me off. Now start the car and move!"

"You listen to me, you little fuck! I said I'm done. Understand? You'll get your money and then it's over. No more deal! No more partnership! No more nothing!" And although he hadn't wanted to, he exploded. "And one more thing—if you even think about laying a finger on me I'm going to rip your balls clear out of your scrotum!"

TJ laughed.

"What's so goddamn funny?"

"You threatening me?"

"Yeah, I'm threatening you."

"You're one fucked up dude. You know that?"

"And you're what? Huh? The voice of reason?"

"I'm gonna say it one more time: start the car and get a move on."

And Millard really wasn't a violent man. He wasn't. But something happened. Sound stopped. Time stopped. And TJ's crooked smile needed to be wiped from his face. So Millard smacked him. A backhand. As hard as he could. He cut his knuckle on TJ's teeth.

Sound resumed. Time resumed. And TJ punched Millard in the nose. They both heard the pop of the bone breaking. They both saw the blood. Millard grabbed a T-shirt from the backseat and pressed it to his face, leaning his head back, trying to stop the bleeding. TJ looked out the window. He had never been to the ballet.

This was a long way from Wall Street.

TJ was getting old. He knew it. The problem with being a hood, a convict, was that before you had a chance to do something, to make a change, you got old. What was he gonna do now? He couldn't go back to the streets, the drugs. He was a wanted man. He'd be caught in no time. Hoods, convicts, dope dealers—they didn't think about the future. The future was a bullet. Eventually. And you didn't need a plan for that.

Millard was squeezing hard on the T-shirt. The blood slowed but didn't stop.

"You don't think I can do it," TJ finally said.

"I know you can do it, TJ, I can't do it. That's all. Me. You're right: I'm a pussy."

"What happened to us?"

"We grew apart."

"I don't feel that way."

"Like I said, it's me. I'm sorry."

"Someday someone is going to quit on you. Let you down. It hurts."

"I know."

"You don't know shit."

"I think my nose is broken."

"I think you're right."

"It won't stop bleeding."

"Sure it will. Everything stops bleeding. Eventually."

TJ opened the door and stepped out of the car. He looked around. What in the fuck was he going to do now? Where was he going to go? How was he going to get there?

Millard opened his door and struggled to get out. The blood wouldn't stop.

"Listen, I'm serious, you'll get your money."

"What am I going to do? Where am I going to go?"

"You can have the car."

TJ didn't want the car. He wanted a friend.

"Hey," Millard said, walking around to TJ, "what's one thing, besides the money—what's one thing you really want? Name it. Anything."

TJ stared at the swaying ballerinas, thinking. He took a deep breath. He exhaled the first thirty-four years of his life. It stank. It smelled like spoiled meat. He licked his lips.

"I want to get laid."

When She Got Drunk, She Got Loose

So—

She was lying on the floor giggling at nothing in particular. Weezal was busying himself with the last dribbles of the Jim Beam. It was good.

Maisey rolled onto her belly and propped her head up on her right hand, tilting her head toward Weezal. She watched him swallow. His Adam's apple bobbing, rising up to greet the whiskey, falling drunk down his throat.

"You got a big Adam's apple."

"Yeah."

"I think it's sexy."

Christ! Weezal thought but there was no more whiskey left to hide behind. He looked to the kitchen. Nothing there. He looked to the ceiling. Nothing. He looked back at Maisey who was smiling, about to giggle again.

"I think your ass is sexy," Weezal said. He meant it. He just didn't mean to say it out loud.

"Yeah?"

"Yeah."

Maisey rolled onto her back. Her shirt pulled tight across her breasts. She felt warm and relaxed. It had been a long time since she felt relaxed. And she was scared. But not frightened. She was scared the way she was scared on the tilt-a-whirl. She liked it. She unbuttoned the top button of her jeans.

CHRIST ALMIGHTY! Weezal thought and had to get up off the couch and leave the room for a moment. He circled the kitchen table and returned.

"How'd you get so bad, Weez?"

"Hard to say. Just kept forgetting things."

"That must be nice. Forgetting things."

"I don't know about that."

"I can't seem to forget anything."

"You don't drink enough."

"I'd like to forget a lot of things."

"There's a lot I'd like to remember," Weezal said, setting the empty bottle of Jim Beam on the coffee table.

He stood over Maisey looking at her body. CHRIST! He laid on the floor next to her. Christ again! He didn't touch her—just got close enough to smell her. She smelled like whiskey and cigarettes.

"What sort of things would you like to forget," he asked, inhaling deeply.

"Why I'm here with you. What would you like to remember?"

"What you remind me of."

Weezal rolled onto his side. Maisey rolled onto hers. Their knees almost kissed. The molecules were making modern dance pieces about his nervous system. Maisey wouldn't have suspected anything out of the ordinary but, unable to take the pressure, Weezal shouted: "Isadora Duncan!"

Maisey didn't know who that was. She was deep in thought.

What was she doing?

On the one hand (her left hand, which, twice before, had carried golden rings of marriage), she had matured. She'd learned not to believe in love. She was interested in wealth and security.

On the other hand (her right hand, which owned a trigger finger and had once gripped a steering wheel tightly as she drove into husband number two), Weezal was a mess.

"Dorothy Humphries!" Weezal shouted and rolled onto his back.

"Who?"

"A dancer."

"Oh."

She wouldn't be jealous. How could she be? She didn't love Weezal. Didn't even want to love him. Maisey rolled onto her back and held her hands high in the air, inspecting them. These hands had changed many soiled sheets at the honeymoon resort. They'd scrubbed those bathroom floors. They'd collected used condoms left on nightstands, rolled into sheets or hanging over the edge of the wastebaskets. These hands had been cleaning other's messes for a long time.

Weezal was also inspecting her hands. Long, bony fingers. He imagined those hands softly stroking his belly, moving down, down...

"Trisha Brown! Trisha Brown!" Weezal jumped up and started heading to the bathroom.

"Where are you going?"

"To take a shower."

"Want company?"

"Bill T. Jones!" was all Weezal said as he stumbled down the hallway and into the bathroom.

Maisey stood and pulled her shirt over her head. It was cold and damp in the trailer but the whiskey had warmed her up. The chilly air felt refreshing. She looked down at her breasts. She smiled at them like a mother watching her children open presents on Christmas morning. She came and stood in the bathroom doorway. Weezal was sitting on the edge of the tub, letting the water warm. When he looked up and saw Maisey's naked breasts, his modern dance piece ended. His mind went blank. And he fainted, smacking his head lightly against the bathroom sink as he crumpled to the floor.

Something to Cry About

One winter day blends into the next. One gray sky followed by another followed by another and so on.

Time slows, maybe it stalls, as the sun sets in a purple afternoon sky. And darkness always brings the bitter cold and quiet. No leaves rustling. Everything is dead. Buried. Wind chimes frozen. Birds down south. No music.

Ten minutes after the first snowfall of the winter season the heart begins to ache for spring. For a warm sun. Not the hypocritical orange flame in a winter's sky, shining bright but delivering no warmth, arriving each day a glorious tease—this wicked winter sun.

The heart aches for the mud of a thawing dirt road. For the river rushing high and fast, carrying the December, January, February ice far away. The heart aches for a single blade of dead, yellow grass finding its way through the melting snow, taking its first breath in months. The thick smell of the waking earth. The heart aches. The living earth.

One winter day blends into the next and so on.

Delivered from the warmth and safety of the womb into the shock of the coldness of this world. A smack on the ass our first hello.

So fucking cold. Forget it. Forget it not.

And one winter day blends into the next and so on—reminding us that this isn't paradise. Is it? That this world is not our home. Is it?

And sleep, our only refuge from the indignity of this life. Sleep, our only escape from one winter day blending into the next. And when we can't sleep, there's always the alcohol. Or the sex. Or the television.

Make no mistake

Everybody is lonely.

You are lonely.

Your lover is lonely.

Your family, friends and neighbors.

They're all lonely.

Rich or poor.

Lonely.

Healthy or sick.

Lonely.

Good or bad.

Lonely.

God made man because he was lonely.

And, returning the favor,

Man made God because he was lonely.

Okay, Here We Go

Marty frozen to the bone,
Sneaking through his house.
Looking for some supper food,
Quiet as a mouse.
Packing up a duffel bag
With beans and meat and bread.
Maybe steal a little nap
On his comfy-cozy bed.

Maisey laid down on Weezal's bed and waited for him. The sheets were clean. Her hair was still wet. Her body was icing over. She curled herself into a tight ball and covered herself with blankets. Nervous. She let her hand slide down to her sex and massaged her clitoris.

Eeny, meeny, miny, moe
Catch a tiger by the toe,

If he hollers let him go,
Eeny, meeny, miny, moe.

Teenage Jesus was having a hell of time trying to decide which girl he wanted to sleep with. The late afternoon barroom filling with afterwork broken hearts. Lonely souls. Ladies in waiting. Some of them ladies not much more than twenty-one, twenty-two. TJ wanted some of that. Young pussy.

Marty couldn't resist. He kicked off his shoes and fell onto the bed. Christ!

But he'd only rest his eyes. He'd make sure he was up and out of the house before Darlene got home. Didn't want her thinking her hot delicious coffee had lured him back. Take a hell of a lot more than her hot delicious coffee to get him back. Man of principles.

But.

Just a few minutes of peace and quiet. Of comfort. Just a few minutes and he'd...

Weezal walked into the room. Maisey was waiting. He looked at her for a long time. He felt clean.

"Come here," she said, stretching out her hand to him.

Weezal shuffled to the edge of the bed, grabbing her hand, sitting down. He inspected her fingers. He kissed her thumb.

TJ was eyeing a blond with his left eye and a redhead with his right. Either one. Both. What did it matter?

Coughing and rolling over, pulling the comforter up around his fat body which was sinking deeper into the mattress. The pimple on his ass only a slight discomfort. Marty snored.

Cold and shriveled into the size of a peanut, Weezal gave it a flick with his finger.

"I don't even know if it still works."

"Been awhile," Maisey asked, poking her head out from beneath the blanket, only slightly startled to see Weezal's naked body. After all, she'd seen it all before.

"A long while."

"Good. Me too."

TJ squeezing in between the blond and the red.

"I'm horny."

"So go play with yourself," said red, giggling, sucking her piña colada.

"I was hoping one of you would take care of that for me."

"We're gay," blond said. He was cute!

"Bullshit."

"We like pussy," said red, laughing. Blond choking on her daiquiri.

"I've got a big cock."

Red stopped choking and glanced at TJ's tight jeans. He was telling the truth. And he was hard.

"Want me to start?" asked Maisey.

"Yes, please."

Maisey rolled onto Weezal's chest and stroked his neck. She licked his Adam's apple. She let her hand travel slowly down his chest. A finger in his belly button. Weezal began to stiffen. Maisey could feel it pressing against her thigh.

"Seems to be working just fine."

"Seems to be."

Maisey kissed Weezal's chest. And down down down she goes. Her fingers rubbing his thighs, occasionally brushing the tip of his cock. His cock growing, stretching, trying desperately to get into the palm of her hand. Her mouth.

"Oh, boy," Weezal said, closing his eyes.

Weezal took his right hand and placed it on Maisey's hip. He let it slide around to her ass. Her perfect round ass. So smooth. So perfect.

They kissed. Whiskey coated tongues. Thick. Lips swelling. Weezal's stubble scratching at Maisey's chin.

Sleeping.

Seeking.

Drinking.

Fucking.

Where's the magic?

Sleeping.

No magic!

Seeking.

That's the magic!

Drinking.

No Magic!

Fucking.

That's the magic!

And one winter day blends into the next and so on.

Marty still snoring.

Blond and red flirting with TJ. (Yes flirting!) TJ making jokes. Not a one of them funny. The ladies laughing anyway. Who cares what's funny?

Maisey climbing on top of Weezal, pushing his shoulders into the mattress. Kissing, lightly, his neck while reaching down between his legs and grabbing Weezal's cock. Stroking it. Bigger still. Weezal's fingers continue to probe finding Maisey moist and meaty. (Yes, Meaty!)

Somewhere a Ferris wheel is spinning.

A merry-go-round and round.

Somewhere a German shepherd is crossing a highway to get laid but, instead, is surprised by the headlights of an 18-wheeler with no time to stop. The German shepherd is dragged thirty yards. Guts smearing across the road.

This ain't the first time this story's been told.

TJ's cock aching, trying like hell to bust free from his tight jeans.

How many punch lines must be told? How many drinks must be drunk? How many cigarettes must be smoked to get to the center of a tootsie's twat?

Pussy will kill you.

Just ask...

One winter day blends into the next and so on.

Ferris wheel. Spinning somewhere.

Merry-go-round and round.

Maisey lifting her hips, guiding his cock. Moistening the tip of it with her wetness. Easing it in. Lowering herself. Swallowing it. Falling against his chest. Weezal with a wiggle.

"Wait," she says.

"What?"

"Don't move."

Wanting to stay where she was. Perfectly still. Feeling Weezal inside of her. Right? Wrong? Who cares? They were fucking.

"Oh, boy," Weezal said, his eyes widening.

"What?"

"I just came."

Well, they were almost fucking.

Maisey burying her head in his neck, closing her eyes. Trying hard not to laugh. Not being able to control it. Laughing. Laughing for a long time. His cock softens and sneaks away. An embarrassed retreat.

Everybody's lonely.

Just ask...

Marty was deep into it: the sleep, the comforter, the pillow. He was deep into it all. Darlene was standing in the doorway smiling at her lump of flesh. That's right—HER lump of flesh. She owned him.

"Poor son of a bitch."

For better or worse, rich or poor, strong or weak, this or that, she owned him. She quietly shut the door and called her mother.

"Can you keep Rose tonight? Yeah. He's sleeping. I'm sure it will be, Ma. No. I'll bring them first thing in the morning. Thanks. I love you."

After all, he promised the goddamn farm and delivered!

But.

Small farms fail in America. Maybe everywhere. But this is a fact: In America, small farms fail. That's the way it is.

Weezal's penis had shriveled into a deep winter's sleep. Neither Weezal nor Maisey tried to disturb it. It had been a long day. A long couple of years. He'd done his best. Little fella.

A shit-green Dodge Dart swerves this way and that, struggling to get up a snow-covered mountain road. TJ at the wheel, his teenage date laughing. Who cares what's funny? Who cares what's dangerous? Who cares when pussy (and this goes for the ladies too), when pussy is the carrot dangling in front of your nose? Who cares what price? Teenagers. Fearless. Eventually a frozen teenage finger will reach under that delicate formal dress and grab a frozen teenage nipple. A finger might get stuck with a corsage pin. Blood. It's been going on inside American cars for a long time. Flesh. Blood.

Weezal felt a failure and he was falling in love. Nothing worse than falling in love while feeling a failure. Maisey was sleeping.

Drinking.

Fucking.

Seeking.

Sleeping.

Where's the goddamn magic?

Here's another one:

A woman, let's say about thirty, is flirting with a twelve-year-old boy. She's the secretary at the public school the boy attends. He's an office helper. She asks him to make some photocopies of something. While he's at the Xerox machine she passes by, her ass rubbing against his. She turns and leans over the boy, over the machine, her breasts pushing into his back.

"Need any help," she sweetly whispers in his ear.

"No."

Her hand accidentally falls, landing on his crotch. She gives it a gentle squeeze.

Man, everybody's lonely.

Weezal staring at a green stain on the ceiling. What in the hell? Puke? But the ceiling?

Four piña coladas. Four daiquiris. Six whiskey doubles on the rocks.

Macaroni and cheese made from scratch. Darlene's signature dish. A fresh pot of coffee brewing. Hot dogs being fried and chopped into little chunks. Sprinkled into the macaroni and cheese. The whole feast baked until golden brown.

Millard smiling as he sleeps. A free man. The car parked behind the bar. Waiting for TJ to take care of his business. Then it would be off to the train station—catch the first train to Philadelphia. Look up Tony Carlson. An old friend. A true friend. An attorney. He'd helped Tony once. Tony was the type that wouldn't forget something like that. Tony was a sports fan. Millard sleeping with a smile on his face. A free man. A fresh start. Begin again.

A quick nightmare: Can you ever really begin again?

Maisey staring at a green stain on the ceiling. What in the hell? Puke? On the ceiling? She gets out of bed and goes to the bathroom. The drunk fading. What time was it anyway?

Five piña coladas and three buttons from a blouse undone.

Five daiquiris and the lipstick smears.

Seven shots of whiskey and TJ's dick still as hard as the truth that your best friend is fucking your wife.

The laughter continues. Always the laughter. To keep from talking. To keep from facing the fact that the sex will not be good. Will not be satisfying. That the sex will feel dirty and cheap in the morning with your head pounding and your nose all stuffed up. Aching. Your throat sore from cigarettes and sour from the lingering taste of jism and cunt juice and beer and whiskey and, oh yes, piña coladas. Keep laughing. Who cares what's funny?

Buried treasures.

Pots of gold.

Falling stars, birthday candles, pennies in a well.

How many drinks does it take?

to lose your fear

to dare to dream

to laugh

to know yourself

to fall in love

Macaroni and cheese now steaming on a couple of plates (the good stuff, the holiday stuff) and candles are lit. A couple of glasses of wine (the good stuff, the red stuff) suggesting a possible romantic situation (how many glasses will it take?)

"Marty," whispered so softly, so sweetly. "Marty."

"Mm?"

"Dinner's ready."

"Mm."

"Macaroni and cheese."

"Mm."

And she kisses him on the neck. She kisses him on the mouth.

"Marty."

"Mm?"

"I missed you."

"Mm."

"I'll be downstairs. Waiting."

"Ok."

His eyes still closed. There's nothing to think about. So, sh. No chicken book. No farm. No tent in the backyard calling. So, sh. Just a cozy winter's evening. Just dinner with his wife. Why should he want anything more than that? Sh. Sh.

"Curious business," said Maisey, holding a piece of the paper bag that Weezal had torn from the whiskey bottle.

"Let me see that," Weezal said grabbing the paper, a bit too aggressively. He read the note. He handed it back to Maisey.

"I thought they were finished," he said

Maisey read the note out loud: "I love you." Then, to Weezal, she added, "You're very sweet."

"I didn't write that."

"Of course you did."

Weezal turned away and headed into his room. He came back out with his coat on, carrying a shovel.

"Where are you going?"

"To look for the money."

He walked past Maisey, pausing at the door.

"I really didn't write that."

"It's okay if you did."

"I wish I could have."

And he left. Maisey, excited about the money, pulled on her coat and followed.

Candlelight. Good food. Fresh flowers. Romance is easy.

These are facts: Darlene makes a mean macaroni and cheese. Marty feels like a real shit.

"How can you still love me," he asks.

Darlene is sipping her wine. "How can I not?"

TJ was one whiskey away from a drunken dick and he knew it.

"Ok, listen: I need to get laid."

"Yeah?"

"Yeah."

"Well, maybe you need to say the magic word."

"Fuck me?"

"No."

"Suck me?"

"No. Tell him, Red, tell him the magic word."

More laughter. Always more laughter.

"Please."

"Oh, for fuck's sake. I need to get laid, please."

"Well, we need to freshen up."

"You need to hurry up."

They stumble away. Red and blond asses swinging. Swaying.

The bartender sees TJ putting on his jacket and asks him for forty-seven dollars. TJ looks through the red's or blonde's purse but doesn't find any money. He scratches in his pocket, it's a show, he doesn't have any money. Bartender gives him a look like, "Pay up. Now." TJ would like to smack that look off his face. He's seen that look before. Shit, he used to have that same look. Back in the day. When he was dealing. He looks around the bar. Drunks. All drunks. Heads hanging over beer glasses. Everything slow and quiet. Broken hearts.

"Look, I left my wallet in the car."

"Bullshit. Pay up."

"Excuse me?"

"I said, bullshit. You didn't leave anything in the car. Now pay up."

"Look, Cuz, you don't have to get rude."

"No, you look, asshole, you've been sitting here for three hours and I haven't asked you for cash once. Now pay the bill or I call the cops."

TJ pushes himself away from the bar, smiling, a laugh leaking out.

"The cops? Why you wanna do something stupid like that? You don't wanna call the cops over forty-seven dollars. Now let me go out to the car and I'll bring you back the money. Scout's honor."

"You take one step out that door without paying and I'm calling the cops. You can explain to them how you left your money in the car. And

I'm sure they'll be curious as to how you're gonna drive home after all that whiskey."

"Now you're starting to piss me off, Cuz."

"Fuck you. Pay the bill."

"You got a filthy mouth, you know that?"

"Fuck it. I'm not playing with you."

And the bartender reaches under the bar and grabs the phone. TJ panics. There was a time when he never panicked. But he wasn't as cool as he used to be. Wasn't as fearless.

He panics. He jumps over the bar and punches the bartender in the forehead. Breaks his hand. Hurts like a motherfucker. The bartender falls back against the shelves under the bar. Breaking glass. Whiskey spills. Blood.

The Bartender grabs a bat he keeps stashed beneath the bar. He jumps to his feet and takes a swing. A wild swing, he misses. Strike one. TJ throws another punch that connects with the bartender's left ear. It knocks him down. As he's falling, another wild swing. Strike two. TJ Pounces. He reaches up and grabs a knife. The lemon and lime knife. He jabs it into the bartender's throat. The citrus burns. Blood squirts. Strike three.

The drunks look up from their beers. One of them turns and slowly walks out of the bar. He doesn't want to get involved. And the jukebox plays. The bartender stops moving.

TJ sweating. Pulling the knife from the bartender's throat. Self-defense, right?

The girls heard exiting the bathroom. Still laughing. Always laughing.

And then quiet.

And then a scream.

Little boys disappear.

Weezal was swinging the pick, breaking up the frozen ground. Maisey was shoveling away the dirt.

Some little boy is sitting on a bar at ten o'clock in the morning watching his mother mop the floor. Maybe some old drunk tries to make conversation with the little boy. The little boy has nothing to talk about. He's four years old. Maybe the old drunk takes out his false teeth and pushes them into the boy's face. Maybe the boy just stares at them. The teeth, the drunk. Maybe the little boy is frightened. Maybe the little boy's mother says something like, "Charlie, put your teeth back in and leave the boy alone. Can't you see he's scared." Maybe the little boy says, "I'm not scared." He knows. He knows what to say. Maybe the little boy eats a pickled egg from a jar behind the bar. Maybe he eats a Slim Jim or a bag of chips. Maybe he drinks a cola. Or a Fresca. Maybe that little boy wonders why his mother cleans the bar. Maybe that little boy will have odd-jobs one day, too. Like his mother. Like his father.

That little boy will disappear, like all little boys, into a man.

"It's not so deep down," Weezal said, sweating, staring at his four-foot ditch.

"Maybe it's in another spot."

He takes three steps to his right and starts swinging his pick again. Maisey starts shoveling. Working hard for their money.

Marty and Darlene chewing their food.

"It's going to be a long winter, Marty"

"A hard one."

"We'd do better for ourselves if we helped each other through it."

"That's the damnedest thing."

"What's that?"

"I was thinking the very same thing. Word for word."

"We've been together a long time, Marty. That'll happen when people are together for a long time."

More wine poured. More tenderness follows. And sure, sometimes wine works that way—tenderness. Sometimes it doesn't.

Where's the goddamn magic?

There wasn't much time. The police. TJ opens the driver's side door and pulls Millard from the car. Millard, half asleep, fights back. Then he sees the blood on TJ's hands and shirt.

"Oh, fuck, TJ! What did you do?"

"Get out of the car!"

"What did you do? Goddamn it!"

"Get out of the fucking car!"

"Why?"

"Listen, I don't have time. Things went bad. I hurt someone..."

"Jesus Christ, who?"

"Get out of the car. I'm stealing it. You don't know me. When the police come, describe me, tell them I jumped you, I stole the car. You don't have to get involved in this."

"I am involved, asshole. Now, what did you..."

"Millard, GET THE FUCK OUT OF THE CAR!"

"No!"

And TJ didn't want to have to do it. His broken hand was swelling, aching. But he did it anyway. He punches Millard in the mouth. Millard falls to the ground. TJ screams in pain. Bones shatter. Jaw bones. Hand bones. Millard tries to shake off the pain. TJ has the car started and is pulling away by the time Millard gets to his knees. Taillights of the Rolls Royce dancing down the highway.

One long winter night blending into the next and so on.

Weezal's arms starting to feel like rubber. The strength gone. The whiskey wearing off, sweating out of him. And then the pick sticks into something. A box. A UPS box full of money.

"Bingo."

"That's it?"

"I hope so."

Maisey shovels the dirt away. They look at the box. It's corroded. They pull it from the ditch. It tears. Rotten soggy clumps of something fall through the bottom of the box and into the hole. The box now empty.

"Jesus Christ," Maisey says, "go get a flashlight."

"I don't own a flashlight."

"You got extension cords?"

"Yeah."

"Well run them out the kitchen window and bring the lamp from the living room."

Some little boys are taught to obey the women in their life. Some are taught to teach them a lesson. Some are afraid of women. Some are not.

How cold. How silent.

Somewhere, probably a hundred yards away, a creek is shivering, chattering teeth. How black the sky. How the pasty moon will follow TJ wherever he goes. Keeping pace. How that same moon will sit, quietly still, waiting with Millard for the police to arrive. How this one cold winter night will blend into the next and so on.

And the wind is drunk.

And the trees are dead.

And the ground is hard.

And sometimes the joke goes like this:

Weezal turned on the lamp and they peered down into the hole. Soggy, wet paper. They grabbed the clumps and pulled them out. Maisey's heart was racing. This was bad news. She held one stack under the lamp. This wasn't money. Not anymore. This was mud and paper. Just paper. Was that Franklin? Jefferson? Jesus Christ! Who could be this fucking dumb? Who could be this fucking selfish? The world in pain. The world seeking

Buried treasures

Pots of gold

The world making wishes on

Falling stars

Birthday candles

Pennies in a well

And this crazy motherfucker buries his money in a pocket of mud. She couldn't. That's all—she just couldn't. In fact, she said, "I can't."

Weezal was embarrassed.

Where are you running to?

Who is going to take you in?

Covered in blood.

Your hand broke.

Your dick. That goofy son-of-a-bitch. Your dick still hard.

So much folly.

A blue Rolls Royce. License plate: PENNINK7. Dyed blond hair. White T-shirt. Blue jeans. Armed. Heading south on Route 209.

"Maisey, Maisey, give me your answer do," Weezal sang softly. "For I'm half crazy, all for the love of..."

"Shut up, Weezal."

"Sorry."

"I can't. I just can't. What were you thinking?"

"I don't remember."

Somewhere a premature baby is struggling to survive. Underdeveloped lungs burning with every breath. Crack cocaine coursing through his seven-month-old veins. Sometimes it's hard to breathe.

One winter day blends into the next and so on.

Cars bounce down country roads, coughing and choking.

Small towns.

Failing farms.

Rotting teeth.

Missing toes.

Darlene was drunk on the wine. Marty was fat on the macaroni. Rose was nowhere to be heard. Ingredients for sex or television or a good book.

TJ's right hand was throbbing. His left hand gripping hard at the steering wheel. No need to speed. Stay the limit. Obey the law. Always obey the law. Especially after breaking it. Dick still hard. Dick always hard while making an escape. Wanted to rub it but the broken hand too tender.

Pain. Thirty-four years and have never been satisfied.

This small town, Goddfree, getting ready for bed. No different from any small town in Pennsylvania. This small town blending into the next small town and so on.

Knowing when it's time to die.

Seeking.

Fucking.

Marty was deep into it: Darlene, the sex, the orgasm. Deep into all of it when he heard the sirens screaming past his farm.

"You see," Darlene asked,

"What's that?

"You fucked me so hard it was illegal. They're coming to get you."

He had, hadn't he? Fucked her hard. Villainous. He was a goddamn man.

The radio playing an old-timey tune that TJ didn't recognize. A doo-wop ditty. So fucking puerile. Where in the hell had he learned that word?

Millard. Released after questioning. Released with no one to call. Nowhere to go. No how to get there.

Chickens Come and Chickens Go,
How Long I'll Stay, I Just Don't Know.

The chicken book was heading into dark places. Marty was afraid of the dark places. Death and destruction. Always and again, death and destruction.

Always and forever.

Forever and a day.

Another honeymoon. Another valentine. Another anniversary. All blending into the next and so on.

Maisey would have liked more whiskey but she was too tired and weak to drive to the liquor store.

Where's the magic? No magic. That's the magic.

"Why did you bury it?"

"To hide it."

"What about under the bed, maybe a closet."

"I guess I was drunk."

She couldn't. She looked at Weezal's bad foot. A puss stain on his sock.

"You gotta get that foot fixed."

"Yeah."

She smoked a cigarette. A mobile home. She should have known better. Sometimes the cover is all there is to judge. Nothing on the inside.

No magic.

"I can't stay, Weez."

"I know."

Hundreds of thousands of dollars spoiled by the earth. The mud. The dirt.

So close.

So fucking close.

TJ riding through the Delaware Water Gap. The road curving. The moon, like a ping-pong ball, bouncing off the mountain peaks.

A red light spinning, swirling in the rearview mirror. A siren screaming. A deep breath.

Knowing when it's time to die.

State lines diminish and the world gets smaller. People blend into more of the same and the world gets smaller. Time, the moon, the sun, all of it blending into itself, diminishing. No distinction. No horizon. No thing. No magic.

That's the magic: No thing.

Marty heard what he thought sounded like a branch snapping in two. It was his heart. Breaking. Darlene smeared her breasts across his hairy back.

No more promises. No more attempts. No more. No thing.

Millard shuffled down the road, his jaw tightening in the cold air. Sore as hell. That stupid son-of-a-bitch. A long winter. Not the first. Just another one blending into the next and so on.

The light from a farmhouse flickering in the distance. Another light coming on in a different room. Two lights lit on opposite sides of the house. He'd ask for help. Hopefully they'd be kind. He could use some of that right now. Kindness.

Now three red lights swirling and a chorus of sirens singing. More on the way. A party. Drunk on speed. Drunk on knowing when it's time to die.

How strong to fear nothing. How light. How giddy.

Racing along. Old-timey tune doo-wopping at full volume, drowning out the sirens.

Who wrote the book of love?

Everyone is lonely.

One winter night blending into the next and finally blending into nothing.

No thing. That's the magic.

Mile marker twenty-five. Stanhope, New Jersey.

Now and at the hour of our death.

Red lights smacking roadside trees, making them dance.

A party.

A carnival come to town.

Bells and whistles.

Maisey packing her suitcase. Weezal sitting quietly on the couch, smoking a Pall Mall. Her perfect ass. So round. Her perfect lips. So fat.

The wind will blow it all away.

Goddfree.

Monkey's Paw.

Joe's.

Dunkleville.

Big Bass Lake and Mobile Homes.

Seeking.

Dying.

One winter night blending into the next until it all blends into nothing.

Everything disappears.

Always and forever.

Forever and a day.

Disappear!

That's the magic!

Marty was going through his filing cabinets. The trashcan was filling with every short story, every false start, every scrap of research, every journal, every birthday card. Darlene was propped on a few pillows, grading papers.

Blend. Blend.

Bleed. Bleed.

Burn. Burn.

Burn the house down. Burn the papers down. Burn the past. Burn the promises. Burn the failed attempts. Ashes cooling, turning to dust.

The wind blowing it all away first thing in the morning.

TJ lit a cigarette. His last. Yabba, dabba, ding-dong.

Sirens. Speed.

Millard stood on the front porch peering in a window. Practicing.

"Sorry to interrupt, but my car was stolen and I was wondering if you could possibly point me in the direction of the nearest bus or train station."

Maisey was smoking a cigarette. Weezal's last.

"This was dumb, huh?"

"How's that?"

"Coming here. Looking for something that can't be found."

Falling stars. Birthday candles. Pennies in a well.

"You're pretty, Maisey."

And Maisey had to laugh. Even though nothing was funny.

"Trailer doesn't look half bad all cleaned up. It was a fucking disaster when I got here."

"Yeah."

She crushes her cigarette, Weezal's last, into the ashtray. She stands. She sticks her hands into her back pockets. And what if he asks her to stay? What then?

"Well. You take care of yourself," she says.

"Yeah. I will."

She picks up her suitcase. She walks to the door. She couldn't, of course. But what if he asked?

"Okay. Bye," she says.

"Bye."

And she leaves.

Weezal listens as the Valiant fires up. He listens as it drives away. He listens and hears the sound of a branch snapping in two. It's his heart.

Breaking.

TJ slams on the brakes. Red lights swerving to the left and right of him. Cops jumping from their cars, hiding behind the doors, pistols drawn. TJ staring into the headlights of more cop cars approaching. Finishing his cigarette. His last. Cops yelling something. Can't be heard over the doo-wopping. Over the heart pounding.

He reaches over the front seat for the bow and arrow. But that's as far as it gets. Bullets shatter the windshield. They shatter the driver's side window. The first bullet catching him in the hip. The second in his right arm. The third bullet is the one with his name on it. It enters through his left ear and exits through his cheek. The fourth bullet and more all arriving too late. But they keep arriving. Metal sparking. Glass shattering. And finally silence. Just dancing lights.

And a lot of blood. Spilling.

She had herself. She had her limited education. Her limited skills. It would be enough. For this life. Herself and her limitations.

Weezal ran the bath water. His foot was sore. It was oozing with puss again. Forget it. Forget it not. Yeah, he needed to take care of that foot. The bath water rising. Steam. Taking care of his foot. Knowing when it's time.

Millard gently knocked on the door. The noise startled Darlene.

"Marty."

"I'll get it."

Marty sweating. Throwing away the past. Hard work. He lumbered down the stairs and peered out the door window.

He opened the door.

"Can I help you?"

"I'm sorry to bother you but..."

"You're cut."

"Yeah, it's been kind of a long night."

"You drunk?"

"No."

"Come on in."

"Marty?" Darlene calls from the top of the steps.

"It's nothing, Darlene. Have a seat."

"I appreciate it."

"Coffee?"

"I would love some."

His foot stinging in the hot water. His body aching for no reason at all. Sinking down low into the tub. Going under. Coming up for air. His pecker floating. His pubic hair swaying this way and that.

The tub so clean and bright. Like Maisey's teeth.

The dirt under his fingernails loosening. The puss still oozing from his missing toe.

Going under. Only the sound of his heartbeat—beating. Staying under. A long time.

Coming up for air. Lots of air.

Sarah.

Strawberries.

Illusive, this life.

Someone's big hands. His father's? No. His own. His own hands now big and strong.

A man.

Hadn't even noticed that he'd become a man.

A razor.

A man's razor.

Slicing deeply along a vein in his wrist. The left wrist. The blood pouring. The wrist falling into the water.

Going under. His heart still beating.

Blood running. Draining.

Emptying himself.

"I'm just gonna take him to the bus stop, Darlene. He's had a rough night."

"Just be careful, Marty. He could be a nut."

Marty walking away.

"Hey Marty."

"Yeah?"

"Do you love me?"

"Yeah, Darlene. I love you."

"Well, you be careful."

"Okay, Darlene. I'll be careful."

Weezal floating. Gently swaying. A crimson tide.

Begin Yet Again

"I'm gonna stop by a friend's house and see if he wants to come along for the ride," Marty said, pulling past the great big sign at the entrance to the trailer court.

Millard didn't care because he was already there, in Philadelphia. He was there eating a fine meal, recently showered and shaved. He was in the bustle of the city. He was there and he was beginning again. Old friends. Music. Who would he call first?

He smiled at Marty. Marty thought that was creepy.

Marty killed the engine.

"I'll just be a minute. You wanna come in?"

"No. I'll wait."

Marty waddled to the front door and knocked. No answer. The lights were on so he tried the door. It was unlocked. It was always unlocked.

"Good God!" Marty shouted, too loudly. But the shock of the trailer's cleanliness stunned him.

That crazy son-of-a-bitch had gone ahead and made a fresh start.

"Weezal?"

And wasn't that the shits? The damn trailer smelled fresh. Something wasn't right.

"Weezal," Marty called, poking his head in through Weezal's bedroom door.

He walked down the hallway to the bathroom. The door was ajar. Marty kicked it gently with his foot.

"Weez?"

He'd begun to bloat. The bath water thick and red.

Marty's knees went soft. He fell.

He couldn't breathe.

The smell of blood.

A note was sitting on the toilet seat.

End Note

Rain falls and falls again.
Landing always on a tin shack.
A tin shack with wheels.
All holes in the roof and rusted pipes.
The alcohol.
The rain.
The alcohol.
The rain again. Always the rain again.
Everything blending into everything else.
And always more blood spilled in the name of love.
Hey Marty—I wrote this one.
Love,
Weezal